A TEASHOP IN KAMALAPURA & OTHER CLASSIC -KANNADA- STORIES

OTHER BOOKS IN THE SERIES

Maguni's Bullock Cart and Other Classic Odia Stories
The Second Marriage of Kunju Namboodiri and
Other Classic Malayalam Stories

A Teashop in Kamalapura & Other Classic Kannada Stories

Series edited by Mini Krishnan
Translated by Susheela Punitha

HARPER**PERENNIAL**
An Imprint of HarperCollins *Publishers*

First published in India by Harper Perennial 2025
An imprint of HarperCollins *Publishers*
4th Floor, Tower A, Building No. 10, DLF Cyber City,
DLF Phase II, Gurugram, Haryana – 122002
www.harpercollins.co.in
2 4 6 8 10 9 7 5 3 1

English Translation © Susheela Punitha 2025
A Note on the Series © Mini Krishnan 2025
Copyright for individual stories vests in their respective writers

Though every effort has been made to trace the copyright holders of the stories published in this volume, it has not been possible to do so in all cases. Any omissions brought to our notice will be rectified in future editions.

P-ISBN: 978-93-6569-342-3
E-ISBN: 978-93-6569-818-3

This is a work of fiction and all characters and incidents described in this book are the product of the authors' imagination. Any resemblance to actual persons, living or dead, is entirely coincidental.

Each individual writer asserts the moral right to be identified as the author of their work.

All rights reserved. No part of this publication may be reproduced, stored in a retrieval system, or transmitted, in any form or by any means, electronic, mechanical, photocopying, recording or otherwise, without the prior permission of the publishers.

Typeset in 11.5/16.2 Adobe Caslon Pro at
HarperCollins *Publishers* India

Printed and bound at
Thomson Press (India) Ltd.

This book is produced from independently certified FSC® paper
to ensure responsible forest management.

To the many forgotten translators who forged the paths we tread.

CONTENTS

A Note on the Series		ix
Introduction		xv
Translator's Note		xxi
1900	Panje Magesharaya: AT A TEASHOP IN KAMALAPURA	1
1912	Kerura Vasudevacharya: MALLESHI'S SWEETHEARTS	12
1931	Ajampura Sitaram (Ananda): THE GIRL I KILLED	28
1914/15	Nanajangudu Thirumalamba: THE CHILD, A TEACHER	54
1933	Srinivasa Kulakarni: A NEW TONGUE	58
1934	Kadengodlu Shankarabhatta: MY ALARM CLOCK	67
1938	Koradkal Srinivasarao: THE MASTER'S SATYANARAYANA	81

CONTENTS

1938	Saraswathibai Rajawade (Giribale): THE BATTERED HEART	89
1939	Shymaladevi Belagoankar: THE SCION OF THE FAMILY OR A SECRET GIFT	108
1939	Kodagina Gowramma: VANI'S CONFUSION	123
1941	Mundkur Narasimha Kamath (M.N. Kamath): WHO'S THE THIEF?	138
1946	S.G. Sastry: A GIFT FOR THE FESTIVAL	161
1945–55	Dr Masti Venkatesha Iyengar (Srinivasa): THE STORY OF JOGI ANJAPPA'S HEN	171
1953	Yarmunja Ramachandra: THE IDOL THAT CHENNAPPA DESTROYED	185
1965	H.V. Savithramma: AN EPISODE	195
1955–65	Triveni (Anasuya Shankar): TWO WAYS OF LIVING	206
1985	Shankar Mokashi Punekar: BILAS KHAN	217
1985–95	Sara Aboobacker: BETWEEN RULES AND REGULATIONS	247

Notes on the Authors   259

A NOTE ON THE SERIES

A POEM ABOUT READING begins 'I opened a book and in I strode / Now nobody can find me' and ends by saying 'I finished my book and out I came ... But I have a book inside me.' Anyone who has read a work of fiction (is it ever wholly fiction?) knows what it is to return repeatedly to the memory of this or that character or event. Sometimes everything is forgotten except the impression and emotion those pages conjured up. This is particularly true of short stories: literary lightning that tears through you and exits leaving a wordy high.

I collect translated stories the way other people collect watches or potted plants, recipes or paintings, or something that gives them the pleasure of possession; my collection of stories belongs to their writers and translators. They possess me. That's just how literature is. Along the way, I have had a whole lot of unoriginal thoughts: Is our portmanteau of words enough to convey the complexity of our lives? Why do some languages appear to have more words than others? How might we convey what cannot be said? Coincidentally, all these questions about language and life apply to the art and effort of translation—some might say trans-adaptation—as well.

The idea for this series came from a collection of Malayalam stories I received from Dr M.M. Basheer, who edited and published *Aadhya Kaalathe Stree Katha* in 2010—stories by early women writers. Why only women, I thought to myself, but there were too many other things to do and deadlines to meet and the moment faded. But the seed was sown. For a while, I rattled along with the idea of a most neglected genre—the long story, which fell between the short story and the novella—until David Davidar published a collection I put together for Aleph Book Company: *Tell Me a Long Long Story* (2017). Five years before that, through Oxford University Press (India), I edited a series of novellas. After I retired, I tried to secure the interest of publishers in volumes of long stories from different Indian languages. Again—closed doors. Very slowly, and around the same time, it became clear that all the big prizes for translated fiction were reserved for novels by living writers. Naturally, publishers shifted focus to the map of that heaven. What, I thought to myself, will happen to those writers who were no longer with us but were the reason we are where we are in terms of tastes, styles, experiments and themes? The sun setting on our literary past, where pre-modern met modern, began to bother me. So, I came up with what I thought was my next big idea—anthologies of EISET: Early Indian Stories in English Translation. Fortunately, my editor, Rahul Soni, saw some potential in this apparently forgotten zone.

The evolution of fiction in Indian languages is linked with the development of prose—in some languages, a relatively recent medium for literary expression. To be sure, storytelling itself evolved from the earliest human societies and is the oldest form of enchantment through entertainment, closely linked with song and India's long culture of orality. India had sophisticated poetics and complex orature at a time when modern European languages were just emerging. Tamil, for instance, was a fully developed language thousands of years ago, well before Sanskrit became the power-and-prestige lingua franca. But printed fictional works came to be evaluated largely in terms of their closeness to Western models, and at least eighty years of Indian short fiction from the last quarter of the nineteenth to well into the sixth decade of the twentieth century were strongly influenced by Western norms riveted in place by British models or translations of European works into English. As schools, colleges and popular reading materials proliferated, maintaining the complex balance between the intimate and the universal fell into the hands of the writers and promoters of fiction, projecting as they did an illusion of life and truth, which is the function of literature. For a very long time in social and academic contexts that reverenced the classics as the only things worth studying, fiction was seen as second-class literature. With this stands the raging question of plural heritage, both local and imported. Was there a conflict? Or a smooth hybridization swallowed whole by a readership from which the writer himself or—on rare occasions—herself originated?

In an interview, Dorothy Figueira said that though early translations were inspired by pragmatic colonial needs to understand Indians better in order to rule and control, it was not entirely unidirectional; Indians responded to commentary from the West. It was a dialogue from the beginning. This was possible probably because the translingual sensibility lies deep in Indians educated in any language, though that immediately reminds me and everybody else that even illiterate populations in our country are effortlessly bilingual. E.V. Ramakrishnan does not agree. In paper after paper, he discusses the massive shifts in the cultural domain when English began to displace Sanskrit as the Indian subcontinent moved towards colonial modernity. He calls this time of cultural and linguistic violence a time of rupture.

It is routinely said and printed that there are more speakers and readers of English in India than there are in the Anglophone world, and the pressure this single language applies today upon our language empire is incalculable. There can be no argument about the fact that the biggest intervention in the social energy of our languages was the arrival of English. At some cost to our languages, while simultaneously enriching us with outside influences, it has nudged us into a sense of needing to keep up with world literature—a trend, which has led to a sudden visibility for translations of Indian literary works.

Languages are like opposing reigning powers, and translators are the ambassadors who flit between two kingdoms. The encoding they pack at one end and unpack at the other for another language readership naturally calls for great skills. Translation is a deep reading of a text. Every story or poem has a voice. Inward, human. It asks you to believe the feeling locked into the printed word, and it reaches you through your reader-ear. We read as listeners because the origin of stories is orality. Imagine the translator's workshop, created in a phantom space between two languages, in some sense, a linguistic outer space where there do not appear to be any recognizable norms. Monolingual people have tried hard to

A NOTE ON THE SERIES

arrive at rules, many of which suit them but most of which break down when translators function in a multilingual context such as ours in India.

Let me say something else here. The multiple flavours and successes of a translation depend a lot on the personality of the translator—how ethical, how vain, how patient, how adventurous s/he is—to say nothing of that invisible meddler called the editor or facilitator. To plunge within, in order to extrapolate outwardly what another said, calls for utter honesty. No grandstanding or vanity must be allowed to intervene and contaminate the rendering. Is the translator competing with the original or seeking to supplant it? I can never decide, but I do think successful translations run just a little ahead of their originals as if clearing the way for the author, becoming in fact a third entity that is neither the source nor the target language. Gustave Flaubert said that a translation should free itself from the translator; is that—could it be—true? At a time when identities are not only plural but fluid, and we are continuously told what to think and how to think, our translated literature should be seen for what it is and can be: not just a part of history, but a bank, a treasure house of our own pasts because memory is the cement of our identity. The translations in this series offer a rich mix of the music and sounds of some of our languages.

As we age, as technology inexorably overtakes us, as we balance the intimate with the universal, with what might we fill our memory baskets given the extreme fragility of the past? What but stories about ourselves and others by writers who were both like us and unlike us?

—Mini Krishnan
Series Editor

INTRODUCTION

IN KANNADA, THE modern short story is known as *sannakathe*, virtually a literal translation from English: *sanna* for short, and *kathe* for story. Differing from the didactic intent in stories of ancient times, the newer form is closer in theme and treatment to Western short stories. Modern Kannada stories are divided into distinct phases of development: *Navodaya* or Renaissance, *Pragatishila* or Progressive, *Navya* or New Age, representing Modernism, and, of course, the experimentation in newer pathways carries on.

The earliest collection of Kannada stories is *Vaddaradhane* (The Worship of Elders) written in the tenth century by Shivakotiacharya. It is a collection of nineteen long fables and parables exemplifying the precepts of Jainism. Later, there were the *Panchatantra* fables by Durgasimha in the eleventh century, and *Dharmamrutha* by Nayasena in the twelfth century. Since they were didactic in purpose, the style is formal, with strong overtones of Sanskrit. Later, Kannada, as a *desi* or local language, developed its unique identity while integrating the influence of Sanskrit—considered as the *marga* or classical language.

Over time, Kannada fiction has been reinventing itself by internalizing foreign influences too, predominantly from sources such as British, French and Russian fiction, to rejuvenate the language to refurbish local sensibilities.

Kannada literature of the early 1900s is known as the *Navodaya* or the Renaissance phase. With exposure to Western philosophy and literature, significantly British, Navodaya writers explored local realities from new, uncommon perspectives. Themes for stories were from real-life situations and the style, therefore, moved from formal to casual. Eventually, the somewhat naive representation of local culture by most of the Navodaya writers led to the *Pragathisheela* or the Progressive phase. As the ideological stance moved from the Conservative preoccupations of representing local situations towards Leftist social concerns, stories tended to become introspective in style to deal with questioning prevalent conditions and trying to find ways of confronting social evils. This preoccupation with literature as a strong agent for change brought in the Navya phase, with stories dealing with personal and social existential situations, and the narrative style, therefore, becoming more contemplative.

Experiments in early Modern or Navodaya stories trace their beginnings from stories by Panje Mangesharaya (1874–1937) from Bantwal, South Karnataka. He published his stories in *Suvasini*, a monthly magazine. His 'Kamalapuradha Hotlinalli' (1900) is considered the first modern Kannada short story. Typically, it deals with a local, real-time situation, treating it with humour. It is interesting to note that he intersperses his narrative with short dialogues to give it a sense of dramatic immediacy.

Kerur Vasudevacharya (1866–1921) from Bagalkot, North Karnataka, is significant for his use of a casual, colloquial style in a variety of stories that deal with mythological and historical as well as socially relevant themes. He published in *Sachithra Bharatha*, a monthly.

M. Narasimha Kamat (1883–1940), from Mundkur in South Karnataka, published his first story in 1911 in *Madhuravani*, a periodical published from Mysore.

Masti Venkatesha Iyengar (1891–1986), writing as Srinivasa—from Malur in Kolar, South Karnataka—is perhaps the first writer whose stories were brought out as collections, in *Kelavu Sanna Kathegalu*, 1920 (A Few Short Stories) and *Sanna Kathegalu*, 1924 (Short Stories), in *Madhuravani* in 1911. The short story, as a literary form, had an enriching harvest when Masti added some twelve or more collections. With his deeper vision of life, he focused on the growth of insight in his characters, given their limited circumstances. He also experimented with form, interspersing his narrative with dramatic dialogues.

Ajjampur Sitaram (1902– 1963), from Shivamogga in South Karnataka, wrote under the pen name, Ananda, going beyond the preoccupation with characters and situations to dwell on broader issues that arose from changing times and varying perceptions of religious beliefs and their social implications. His *Nanu Kondha Hudugi*, 1931 ('The Girl I Killed'), is significant for focusing on the variety of cultures with conflicting values in our country and questioning the right of modern cultures to 'reform' people with implicit belief in ancient practice.

INTRODUCTION

Sosale Garalapuri Sastry (1890–1955) experiments with a blend of techniques by using extended dialogues while narrating 'Habbadha Udugoray', which, incidentally, has a plot similar to O. Henry's 'The Gift of the Magi'. In fact, A.R. Krishna Sastry, (1890–1968) from South Karnataka, a well-known editor of a periodical, *Prabuddha Karnataka*, goes even further by experimenting with the conventional form of the short story in both theme and technique to develop it like a play. His 'Gurugala Mahime' ('The Guru's Greatness') develops dramatically within the amazingly restricting form of a dialogue between two static characters with opposing views on the Omnipotent Provider. Unfortunately, the story could not be included for want of space.

Koradkal Srinivasarao (1895–1948) and Yarmunja Ramachandra (1933–1955), both from South Karnataka, herald the protest-writing that became one of the major preoccupations of the *Pragathishila* writers of the following generation. Later writers, like Shankar Mokashi Punekar (1928–2004) from North Karnataka, opened out the ambience to include a plot with a Muslim setting, basing it on a historical incident during the Mughal rule and even including an Urdu *matla* to heighten the touch of irony with its double entendre.

Nanjanagudu Thirumalamba (1887–1982) from South Karnataka was the earliest woman writer. She also edited *Karnataka Nandini*, a monthly newspaper for women. She was instrumental in publishing *Sanmarga Darshini*, a newspaper, and *Sati Hitaishini*, a monthly magazine—both for women. She published her novel, *Susheela*, in 1913, in *Sati Hitaishini*. In her story selected for this collection, her plot is ancient but her treatment is current in its concern for what we lose in what we presume we have gained.

INTRODUCTION

Other writers from South Karnataka, Kodagina Gowramma (1912–1939) from Coorg, and H.V. Savithramma (1915–1995) from Bangalore glorify the self-effacing nature of their women protagonists, while H.V. Savithramma goes even a step further in making her lead character an English girl.

Shamaladevi Belgaunkar (1910–1943) from North Karnataka, Saraswathibai Rajawade (1913–1994) from Udupi and Sara Aboobacker (1936–2023) from Kasargod, in the South, were progressive enough in their feministic approach towards questionable ancient social practices that violated the rights of women. Aboobacker as a Muslim focused on the plight of Muslim women. Rajawade has even given a twist to her story with a life-in-death ending, investing the woman protagonist with a regenerative ability.

Anasuya Shankar, from Mysore in the South, wrote under her pen name Triveni. She is famous for her novels, like *Sharapanjara* and *Belli Moda*, which were made into movies. She has even used a variety of the traditional fable form with animals as characters to contrast with human characters with their deeper sense of integrity in relationships.

Significantly, Sara Aboobacker is the only Muslim writer. There seem to be no Christian writers of stories in the Navodaya phase.

Unfortunately, the details of the first publication of some of these earliest stories could not be located as many of the newspapers and periodicals in which they were published could not be traced. Even the family members had not treasured copies of such publications, in some cases.

In the introduction to his collection, *Mareyabaaradha Haleya Kathegalu* (1999) (Old Stories That Should Not Be Forgotten), Dr

INTRODUCTION

Giraddi Govindaraja writes about a project that he and S. Diwakar, then editor of *Malligge*, a monthly magazine, undertook in 1980 to gather and publish some twenty-nine Navodaya stories that had appeared in the magazine. Thanks to their efforts, we have early modern stories also in collections such as *Mareyalaagadha Haleya Kathegalu*, edited by Giraddi Govindaraja and *Shathamaanadha Sanna Kathegalu*, (Short Stories of the Century), edited by S. Diwakar, all of them published by Pranesh Siravara of Prism Books Pvt. Ltd, Bangalore.

—Susheela Punitha

TRANSLATOR'S NOTE

THE INITIAL PROCESS of putting this collection together was exciting as well as bewildering. Exciting in terms of gathering and reading through stories by early modern writers made available, thanks to help from friends who gifted or lent copies from their invaluable collections, and bewildering as to the choice of stories, limited by the number of pages required for this collection. The final selection has a fair representation of writers from both North and South Karnataka and also an equal number of men and women writers. In fact, I have included stories from all the women writers that I was able to secure.

Translating the stories was a tapas, an indwelling in each story as it unfolded, not just in terms of the plot and the characters, but the typically specific Kannada ambience of the setting and its implications that I had to convey in English. And not one story is similar to another. It was as if each writer was telling me a story in Kannada and I was retelling it in English, preserving its local spirit.

TRANSLATOR'S NOTE

The spontaneity of narrating each story was threatened to be stalled as I sought to close gaps in meaning, significance and flavour by retaining local expressions and making them intelligible to the non-Kannada reader while, hopefully, not interrupting the flow. Thus, each story has drawn from both English and Kannada with felicity to create a seamless blend so that the ambience is specific to a Kannada story retold in English. Expressions familiar in Kannada have been retained with footnotes to facilitate an aesthetically wholesome reading experience. It was indeed a tightrope walk to find a balance between being faithful to the flavour in each story and being concerned with its intelligibility to the reader.

I have tried to be true to the intention of the writer in each story. But in 'Bilas Khan', the spirit of the story gains significance through the images it creates; and these images seem to focus on a new beginning, beyond the intention of the writer Shankar Mokashi Punekar. The title focuses on the grief Tansen endures upon the death of his son, Bilas Khan. And yet, the story concludes, not with the death but with the birth of the raga, Bilas Khan Todi, the first that Tansen composed out of that anguish. This image enabled me to interpret the story as narrating not only a death but also a birth. As I had done previously while translating Vaidehi's *Asprushyaru* and S. Diwarakar's short story 'Kraurya', had Punekar been alive, I would have transcreated the title to 'Bilas Khan Todi' with his permission, to focus on the life-in-death viewpoint that arises from the story.

Way back in 2008, when I sent my translation of the first chapter of *Bharathipura* to Prof. U.R. Ananthamurthy for his comments, he called me up and said, 'I've read it. I don't know how to tell you how good it is ... I couldn't've written it this way.'

TRANSLATOR'S NOTE

'But it's yours,' I protested. That was my first attempt at translation, and I did not know any better.

'Yes, that's true,' he said, 'I can write this way in Kannada but I can't do it in English. My English is academic. You've written from your heart, from your spirit.'

That was an invaluable insight. It enabled me to see my mission as a translator. I was to transport the spirit of the story in Kannada into its English version to keep it alive. I have endeavoured to do just that and hope that I have succeeded.

I am deeply indebted to Mini Krishnan, my editor, for inviting me to translate *Bharathipura*. She trusted me at a time when I did not know what it was to be trusted as a translator. And she has been steering me through each experience including this present collection. As Mini Menon, she had been my student. And as my editor, she has guided me as I used to mentor my students; lead them to the tip of the cliff and give them a gentle nudge to see them take wing.

This project was formidable in some ways. I was used to translating writers whom I could consult whenever I encountered problems with local cultural or religious signifiers. But now, I had to rely on Vaidehi, S. Diwakar and Pranesh Sirivara to procure the stories and help me through such hurdles.

Also, while previously there was no problem with getting the writers' permission to translate, trying to locate relatives of writers from a bygone era was a Herculean task and nearly impossible—but for help from Mini, Vaidehi, S. Diwakar and Pranesh Sirivara. The only exception was Sara Aboobacker with whom I could talk over the phone and who sent me her consent through a message from her daughter-in-law's cell phone before she passed on. This permission seems doubly precious in the context.

TRANSLATOR'S NOTE

I would like to add a bit of personal history before I close this note. My late husband David's great-grandfather, Rev. David Punitha—whose name he bears—was a member of Rev. Kittel's Committee that compiled a Kannada–English Dictionary in 1894. We have the copy of the dictionary that was gifted to him. And my grandfather, Rev. Chintamani Caleb, worked as a translator from English to Kannada at the Wesley Press, Mysore. He lived with us when I was in college and used to tell me about meanings becoming so stratified in Kannada that it was impossible to recreate them to make them more relevant. He gave me the example of 'Rathri Bojana', a translation of Last Supper, to refer to Holy Communion. He wanted to change that expression to something more relevant but the British pastors of the London Mission felt that that was unnecessary. Now, the Holy Communion Service is known as Karthana Bojana, implying Christ's Supper. I guess, we translators are trying to transfer from one language to another, the intention behind the cultural and connotative implications of expressions.

Ultimately, let us hope that the connections we make through translations will enable us to see more similarities than differences in our pluri-cultural milieu. That would serve to make translation a powerful tool for cultural confluence.

—Susheela Punitha

PANJE MAGESHARAYA

At a Teashop in Kamalapura

THE HARBOUR AT Kamalapura basked in the warmth of the evening sun during one of the two balmy months of vasantha.[1] A few boats from Virapura tethered to the dock danced gently on the ripples. A boatman held the blade fixed to a cutting board firmly between his toes, scaled fish deftly and tossed them into a mud pot of water near at hand while shooing away the crows that came swooping down. Fisherwomen stood waist-deep in water, watchful, diving suddenly to the surface with crabs that they tucked into the pouch-like folds of their sarees. A Mappila[2] youth on the bank stole secret glances at these dark-skinned beauties giving free rein to his imagination.

---

1 Spring
2 Malayala Muslim

The first Navodaya story to be published. Originally appeared as 'Kamalapurada Hotlinalli' in 1900 in *Suvasini*, a monthly magazine.

There was hurry and bustle everywhere, with the screech of vehicles and the clamour of coolies adding to the din. A merchant in a corner took stock of the bags of coffee seeds from the ghats, calling out to the labourers to stack them. Men unloaded goods from a ship from Bombay. An old clerk—writing the manifest of goods in a shipment—supervised the proceedings with the fingers of one hand holding his glasses in place, and tugging at the pen stuck behind his ear with his free hand. An English officer held on to the helm of a white boat as he made his way towards the seashore. His foot soldier stood in the boat, holding a rifle. A group of retired gentlemen walked down the promenade praising each other. It was a bit too early for government officials to come out to refresh themselves. The few who were out wended their way towards the 'three-paisa' teashop. Some who had already eaten patted their moustaches delicately with their handkerchiefs. Some others filled the air with cigar smoke. Yet some others struck matchsticks to light their beedis. Quite obviously, all of them valued money.

The manager of the teashop was Poornaswami Iyengar, shortened to Ponnuswami. People also called him Ponswami, naturally, or even Pennuswami—Pennuswami because some twenty years earlier this Iyengar had left town all because of a woman, a penn. He had gone on a pilgrimage to Shriranga, Thirupathi, Jagganatha and Rameshwara, acquired some money in the bargain and returned to Kamalapura to set up the 'three-paisa' teashop with a philanthropic intent. He maintained that there were benefits in pilgrimages.

Iyengar knew how to make sweets, both local and foreign. He spoke a smattering of quite a few languages and had an amazing collection of yarns to delight his customers. He had no children of his own, though Nelluru Neelambe's younger son did call him, 'Appa! Appayya!' and stopped by twice a day for petty cash. Iyengar often muttered—for whatever reason—that he had set up shop only to be self-sufficient; not for profit. Nevertheless, his clientele grew from day to day. Someone dropping in for a quick one-paisa cup of coffee might well stay on to empty his pouch on eatables, only to keep listening to Iyengar's travel tales, hardly aware of what he had eaten. Some cajoled Iyengar to open his bundle of yarns only to give him the slip while he was caught up with his storytelling. Iyengar would gather his wits immediately, go after them and claim his dues.

Initially, Poornaswami Iyengar had a good impression of the young men in Kamalapura. But it had changed in recent times for many of them had tucked into his coffers instead of his delicacies. He tried ways to rid them of this malaise. He kept an account of the dues; he wrote to those who had gone out of town asking how they were doing. He put up a sign: 'A Poor Man's Request', listing the names of his creditors. Somehow, he managed to retrieve his dues, sometimes by underscoring in red the names of people who owed him for as long as six years.

That day there was quite a crowd at the restaurant. Shyamaraya soaked bits of chappathi in his coffee. Malenaadu Kuppanna sipped his cup of tea. Iyengar could not stand either of them; they teased him deliberately. Two days earlier they had eaten and drunk their fill and walked away in a huff.

'Everything this Iyengar says is a lie,' they had said while he was spinning a colourful yarn of so-called personal experiences among the clientele. 'He cooks up these extraordinary stories just to get his customers to spend more, knowingly or unknowingly.'

Iyengar decided on a plan to reclaim his credibility.

So, on that day as a prelude to a quarrel, Kuppanna said to Shyamaraya, '*Rayare*, have you heard of the time Iyengar swam the Arabian Sea at Rameswaram?'

Poornaswami Iyengar did not pucker his eyebrows as usual. He could barely contain his glee.

SHYAMARAYA: Who was with you on that day, Iyengarare? Did that Gundacharya save you from this danger too?

KUPPANNA: Yes, that must've been it. How else could our Iyengar have swum all the way to the Andaman Islands?

Iyengar was silent.

SHYAMARAYA: Where's your Gundacharya these days, anyway?

Someone stepped into the restaurant right at that moment and stood in his tracks since Iyengar had gone inside for some purpose and the newcomer did not know anyone else.

Iyengar entered, beaming to see a long-lost friend.

'What Iyengarare? All well?' said the stranger.

'Arre, when did you come, Gundacharyare?'

The regular patrons stared at the outsider.

'What can I say, Iyengarare? I've been looking for you the last ten years. I was destined to be blessed with your darshan today.' He sat down to rest.

'We haven't met since that day, have we?' said Iyengar, pretending to be thinking of something but looking slyly at Kuppanna.

'Since when?' Kuppanna took the bait.

'We haven't seen each other since that day. True.' Iyengar continued as if Kuppanna had not spoken, 'Not since that day when I swam the sea at Rameswaram, shouldered the sinking ship to help it float again ... and reached the top of the hill at Kanyakumari. True.' He stared at Shyamaraya.

'True, but those days are all over. And there's no one who'd even believe our stories now,' said the stranger. 'Who's this person?' he asked, noticing Kuppanna staring at him.

That was just the break Kuppanna needed.

'Acharyare?! We know your name because we've heard it a hundred times a day every day from this Iyengar. The day our Poornaswami Iyengar was bathing in the Kaveri ...'

'Yes, yes, I'm the Gundacharya who saved him. Hadn't I been there, our Iyengar would've been an oblation to a crocodile. Iyengarare, what was your handful of sacred kusha grass for that fifty-foot-long croc? It would've preferred you, for sure.'

'That's broker Kuppanna, the gentleman who says I spin yarns. Why bother about such people anyway, Acharyare? Is there anyone here who knows those days?' Iyengar pretended to sound indifferent.

SHYAMARAYA: So, is this *that* Gundacharya?

GUNDACHARYA: Yes, yes, I'm *that* Gundacharya who saved Iyengar from the croc's mouth when he was having a ritual bath in the Kaveri. I'm also the same Gundacharya who nursed him back to health when he was ill in Kerala. 'I'll never forget you. I'll never let you go,' he had promised me then. I've thought of him every so often in all my lonely wanderings. I thought I'd see the end of all my troubles if only I could meet him again. It's Sri Krishna's grace that I've been blessed today. Iyengar, have you forgotten?

'Oh, no, swami! You saved my life. I can't forget your help for many births to come. I'm ready to return your service in any way I can.'

KUPPANNA: Now, if he were dying, your help in his time of need would truly be a return of favour.

As if on cue, a waiter brought metal tumblers of coffee and leaf-cups of snacks.

'What was even worse was when three wild elephants chased Iyengar on the island of Sri Lanka ...' Gundacharya continued with one eye on the audience and the other fixed on the refreshments.

Kuppanna and Shyamaraya had already eaten whatever they had ordered, but now they gathered closer to Gundacharya on the pretext of listening to his stories. As soon as Iyengar prodded his guest to eat what had been served freshly, Kuppanna dug his right hand into a donnay,[3] picked up a snack from the leaf-cup, and secured a tumbler of coffee with his left. Iyengar looked as if he had been stung by a scorpion.

The snacks vanished in a moment.

'I'm still famished,' said Gundacharya.

Iyengar brought a refill and placed it close to his friend.

'Maharayare, do you believe now that my stories about my expeditions were true?' he asked the other two, eyeing them with irritation.

KUPPANNA: Well, with the spread we've enjoyed today, we're convinced that the one about the crocodile is true. How long will you be staying here, Gundacharyare?

GUNDACHARYA: For as long as our *runaanubandha* lasts. This bond from our past lives—let's see how long it lasts.

Iyengar did not like what he was trying to insinuate. Gundacharya rinsed his hands and asked for some snuff. Iyengar

---

3   Banana leaf cup

held out his snuffbox. Gundacharya tipped snuff generously into the palm of his hand and tried to stuff a pinch or two up his nostrils. He then filled the remaining snuff into his own snuffbox and passed it around. Iyengar was as nervous as a defanged snake.

'See you tomorrow,' said Kuppanna and Shyamaraya at last, as they wended their way out.

'Iyengarare! How was I? Did I make those scoundrels believe your yarns or not?' Gundacharya asked, twirling his moustache after all the customers had left.

IYENGAR: You talked too much! You should've stuck to what I had told you. You added too many lies.

GUNDACHARYA: Those blackguards believed you only because I did so. I may have made my stories more colourful than yours but, at least, none of them will say I'm lying.

IYENGAR: You've been generous with my snuff and left me with an empty box.

GUNDACHARYA: I guess I got a little excited while talking. I forgot what you had told me.

IYENGAR: True. Even I forgot to tell them you were sailing back the day after tomorrow.

GUNDACHARYA: Never mind. You can always tell them tomorrow. Our game hoodwinked them, didn't it?!

IYENGAR: You better keep telling them right from the morning that you'll be leaving. Tell them you're going to your son-in-law's. If you leave the day after, I'll give you a gold coin as promised.

Even before Gundacharya could stifle a smile, someone called out to Iyengar from the door.

'No coffee at this time of the day, ayya!' responded Iyengar from inside presuming it was Kuppanna. Gundacharya stretched out on

Iyengar's cot; he was not hungry, anyway. Iyengar finished his lunch and came outside to see Gundacharya fast asleep. He ground his teeth and went inside, seething.

The tugboat reached Kamalapura on Sunday. Iyengar told Gundacharya about it some three or four times; he did not seem to hear him. The customers had heard that Gundacharya was leaving by the boat that day, but the man never once hinted at his departure in his conversations with them. Iyengar did try to bring the discussion around that topic. But when he puckered his eyebrows talking about the upcoming chariot festival in Hennur, Gundacharya diverted the talk to some medicine for the plague. Iyengar bore this patiently.

'What's the meaning of all this?' he exploded with fury after the last of the customers had left.

'Of what, Ponnuswami?' asked Gundacharya.

'Don't you dare call me Ponnuswami! You'll have to leave by tomorrow morning. Understand?'

GUNDACHARYA: Leave? Where to?

IYENGAR: Go where you will. Just get out of here.

GUNDACHARYA: Iyengarare, you're ranting! Couldn't you sleep last night?

IYENGAR: You better leave tomorrow morning. Or else I'll neck you out. You remember the contract, don't you?

GUNDACHARYA: What contract? In fact, I was thinking of having an oil bath tomorrow …

'Will you get out tomorrow or not?' Iyengar was beside himself with fury. 'I got you here only for a prank, only to convince those good-for-nothings that my yarns weren't baseless. And you're sticking on.'

At a Teashop in Kamalapura

GUNDACHARYA: Have you forgotten my help? That day when the crocodile got you, didn't I save you with my pavithradarbe of kusha grass?

IYENGAR: Don't bother me! There was no crocodile, and you didn't save me from any. Your holy kusha grass indeed!

GUNDACHARYA: There's no cure for ingratitude. Have you forgotten that I saved your life?

Gundacharya wiped his tears. They heard voices outside.

IYENGAR: Fine! I'll give you fifteen rupees. Will you go?

GUNDACHARYA: Iyengarare. Go to sleep now. We can talk about this tomorrow. The mind does play tricks when you miss sleep.

News spread like wildfire all over the town that Iyengar and Gundacharya had had a fight.

Kuppanna and Shyamaraya wanted to talk to Iyengar about it. But they did not have the nerve to enter the restaurant; Iyengar had stopped giving credit.

'Le, Gunda! You better leave by the boat tomorrow. Or else, I'll tell them myself that everything's a hoax and neck you out.' Iyengar was scared Gundacharaya would drain his restaurant business.

'Can't I leave on Monday? The fifteen rupees you're giving me will barely cover my travel expenses. Che, I ruined my reputation telling those lies.'

'As long as you clear out of here!' Iyengar handed him sixteen rupees.

News went round: Gundacharya was leaving at ten on Monday morning. When Kupanna and Shyamaraya entered the restaurant, Gundacharya was all set to leave.

'I've been to many towns,' he said, looking at the two, 'I've seen many people. But I've never seen a place as good as this or people as fine as you.'

'Don't forget us,' Kuppanna pleaded.

GUNDACHARYA: When I'm wandering aimlessly in my old age, won't I remember you? When I struggle to fill my belly, won't this restaurant ...'

'You're going to your daughter's father-in-law's house in Hennur, aren't you?' asked Shyamaraya.

Gundacharya shook his head, smiling sadly.

'I've neither a daughter nor a daughter's family. I'm alone in this world except for those few I've helped.'

Everyone looked at Iyengar, filled with pity for his friend.

KUPPANNA: But Iyengar told us you were going to your daughter's house!

Iyengar stood up making a wry face.

SHYAMARAYA: He also told us you were bent on leaving though he wanted you to stay on.

GUNDACHARYA: Lies! I would've surely stayed. He had only to ask me. But he doesn't like me here. He grudges me the one meal he'll have to give me. He's the one who spread the rumour that I was going to Hennur. I didn't like him telling a lie. But he insisted. One lie must be firmed up only with another lie, he said. And so, I decided I'd go away somewhere else. But why should I lie to you before leaving?

Everyone was stunned.

GUNDACHARYA: I have no children or family. Iyengar threatened to throw me out and so, I'm leaving. I'd have stayed on if he had asked me to.

At a Teashop in Kamalapura

Gundacharya looked at Iyengar with laughter in his eyes and walked out of the restaurant.

Even today, no one knows where he went ... When Kuppanna and Shyamaraya tried to locate his antecedents, they discovered that he was Nelluru Neelambe's younger brother. Even now whenever someone comments on Iyengar's life story, they do not fail to mention, as a footnote, the events related to Gundacharya's visit.

KERURA VASUDEVACHARYA

Malleshi's Sweethearts

HEMAREDDY PRABHU DESAI was the head of quite a few villages that raised some six to seven thousand in taxes. Apart from the fringe benefits, he also earned well from the tenant farmers on his land.

When Desai visited his private garden one day, Malleshi, his gardener, took him around. Thanks to Malleshi's keen eye, not a crow, nor a sparrow could enter looking for fruit or worm. The fencing was as firm as the walls of a fortress. Even the cows and cowherds who had to cut across kept to the neatly paved pathway. Desai was pleased to note that the vegetable patch, the sugarcane plot and all the trees in the orchard were laden. Even he, as the owner, could not have plucked a single flower or fruit without his gardener's knowledge.

From *Toleda Muttu*, *Manohara Granthamaale*, Dharwad. *Malleshiya Nalleyaru* was first published in 1912.

Malleshi's Sweethearts

After wandering about his estate, Desai came to rest on a stone bench under a mango tree laden with fruit.

'Malleshi, it looks as if we'll earn a lot more than we did last year. You've tended the garden very well.' Desai was lavish with praise.

Malleshi was overwhelmed. He moved his rifle from his right hand to his left and saluted his master with a smile of self-esteem. Desai removed his turban, wiped the sweat from his head and said, 'Malleshi, ever since Baram died, I don't have a tonga-driver, my boy.'

'True, devaru,[1] I don't know if we can ever get a tonga-driver as good a Baram,' was Malleshi's unbiased opinion.

'Can you drive my tonga?'[2]

'I'll drive it if you ask me to, devaru. When I was in Kanakanuru, working for a white dore,[3] I used to drive his tonga.'

'Really? But his horses were mere ponies. Mine are like elephants in heat. They wouldn't heed even Baram.'

'Why won't they back down, devaru? Even the mother of all horses will submit. We just have to get on the tonga and give the tail one twist to let the horse know who's the master ... and to let ourselves know too. The only mysterious creature is a woman. No one has been able to gauge *her* depth.'

'Good that you talked about a woman, Malleshi. My wife needs someone to help her in the kitchen. Why don't you look for a bride?

---

1   Literally, God; term of respect
2   Horse-cart
3   The British boss

If you get married, we could keep both of you. If you ride my tonga, I'll pay you four gold coins a month.'

'Please don't ask me to get into that, devaru, I beg of you with folded hands. Can any married man enjoy the freedom he had as a bachelor? "Buy me a sari, buy me a blouse piece, buy me bangles …" the buy-me never stops. If she goes to the fair, I'll have to go with her, whether I like to or not. If she brings back a quarrel, I'll have to fight back, taking her side, whether she's right or wrong. Isn't it much better to give up all thoughts of marriage and live in peace, chanting *"Shiva, Shiva"*?'

'You crazy boy! If men refuse to get married, how can the world move forward? Your father was married, your grandfather was married. Even his father would've been married.' Desai tried to din some sense into the boy's head.

'It may be easy to get married, ayya.[4] But who knows how the marriage will turn out? My parents didn't spend one day without fighting.'

'Malleshi, just listen to me. Get married. Don't keep arguing.'

'You're my father, ayya. If you ask me to get married, I'll have to. But you're also asking me to find a bride for myself!' Malleshi sounded nervous.

'I'll meet the expenses. Can't you go about and find a bride? Where's the shortage of girls for a boy like you?'

'There's no shortage, ayya. Half the town is full of girls. But they're beyond our grasp when we try to catch any of them. Anyway, give me leave for two days. I'll get one.'

'Go. I'll grant you leave for two days. Get a good bride for yourself.'

---

4   Master

The next day, Malleshi woke up early, shaved and bathed. He wore a pair of clean, brown pyjamas and a white shirt. He tilted his turban to the right, stylishly, and stuck a few jasmines above the ear. Slipping his feet into a smart pair of slippers, he strutted out of his house towards the town, looking like a prospective bridegroom. On the way, he strode into the Charanthaya Mutt.

'Erasangayya Swami!' he called out.

'He has gone out,' said a young girl, peeping out from behind a curtain. Her voice was melodious.

'Quite pretty,' said Malleshi to himself, wondering if he could stop to talk to her.

'Why have you come? Did you need a drink of water or … something to eat?' she said, smiling at his outfit.

'No, I'm not thirsty,' replied the idiot.

Malleshi was new to such an experience. He could not guess her deeper intention. Though the girl was providing him with an excuse for conversation, he could not take the hint. He would not take advantage of the situation. The girl was tickled. She got bolder.

'Then, why have you come here?' she asked, stepping out from behind the curtain. 'Is it anything to do with your wedding? You look like a bridegroom, dressed the way you are!' She giggled.

Malleshi was shocked.

'How did you guess what was on my mind? Yes, I want to get married. And so, I came to meet Erasangayya Swami to find out from him if he knew of any girl from any of the families around here. But who are you? You look like a stranger.'

'We belong to Manganuru, the neighbouring village. I wanted a pendant for my chain. My father and Erasangayya have gone to the jeweller on the market street. By the way, what kind of girl do you have in mind? Would a dark girl do? Or one with a squint?'

'I work for a landlord. My master has ordered me to look for a beautiful girl. You look good enough. Will you marry me? To which caste do you belong?'

'We are Reddys from Naravala. My father hasn't yet thought of getting me married.'

'Perfect! I'm a Naravala Reddy too. Look, I'll buy you a pendant. I'll get you a pair of armlets. Will you marry me? Tell me.' Malleshi sounded eager.

'After the wedding, you'll have to stand when I ask you to stand and sit when I ask you to sit. Are you willing?'

'Once I take you as my wife, I'll have to obey your orders, anyway.'

Malleshi did not sense that the girl was teasing him.

'Then come tomorrow morning and ask my father.'

'Why are you stepping back now? What if your father refuses?' Malleshi became nervous.

'What can *I* do about that?'

'Fine. I'll come tomorrow,' said Malleshi, walking away a bit unsteadily.

He took another lane and kept on, singing a folk song to calm himself. Suddenly, a bull came charging towards him from a side track.

'Malleshi! Malleshi! Get hold of that bull, maga,'[5] screamed an old woman, running behind it. Malleshi caught hold of it by the horn with one hand, held it firmly and stopped it.

---

5   Term of endearment; literally, son

'You did a great job, magane. Can you also bring it to the cowshed?' Malleshi obliged. He dragged the reluctant bull to the barn, tied it securely and sat on the steps, chewing on his stock of betel leaves, nuts and tobacco.

'Malleshi, I heard that henceforth, you're going to drive your dore's tonga? Is that true?'

'Yes, Sangavva. But, if I'm to get that job, my ayya insists that I should get married.'

'But why?'

'Ammayya needs a maid to help her in the kitchen, that's why. Ayya will pay me four gold coins a month. We are to live in their lean-to and eat from their house. Avva,[6] do you know of any girl for me?'

'Where's the shortage of girls, Mallanna? I have one right here, in my house; my sister's daughter. She's nearly eighteen.'

'So what if I'm eighteen? Do you want me to marry any odd stranger, Doddamma?'[7] drawled Neelagange, emerging at the front door.

'Stop it, Neeli. If you continue to be fussy, you'll end up a spinster.' Neelagange's aunt sounded angry.

'Who'll marry a man who chews tobacco and spits it out all around him?'

'I may chew tobacco, but I also brush my teeth thrice a day,' boasted Malleshi, spitting tobacco and wiping his moustache, as if ready for a contest of words.

---

6 Term of addressing an elderly lady; literally, grandmother.
7 Mother's elder sister; aunt

'Neela, will you marry him if he gives up chewing tobacco?' Sangavva intervened.

'First, let him give it up. Then we'll talk.' Neela giggled softly. Malleshi noted that she was not one for easy laughter.

'He'll give up. What's the big deal?' retorted Sangavva. And turning towards Malleshi, she said, 'Mallesha, go home now. Her father, Lankappa, has gone to the farm. Let's talk about this tomorrow ... The girl laughed. Didn't you notice?'

Malleshi got up and walked away, talking to himself, 'She talks too much. Should I give up chewing tobacco for *her* sake? And yet ... she's good looking, fair and strong. She'll be just right as a help in the kitchen ... Anyway, let's see where this leads.'

He was feeling a bit thirsty even when he was at Sangavva's house. But there was no way he could have asked her for water, given the situation. So, he went down the lane towards the well near Hanumatha's temple and went down the steps leading to the well, cupped his hands and drank from it. Even as he was climbing up, a girl called out, '*Le*, Malleshi, help me get this pot on to my hip.'

'Why, Ambu?' said a widow standing by, 'Aren't we women here? Was Malleshi the only person fit to help you? Did you have eyes only for this tall, graceful sugarcane? He'll help you only if you promise to marry him. Who'll help just anyone to lift her pot to her waist?'

Malleshi did not get the implications. He only guessed that the girl was unmarried. But the dart struck Ambu's heart. She blushed. She was hardly aware of Malleshi helping her. She was hardly aware that she was carrying the pot. She just stood there.

'That's done, Malleshi,' said the widow. 'Will you now help *me* to lift my pot?'

Malleshi's Sweethearts

Ambu came out of her trance.

'Chayyakka, who'll help just anyone with her pot?' said Ambu, laughing.

'*Le*, you witch!' the widow shot back, 'Are you saying *this* to me, a widow, and an aged one at that? If I don't get that Malleshi to tie the thali[8] round your neck, my name is not Chayyavva.'

Malleshi did not quite get the drift of their bandying. He believed that Chayavva would somehow get Ambu married to him; he felt gratified. He made his way to Chayavva's house after all the women had gone their way.

'Why have you come, Malleshi? Are you in such a hurry to get married?' Chayavva teased him.

'Yes, Chayavva,' said Malleshi, seriously. 'My master has asked me to get married as soon as possible. My mistress needs a maid. Or else, where's the hurry for me to be married?'

'You don't have a house; you don't have land. Who'll marry you, tell me Malleshi?'

'Is that so?' Malleshi sounded shocked. 'Didn't you vow at the well that you'll get that girl married to me? Why d'you talk like this now, Chayavva?'

'Oh, yes, of course! I said that, didn't I?' Chayavva burst out laughing.

'My wife and I will be living in the bungalow. My master has promised to give me some land in another four years. Right now, he'll pay me four gold coins. Also, he's meeting all the wedding expenses.'

---

8   Symbol of marriage

Right then, Ambu appeared at the door with an empty water pot on her hip.

'Coming to the well, Chayakka?' she called out.

'Come, come in, my bride!' said Chayavva, winking at Ambu. 'Look, your bridegroom has come, eager to be married. Let the negotiations be done by the evening.'

'Can't you come quickly, avva? You're going crazy in your old age,' grumbled Ambu, turning away. Chayavva picked up her pot and followed her.

'The girl seems hesitant,' mused Malleshi, trudging homewards. 'But so what? She didn't say, "No," did she? Whether she says "Yes" or "No", I'm sure Chayakka will surely get her for me … Quite a strange girl, though.'

'Typical village idiot!' said Hema Reddy Desai to himself, as Mallesha bent forward, bringing his palms together to greet his master with respect.

'You seem to be all rigged up, Malleshi,' he said, chuckling. 'What's up?'

'I went out looking for a bride, ayya.'[9]

'Did you find anyone?'

'I've seen three girls from three families. And now I find that I have to get the consent of the father before I get the bride. But holding on to the girls is like holding on to wriggling snakes, ayya.'

'Oh, let them squirm, Malleshi. For how long can they do that? A wife will mellow down in the hands of an expert.'

---

9   Master

'*You* don't say that to me, ayya. You are the Patel. You lord it over the villagers with an iron hand. But you're a mouse in your own palace.'

Hema Reddy Desai felt like laughing. Yet, he pretended to be angry.

'You crazy son of a bitch!' he said.

'Am I lying, ayya? Why're you angry with me?' Malleshi sounded confused.

'No, Malleshi, you're right. If you don't want the problems of marriage, just forget about it.'

'But ... but, you said you need someone to help avva with the housework ...'

'Don't worry about that. Our cook, Bhimavva's daughter has come from their village to visit her. We've appointed her to help in the kitchen.'

'So all my efforts are like washing curry in a lake ...' Malleshi looked despondent.

'Don't get disheartened, Malleshi. If *you* want to get married, get married. I'll meet the expenses.' Desai looked kindly at Malleshi; super efficient as a watchman and yet so innocent.

'Where's the need for me to get married, ayya? I would've got married if that would've helped avva.'

'Right now, there's no job for your wife in our kitchen. So, you can get married whenever you want to.'

'That sounds good, ayya, but now, I have a problem.'

'What is it, Malleshi?'

'I've given my word to three girls. What will I tell them?' Malleshi looked troubled.

'Of the three of them, how many can you marry? One or two?'

'Only one.' Malleshi was sure about that.

'Fine. Let's say you'll get married to one of them. What will you tell the other two?'

The idiot shook as if he had been struck by lightning and then stood staring at his master. Hema Reddy Desai shook his fist as he questioned him, 'Tell me, Malleshi. What is your reply to my question?'

'What can I say, ayya? This is driving me crazy ... All I can say to the other two is that I'm married; I'm helpless.'

'Will they be satisfied with that, Malleshi?'

Malleshi thought for a while and then shook his head.

'If that is so, let all the three be dissatisfied. Why just two? But let that be. How did the three give their consent? Tell me.'

As Malleshi narrated the day's exploits, his master could not control his mirth. He laughed until his sides hurt.

'You idiot!' he said, when he could control his mirth, 'You know nothing about women. Those charming girls were only making fun of you. And you were taken in. Not one of them wanted to marry you. If you go tomorrow and tell each of them that you don't intend to marry her, they'll be relieved, not even a bit disappointed. Go, go and see for yourself.'

Malleshi sighed with relief. A boulder had been lifted from his shoulders.

'Now, I can sleep in peace, ayya,' was all he said.

And once he learnt that his horoscope did not match with that of any of the girls, he gave up all thoughts of marriage and relaxed.

Malleshi's Sweethearts

Anyway, he was eating with his Master's household, thanks to his bounty. He hardly had any other expenses. So he believed that this was far better than being married. As for work, all he had to do now as a tonga-driver was to drive his master around his lands in the cart, for about an hour or more. And drive him to the District Office in town once or twice a week. Some of the outcastes working for Desai scrubbed down the horse and cleaned the stable every day while a servant girl came to boil some beans for its meals. But Malleshi himself took care of its timely feeding of beans and grass with water.

Malleshi was naive and able-bodied. He was not quite satisfied with his new position as his Master's tonga-driver. He did not care much for sitting in the cart, whiling away his time, waiting for his master. He tagged along even when there were attendants at the Taluk Office carrying the records and walking ahead of Desai, whenever he went there on duty. And at home, if ever the lady of the house called him to see to something, he felt favoured. He did not feel belittled even when Bhimavva, the cook, gave him an odd job or two. And he was quite willing to pitch in with Bhimavva's daughter, Giribai, to help her with *her* chores. And thanks to Giribai's guidance, Malleshi slowly learnt to handle other responsibilities as well. He may not have survived as a student of arithmetic in a classroom, but slowly, he learnt to shop, to calculate the price of fruits and vegetables and to bring back the right change. Day by day, Malleshi became more and more responsible, and more and more endearing, now that he was losing his naivete.

Since Giribai was in charge of seeing to the grocery shopping, she would sit with him, explaining the details of quantities to buy, amount to be paid and change to be expected. Malleshi was eager to learn and soon became quite competent. Giribai did not mind that he was known as a blockhead. Thanks to her help, Malleshi became quite capable of handling greater responsibilities about the house as the months rolled by.

One day, the lady of the house called out a long list of items to be bought for some festivity: betel leaves and nuts, coconuts, bananas, honey, dry dates and camphor.

'Malleshi,' said Giribai, giggling, 'These are quite a few items. I'm not sure you'll be able to remember every one of them. It would've helped if you could read. I could've made a list for you.'

'Why do you worry so much about such a simple thing, Giribai? Even if I don't know how to read, I can make a list of all those items. Try me out,' he said, casually.

Giribai immediately brought him a bottle of ink and a pen, to take a dig at his smugness. Malleshi sat down confidently, as if he was used to doing what he was going to do and began to draw shapes: circles for areca nuts, a tiny swirl for betel leaves, a few ovals for dates, an oval coconut with a tuft, and tiny squares for camphor. His mistress was so amused by his dexterity that she could not stop laughing. But Giribai did not.

'Avva,' she said, 'if Malleshi took this slip of paper, he cannot forget even one item. His clever drawings are doing the job of words, aren't they? He's getting smarter by the day,'

And to Malleshi, 'Malleshi, you haven't marked the honey you'll have to buy.'

'Where's the need? I'll be taking this silver bowl to bring it in any way,' he said.

Giribai was happy to see his face bright as the full moon; the clouds of stupidity had drifted away. From that day, she began to teach him to read and write, away from prying eyes. In about a month or two, Malleshi learnt to write simple words without much effort.

When she had lived with her aunt, Giribai had studied up to the fifth grade and later, had even taught little children in that same school for about three years. She had given up the job and come to help her mother when her favourite senior teacher had left the school and moved to another town. Though she was not highly educated, she could teach Malleshi to shed his uncouth ways and to talk like a well-bred person.

And when the attractive young girl began to talk about other interesting things, he learnt that women were not an alien species, after all. Sweet talk is always sweet. And when it comes from a kind, gentle woman, can it ever be sour? In subtle ways, she deftly taught him the ways of the world. He was grateful to her, seeking and relying on her advice. He had fallen for her but was not aware of it. He was a decent young man, devoid of guile. It is not surprising that Giribai too grew fond of him.

One day, Giribai was cleaning her mistress's hand-held mirror when it slipped from her hand, crashed and broke. She was scared. She brought Malleshi to the room and wept, 'Ayyo, what shall I do, Malleshi?'

He thought for a moment.

'Don't worry,' he said, 'I've seen another just like this one where ayya bought this for avva. I'll get that for you. Just clean up this mess.' Giribai found his tone of confidence comforting.

Malleshi pulled out four rupees from his pouch, went to the market in town, bought the mirror and handed it to Giribai all within an hour. She was delighted and grateful for his help.

Staring at her glowing face, Malleshi felt his whole life had become worthwhile at that very moment. This incident formed a deeper base for their friendship. Giribale felt the day wasted when she could not do something special for Malleshi. And Malleshi thought it was a bad day when he did not make her happy. Saying that love blossomed between the young couple is much like the mendicant with his noisy rattle walking up and down our streets forecasting the obvious; that rain will bring slush in its wake.

One day, Malleshi was in bed with a throbbing headache. Both Hema Reddy Desai and his wife had relieved him of his duties for the day, asking him to rest. That afternoon, after her work in the kitchen was done, Giribai went to his room with the oil of cinnamon sticks, laid her hand gently on his forehead and said softly, 'How are you feeling now, Malleshi?'

Malleshi sat bolt upright, as if an electric current had shot through him, and grasped the delicate hand.

'What a wonder, Giribai!' he exclaimed. 'The magic touch of your soft, warm hand has soothed me … My head has stopped throbbing, but now my heart is, I wonder why?' He laid her hand against his chest and held it firmly with both his hands, lest she should pull it away.

'Malleshi, if you shout that way, what will people think?' cried Giribai in a panic. She was hardly aware of what she was doing when she stood behind him and put her other hand on his mouth.

'You're right,' he said, grasping that hand too, 'I'm lost in a strange bliss. I didn't know what I was doing.'

Love struck them like a bolt of lightning descending straight from the clouds. Giribai felt a tremor all over. She was glowing.

She looked at Malleshi with lovelorn eyes and whispered, 'You crazy man!'

Malleshi stood up, hugged her and nibbled her lower lip.

After this unexpected experience, both of them hardly met, hardly spoke to each other. But their eyes became eloquent. The lady of the house noticed it with pleasure. Everyone had hoped for this. Hema Reddy Desai got them married. He also upgraded Malleshi's responsibilities by making him the treasurer of the household, now that he was fairly literate and eminently trustworthy. Giribai became her mistress's right hand.

Malleshi pretended to grumble that Giribai was high-handed, 'What else can we expect if our role model who bosses over the whole town is a mouse in his own house?'

But in truth, he felt nothing could be better than being married to her.

AJAMPURA SITARAM (ANANDA)

The Girl I Killed

1

THIS HAPPENED SOME six to seven years ago when I travelled all over Mysore during the holidays one summer. I had this craze to capture in photos, the charm of all the sculptures across the state. Whenever I had read tantalizing descriptions of temples in places like Somanathpura, Beluru and Halebeedu, I used to think, 'Fine! If I live long enough, I'll enjoy all of them with my own eyes … someday.'

And so, I was excited when I set out. My dream was coming true! But what I am about to narrate is not a detailed discourse about my travels. It is about something that happened during this tour; something that happened in a village, in just a few days after I set out.

Originally published as 'Naanu Kondha Hudugi'.

The Girl I Killed

The village was Nagavalli.

By the time I reached that place, I can say my dream of wandering was done. Well, almost done. I had already collected some hundred to a hundred and fifty pictures; photos that I myself had taken.

Kariyappa was well respected in Nagavalli. He was the headman of the village. I was staying in his home. My story begins here. Well, more or less.

It was around nine that night by the time I reached the village. I had put my luggage in a cart and trudged behind it. I had not felt like travelling through the night with that cart. I decided to stay back in Nagavalli.

'Is there any place here where I can sleep tonight?' I asked the cartman. He mentioned Kariyappa's name and said, 'Swami, with your permission, I can take you to him and explain your situation. He will see to all the arrangements.'

'Do,' I said.

Kariyappa's house was just a short distance away. I stood by the cart while he got down and went towards the house. He returned a few minutes later with another person.

'Buddhi[1], this is the person, Kariyappanavaru,' he said, respectfully.

Kariyappa came closer towards me and bringing his palms together in a namaskara, said modestly, 'Swami, please come in. Consider this your home.'

'I'm troubling you, forgive me,' I said, greeting him with a namaskara, just as he had done.

---

1 Term of respect; literally, wise one.

'How can you say that, swami? How can you be any trouble? You've decided to come to my house. You're my athithi.² I have the punya³ to have you as my guest. I'm blessed. Please come in, this way.' And turning towards the cartman, he said, 'Le, Thimma, take ayya's things inside.'

Both of us went to the veranda and sat on a mat spread over a stone ledge. Kariyappa's family seemed large. Even as we settled down, some three or four children came running outside to stare at me curiously. My hat and boots might have seemed strange, even funny.

There was a room beside the bench. A servant opened the door, swept the room, spread a mat and brought in a lamp. The cart driver arranged my luggage in a corner. I paid him and sent him off.

'Swami, would you like to change now?' said Kariyappa.

I got up and went into the room, changed into the more comfortable dhothi⁴ and shirt and came outside. Someone had brought some warm water. I felt refreshed after washing my face, hands and feet. In another half an hour, dinner was over. We came outside, sat and chatted awhile, munching betel leaves and nut. I narrated my tour of the temples in vivid detail. I could see from the way he spoke to me and saw to my needs that he was happy I was his guest. As we got talking, I learnt a few things about him too. He was wealthy, paying nine hundred rupees as tax. He had quite a few servants, a barn and cattle, and lived in this mansion,

---

2   Guest
3   Religious merit
4   The length of unstitched cloth tied around the waist and falling to the ankles to cover the lower part of the body.

the largest in the village. More than anything else, what struck me most was his guileless modesty. It seemed to come naturally to him. I felt I would be overwhelmed with his hospitality!

I could not sit for long; I was tired after the day's trek. I explained this to my host, bid him goodnight, put off the lamp and fell asleep.

2

It may have been around six-thirty or seven by the time I woke up the next morning. Water was ready and waiting for me outside the door. I washed my face and sat inside. Kariyappa came with a glass of milk. Perhaps they were not used to morning coffee. And I am not used to milk. But I drank it somehow; he himself had brought it and so, how could I refuse?

And then, making him sit beside me, I showed him the photos, describing each place as well as I could, from what little I had learnt about them from my tour. I cannot explain his surprise and joy; he was overwhelmed.

'Swami,' he said, staring at me, 'if you're willing, I'd like to take you to a temple not very far from here, Rangappa's Temple. It's very old, swami. Intricately engraved.' I was all ears.

'Where?'

'Not very far, swami. Just about three miles from here. There! Can you see that hillock over there? That's Maradi betta.[5] The temple is at its base.'

---

5   Hill

AJAMPURA SITARAM (ANANDA)

I had yet to write notes on some of the photos I had taken in Beluru. And I had to write to Lakshmi.

'Fine! I'll go over to that place tomorrow morning. I've got some writing to do today.'

'Of course! Please do as you wish,' he said.

By the time I could write the notes and fill in the details for the photos, it was around twelve. After lunch, I sat down to write to Lakshmi.

I would write to her whenever I could make time during my travels. Of course, most of my letters were details of my tour of the ancient temples; about the awesome majesty of these monuments in stone as well as the detailed, intricate carving of specific features. Thoughts of Lakshmi followed me faithfully wherever I went. Quite often, I would feel, 'What a shame Lakshmi isn't here to see this beauty! It would've looked even more enchanting, had she been by my side.'

Today, I told her about my stay in Nagavalli and the warmth of Kariyappa's hospitality that I was enjoying; about his mansion, his status, his children and other such details. I even wrote about my plan to visit the Maradi Hill the next day. And I concluded, as usual, on a personal note.

But there was no post office in that village, only a post box. On asking around, I learnt that a postman from Belur collected mail from it twice or thrice a week. But no one seemed to know where the post box was. I stepped outside, hoping one of the servants would know and that I could get him to post my letter. As I came out, I saw a young girl right across from my room, sitting on a stone bench and leaning against a pillar. I thought she could be my host's daughter. I stood there wondering what to do next; none of the servants were around.

'Is there anything I can do for you, buddhi?'[6] said that girl, coming up to me, 'Please tell me.'

She was smiling. I was touched by the naive warmth of that village girl.

'I have to mail this letter, amma,' I said, 'But I don't know where the post box is. Can you show me?'

She took a few steps towards me and said, laughing, 'Why should *you* take all that trouble, odeya? Give that letter to me. I'll go and post it for you.'

Just listening to her chatter was so pleasant, I felt like carrying on.

'But isn't that a bother?'

'*Ayyo*! What kind of a bother, buddhi? You're a great man.'

'Are you *sure* it's no trouble?'

'No, my odeya, give me that letter.' She put out both her hands.

'What's your name?' I asked, handing it over.

'Chenni,' she said shyly and walked away.

'Nice name,' I thought. She conversed easily too, with a naive poise. Her local dialect had a charming lilt to it. Her clear, wide eyes had sparkled with a child-like innocence. Everything about her struck an unknown chord somewhere deep inside me.

I caught a nap after lunch, and it was around four by the time I got up. I came outside my room to wash my face. And again, I saw the girl. She was right where I had first spotted her, sitting on that stone bench and leaning against the pillar. As soon as she

---

6   Term of respect; literally, the wise one.

saw me, she folded her stretched-out legs and began to tug at the loose threads of her sari. Her mind seemed to be somewhere else.

I needed water. There was no one else around. I had spoken to her only once that morning. And yet ...

'Chennamma, I need water to wash my face,' I said with easy familiarity.

'I'll get you, my odeya.' She scurried into the house, with her winsome smile.

I felt Chennamma had brought that guileless smile with her when she was born. Her innocent face beamed every time she saw me. I have often seen young girls smiling in towns. But those were tempestuous generally, like whirlwinds ready to uproot trees; roaring turbulent waves to create havoc in the heart. Chennamma's smile was different. It was like the gentle breeze gliding here and there, through fresh shoots and sprigs, bringing their soothing fragrance, setting up tiny ripples in the heart. While that whirlwind brought dust to the mouth and the eyes, a smile from this peasant girl was, oh! like a jasmine, so clean, so fragrant.

By the time I could sort out these thoughts, Chennamma came with the water. By the time I had a wash, she herself had brought me a cup of milk and some light refreshment. After breakfast, I set out with my flute and camera for a morning stroll. Chennamma sat at her usual place.

After walking some distance, I wondered which way I should head. I remembered hearing that there was an orchard behind the house. I decided to go there but I did not know the way. Wondering what to do, I thought I would ask Chennamma.

'Chennamma, there's a garden somewhere here, isn't there? I'd like to see it but I don't know the way. Can you guide me?'

The Girl I Killed

'Surely, my odeya,' she said, and taking me to the backyard of the house, pointed to a pathway, saying, 'That's the way to our orchard, ayya.'

'I'll go that way, then,' I said and walked on. I had barely gone a few feet when the edge of my dhothi got caught in the fence around the vegetable patch. I turned back to release it delicately. There was Chennamma, standing exactly where I had left her. I wondered if she was worried that I may lose my way.

Beyond a hundred yards was the orchard, a beautiful grove, mainly with areca and coconut palms and a few fruit trees. The golden glow of the setting sun heightened the natural beauty a hundredfold. Even as I ambled on, I came to a wide well with a pulley on one side. On the other, were steps leading right down to the water. Right around was a stone wall, some two feet high. I sat on that low tank bund to savour the ambience.

3

Drunk with the beauty of natural splendour, my spirit felt an indescribable happiness, a state of bliss. The cool of the grove mingled with the breeze as it wafted in waves towards me. All around the tank were flowering trees. Their fragrance too added to my sense of euphoria. I could hear a variety of birdsong from the sky, from the trees and even the bushes. My heart became a bird with the birds, a bloom with the flowers. Why do poets describe a heaven we have not seen? Heaven is wherever there is such contentment, I felt. My heart was filled to overflowing with joy. With that surge, I began to play the flute. Each note burst into a hundred and embraced the orchard. My heart filled with my own melody. I played a few keerthanes,[7] and then, burst into song. Confident that I was all alone, I sang the lyrics as I pleased. Suddenly I heard a sound behind me, gulu, gulu. I stopped singing and looked back. It was that girl, Chenni; she had gone down the steps and was filling a pot with water.

Even as I was staring her way, she lifted her head to look at me. I was greatly embarrassed; these people held me in high esteem as a cultured city-bred, and here I was like a cowherd, playing my flute and screaming away as I pleased! With my back towards the steps, I had not seen her coming. I had not even heard the tinkle of her bangles or her anklets, as I was engrossed in my singing. I felt sheepish. For a moment, I said, 'So what?' to myself. But that was fleeting; it did not pacify me. I placed the flute by my side and took up the camera, pretending to peer through it. I guessed she was coming up the steps with the heavy pot. I could not hear her footsteps once she had climbed all the steps. Instead, I heard the jingle of her bangles. I was embarrassed to see her and yet, I turned and looked up. She had filled two shiny brass pots with water, climbed all those steps with them and was placing them on the wall around the well. That was the moment I saw her; right before the smile at my singing had left her face. I felt ashamed of myself. I turned away and stood up.

I felt she was saying something. I had not paid attention, being too caught up in my own confusion.

'What did you say, amma?' I asked, turning towards her.

'Why did you stop singing, my odeya?'

---

7   Devotional songs

The Girl I Killed

God alone knows how awkward I felt at that moment. I was tongue-tied.

'Aah—ohh ...' I mumbled as I pulled up a blade of grass and pretended to chew on it. 'The song was over.'

Though the question sounded like a ridicule, I was not angry. Why should I be? I *had* done something stupid, hadn't I? And her question may have sounded sarcastic to my frame of mind at that moment. But such scorn was surely beyond that guileless village girl, smiling at me. Anyway, what was done was done. I stood up and, gathering my flute and my camera, I took a few steps.

'My odeya,' she called out.

I turned, wondering why she was calling me. She was lifting one of the pots of water on to her head. The other was on that wall's well.

'Buddhi, will you just help me lift this one?' she asked, shy and hesitant, on seeing me turn towards her.

'Sure!' I said, and putting down the flute and the camera, I lifted the pot and placed it on her waist. This little help may have seemed huge to her. She was beaming. As she walked away, her youthful body swaying gracefully with the weight of the two pots added to the charm of the golden haze of the setting sun. I felt a sudden impulse to take her picture.

'Chennamma!' I called out, adjusting the camera. It did not even occur to me to wonder what she would think.

'Did you call me, odeya?' She turned carefully, weighed down with the weight.

'Huhn! Will you just stand right there for a moment?'

Her surprise showed on her face as she turned towards the fading sunlight; her artless smile mingling with the fading golden rays.

'Now, you can go,' I said, after clicking a photo.

'What did you do, buddhi?' she asked, curious. How was I to explain in a way that she could understand?

'I'll tell you tomorrow.'

She turned around carefully and walked towards the house, slowly.

4

That night after dinner, I went to my room and lay on my bed. I could not sleep. The experience at the well that evening was still on my mind. I giggled to myself, 'What will Lakshmi say when I tell her about this ... she'll laugh helplessly.' Even I laughed helplessly.

It must have been quite late by the time I could wind down and get to sleep; it was past eight when I woke up the next morning. I had a quick wash, hurried through breakfast and got ready to head towards the Maradi Hill. My host sent a servant with me. He carried my equipment as we set out. It was around midday by the time I was done with Rangappa Temple.

On our way back, the path cut through a meadow where cattle were grazing. Farmers were working in the paddy field beyond. Suddenly, the cowherd burst into a folk song. What had he to fear? He was singing with great aplomb. He sounded funny. I wanted to stop and watch him. But the servant was there with me. What if he laughed? I felt embarrassed. Also, my experience at the well the previous evening was still fresh in my mind. So, I did not stop.

The Girl I Killed

The train of memory led me to Chennamma. Her winsome smile, typical of a village girl, danced in front of me. Her graceful stance as she had stood deftly balancing two dazzling brass pots of water was imprinted on my eyes. I presumed that she was my host, Kariyappa's daughter. I knew nothing else about her. Suddenly, I was curious to know more.

'Who's that young girl in your master's house, ayya?' I asked the servant.

'Which young girl, buddhi?' He had stopped to stare at me. He did not know which girl I was referring to, perhaps.

'That girl ... called Chennamma.'

He was still staring at me. He laughed a little when he asked, 'Why, buddhi?'

I felt insulted; I was also embarrassed. He seemed to have misinterpreted my interest in that girl. But how was this idiot to know that my Lakshmi was everything to me? He had sounded sarcastic when he said, 'Why, buddhi?'

'For no reason, ayya,' I retorted, 'Why? Shouldn't I have asked?'

'Ayyo, why not, buddhi? ... Yes, she's the yajamana's[8] daughter.'

There was another question at the tip of my tongue. But I held it back. This man had laughed when I had asked who she was. How would he respond if I said, 'Is she married?' I kept quiet.

On reaching home, I had a bath and lunch and then made some three to four copies of the photo of Chennamma that I had taken the previous day. It had come out beautifully. The whole family was happy to see it.

---

8   Master

AJAMPURA SITARAM (ANANDA)

Lunch had been late, and so, I was not hungry for dinner. I told the family that I would not be eating. I was not sleepy either. I did not know how else to while away my time and so, I stepped out for a walk. It was nine by the time I returned. I was still not sleepy. Lighting the lamp, I spread out my bed, and lay down with a novel. I may have read for about ten minutes when I felt the door rattle. Thinking that it must have been the wind, I went back to the book. Now, I heard a gentle tapping.

'Who's that?' I said, still lying down. No reply. Again, after a few moments, there was the tapping.

'Who's that?' I repeated, sitting up. I heard the tinkle of bangles. And Chenni's soft voice.

'It's me.'

I was shocked. What would she have to do with me at this time of the night? Whatever. It was best to find out.

'What, amma?' I asked, opening the door wide enough to put out my head. The light from my room was shining on her, hazily. In her hand was a plate with a few bananas, some sugar candy and a cup of milk.

'Buddhi,' she said, in response to my question, 'You didn't have your dinner. And so, I brought you these, my odeya.'

Saying, 'That's nice of you, amma,' I took the plate from her and went towards the bed to lay it down. Chennamma came inside, right behind me. My heart missed a beat.

'I don't need anything else, amma. You may go now,' I said, placing the plate by my bed.

'Why, buddhi? Can't you eat in front of me?'

'Not that … Of course, I can eat. It's just that I don't need anything else. Also, it's not proper for you to be alone with me …'

Even before I could finish talking, she went to the door, shut and bolted it. Some sort of an inkling that was taking shape in my head as she came in seemed to get clearer. I shivered seeing her shut the door. I broke out in warm sweat. My face was glistening with it. My throat went dry; I swallowed hard.

'Why, why're you closing the d-door?' I said, stepping forward to open it. Chennamma darted across and stood in front of it, smiling. I felt my knees buckling. Now, there was no doubt. Her intention seemed to be etched across her chest.

'*She*? An innocent village girl?' I sighed to myself.

5

My knees could not support me any longer. I went back and sat on my bed, holding my head in my hands.

Here, before I go any further, I feel like talking about something else. So, listen, please.

The one who saved me from the snares of sin that night was Lakshmi. Her love was a fortress surrounding me. From the day we had become one, she had made me feel that what I could see in her, I would not see in anyone else. I never had to look elsewhere either for looks or character or love. And, being in my predicament, when I was feeling vulnerable without Lakshmi by my side, I still feel it would not have been surprising if I had taken advantage of that village belle that night.

I was quite young when that happened; I was sturdy. Though it is a bit awkward to describe my looks, I can surely say I was not ugly. And if I am to recreate that situation for you, it is proper to describe Chennamma too. She could not have been more than twenty, neither tall nor short. Dusky. Quite attractive, with the bloom of youth. I had always seen her smiling, always with a mischievous expression in her eyes. The smile and the twinkle blended to make her disarming. All I can say it that she had the assets to trap the unwary. Also, her very behaviour that night was far from being that of an innocent village girl.

As I sat on my bed, such thoughts churned through my brain as in an oil-press, singly at first and then, in tens and in hundreds. My mind seemed to drown in darkness. My throat and mouth went dry, and I found it hard to swallow. I had not dreamt that I had been arousing that young woman's passion. I was ready to take an oath at anytime, anywhere, that I had never encouraged her in any way. She was not all that innocent; she had shown me in many ways. Only, I had not seen through her guile. She must be crazy. Yes, crazy is the word. What if the family got to know? They treat me as an honoured guest from town. And now, at this time of the night, in *my* room, she and I together ... This was too much. I would lose their regard.

And the way she had come; creeping in stealthily. Isn't she married yet? I felt depressed. I began to see everything she had done in a new light. Why had she crept behind me when I was strolling through the estate? And that incident at the well? That must have been a ploy Why did she ask me to lift that pot and rest it on her waist? Let that be But when I was doing just that, she touched my hand while placing hers around the pot. I had thought it was accidental. And another image When she bent to lift the first pot to her head, the seragu[9] of her sari had slipped.

---

9   The upper end of the sari

The Girl I Killed

She showed no sign of embarrassment that I had seen her in that state. She placed the pot on her head and only then did she pull up the folds of her sari over her shoulder ... slowly. I had put it all down to the ways of a village girl; I never realized that they were but strands of the net she was casting to bait me.

I tried to still the confusion in my mind to think of a way out of this awkward situation as soon as I could. There was no point in getting angry with her. I was scared that it could only make matters worse. I had to get her out, somehow. But how? What should I say to her? Or should I just lie down and cover myself with the blanket, head to toe? That would not do. As long as she was with me, I would feel a huge boulder weighing me down. And then, a plan occurred to me; I felt that was the best way out. I would tell her, somehow, that what she was doing was not right. I would tell her that it was scandalous, that it was a sin. I would impress her mind with its depravity and cleverly send her away. I felt tickled; God seemed to have given me, a city-bred, an opportunity to preach about marital fidelity to this village girl.

I lifted my head and looked at Chennamma. She was still standing there, leaning against the door. Seeing me smile, she beamed. Fearing that she might take my smile as an encouragement, I swallowed and said, 'Chennamma?'

'What, my devare?[10] She took a few steps closer.

'Sit down.'

She sat right on my bed. I moved away, took a deep breath and began again.

'Chennamma.'

---

10 Term of respect; literally, God

'What is it, my odeya?'

Though her actions seemed brazen, I could sense that she sounded innocent.

'Chennamma, look. Can you do *this*?'

'Do what, buddhi?'

'Come like this, stealthily, in the middle of the night ...' I had not yet finished when she cut in.

'I haven't come secretly, devare.'

'Then?'

She did not reply.

'Look, if your family gets to know,' I explained, 'You'll lose your honour, and I'll lose the respect they have for me.'

'They won't say anything, devare.'

I was taken aback.

'What did you say ...?'

'They ... won't ... say ... anything, I said.'

'Look, whether they say anything or not ... I'm not willing to do this. I'm married, Chennamma. I wouldn't want to spoil another man's ...'

'Ayyo, buddhi! Why do you say that? I'm not married, my odeya! I'm a basavi.'[11]

'*Basavi*? ... *Basavi*. What's that?'

'I've been given to God.'

I had never seen anything like this; I had only heard about such a practice. But I had not understood what that implied. My initial fear vanished; I became curious. This was getting interesting. I wanted to know more about it.

---

11   A girl dedicated to God

'Given to God? By whom?'
'My father and my mother.'
'Why did they do that?'
'Buddhi, when I was seven or eight, I was very ill. Then my parents vowed to the god in the temple near Maradi Hill that they would offer me to him if I got well. I got well, buddhi.'
'So ... won't you ever get married?'
'No, buddhi.'
'Will you live like this all your life?'
'Yes, odeya.'
'Like a whore?'

She might have felt a sword piercing her when I said this. In a moment, she was frowning, her nostrils and lips were quivering. Her fury made her look terrible; awesome. Piercing me with her penetrating stare, she said, 'Buddhi, you shouldn't say such things.'

I was bewildered by the sudden change in her.

'What did I say?' I said, swallowing spit anxiously.

'I'm not a whore. Understand that.'

I was confused. She was not married. Her behaviour was definitely improper. And yet she was 'not a prostitute'. My temper was rising.

'What else are you? Instead of getting married and living decently, you've come here ... to foist yourself on me ... in the middle of the night.'

'Buddhi, haven't you understood yet? Basavis can't marry, my odeya.'

'Why not?'

'Shouldn't they fulfil the vow, buddhi?'

'Can't you fulfil the vow by getting married?'

'No, my odeya. If we're married, how can we serve other men, like you? Is that respectful?'

'But why should you serve other men?'

'Then? Shouldn't we carry out our promise to God.'

'Is *this* the way? Whoring in his name?'

She frowned suddenly.

'Buddhi, don't say that to me. Don't ever say that ...' she stressed.

'Look, I'm not your husband. And yet you've come to me in the dead of night ... who else does such a thing? And yet you say you're not a whore.'

'We're not whores, buddhi, we're *not* whores. Whores do it for love of money. They don't mind sleeping with anyone. It's their profession, their living. They are not fulfilling any promise to any God.'

'And you?'

'We don't touch money, my odeya. We don't go about sleeping with just anyone. We only serve someone like you who may come as a guest. In satisfying you, we fulfil the vow our parents made on our behalf. Don't call us whores, my devare.'

'Then, do your parents know about your "service"?'

'Don't they, buddhi? They're the ones who made this vow. Wouldn't they know?'

'Fine, they *know*, and they've sent you. But how do they know if I'll consent to this or not? What courage did they have to send you to me?'

She did not respond immediately. Then, smiling, she cocked her head to a side and said, 'You asked our servant who I was, didn't you?'

Now I recalled asking their servant and him replying with a sardonic smile.

'Ayyo, bhagavantha!' I sighed. 'Yes, Chennamma,' I said to her, 'I did ask him. I was just curious, that's all. I vow on my Lakshmi's name that I had no other intentions.'

'Ayyo, forget about it, my devare. Why are you calling upon God for such a trivial thing.'

'It's not trivial, Chennamma. Listen. Can life come back once it goes?'

She was quiet.

'Tell me.'

'No, my odeya.'

'Then, tell me. For a woman, her respectability is her life. A woman who has lost her respect is worse than a bitch. It's all you women have—your honour. It is said that there's no place even in hell for women who've lost that worth.'

'Buddhi, all that you're saying applies to married women, my odeya. If they do what we're doing, they'll be ostracized. We're not like that, devare. We've been offered to God. For us, serving decent people like you is …'

'Ayyo, Chennamma! You don't know anything. Listen to me. Will God be pleased if a woman loses her honour in his name? If there's a vow to God, go and serve him. Who's to stop you? Why lose your self-respect, instead?'

'Buddhi, people like you are our God. We get punya when we serve people like you.'

Hearing her say that, I groaned to myself, 'Ayyo, devare! What injustice! What sins! Committed in God's name! "To please God", she says!'

I could not speak. I sat thinking awhile ...

What ignorance in these people! Is there such a disgusting practice too in the world? Yes, people do offer their children to God; I've heard about it. It speaks of their devotion. But this? Is *this* the way people fulfil their vows? How can they do such a heinous thing in the holy name of God! What is the plight of women like her? This girl is truly an innocent village girl. She is not like the prostitutes. Their style is different. She is guileless, entrapped in this disgusting custom of her people. She truly believes that the vow of her parents is being fulfilled in what she is doing. Ayyo, deva! To think that her very parents are heaping her life with sin! What is their plight? What is hers?

They might believe that she is alive today because they have fulfilled their vow. But isn't the very essence of her womanhood dying, bit by bit? How will they ever see that? Instead of dying then, as a baby, in a split-second, she is dying now, little by little, day by day. Does she realize that? No, she doesn't! That's amazing! She firmly believes that she is right in what she is doing; that God is pleased with her service in return for preserving her life. As the dharma[12] of her life, she religiously does everything she considers sinful in married women. And her parents support her. But what can *they* do? They too are entangled in their tradition ...

My heart seemed ready to burst with such heart-rending thoughts. I sighed a deep sigh. Chennamma had been standing there, twisting the edge of her sari around her finger. She looked at me when she heard my sigh. Her face showed some uncertainty. She could have been married by now and lived as a happy

---

12 Rightness

housewife, like others. But instead ... to think that this innocent girl was a victim of some disgusting practice! I could not handle my grief. My eyes filled with tears.

'Chennamma, only your God must protect you,' I said, wiping my eyes. She must have been upset to see my tears. She came closer. I did not have the heart to move away. She was not sinning willingly. Only her body was a victim of the guilt; out of sheer ignorance. Just as a pure drop of dew glistens like a diamond on a lotus leaf, her heart was pure. I ached for her innocence. I ached for her life. My tears kept flowing. I wished I could wash her tainted body with my tears. I felt close to her in body and spirit. I reached out and held her hand; trembling. Without letting go, I caressed her fingers.

'Chennamma,' I said softly.

'What, my deva!' she responded, drawing closer. Her face looked clouded. What could she be thinking?

'Look, Chennamma,' I said, staring at her. 'You said I'm your God, didn't you?'

'Yes, my odeya, you're my God.'

'Then, you'll have to obey me, shouldn't you?'

'I'm your servant. Speak, my devare.'

'You shouldn't carry on in this sinful way, henceforth. Understand?'

'Then? The vow? To God?'

'Ayyo, forget about that vow! Today, you said I'm your God. Haven't you served anyone else before this?'

Chennamma did not speak. She lowered her head.

'Look, you've served many others before this. Today, you've come to serve me as your God. Can you give God someone else's leftovers? Isn't this a vow of scraps, of castoffs? This is sin. Chenna, you don't understand. If you did, you wouldn't live such a sinful life. Just think about it. What's the difference between you and a prostitute? This is her livelihood. You don't have to earn your living this way. The sin is the same, nevertheless. God will never accept this sinful offering.'

Chennamma listened to me in silence. The look of bewilderment and anxiety slipped away. She looked weary. She slouched a bit, staring at the floor.

'Chenna,' I whispered, shaking her hand gently. She looked up. Her eyes were like that of a child who had lost its way.

'Chenna, do I make sense?'

She did not speak. She bent her head and even as I watched, tears rolled down her cheeks. They became her silent response to my question. I had done my duty; I had cast away the ignorance that had shrouded her innocent soul.

If someone had covered a long distance, walking down a pathway, step by step, believing that with every step, he was getting closer to his destination, and if he met another on the way who told him that he was on the wrong route and that every step he took was taking him away from his journey's end, how would he feel? I may have made such an impression on Chennamma; more or less.

She broke down and sobbed. I comforted her, 'Look, Chenna, I'm not angry. I don't feel disgusted. Am I angry? Tell me.'

'No, odeya,' she whispered.

'Good, are you, in any way, angry with ...'

'Ayyo, devare! Don't say that. When I look at you, I feel like rolling about at your feet.' She held my feet and was about to touch her forehead to it. I stopped her.

'Good. Then put your hand on my head and swear. Say, "I will give up this vow."'

Chennamma laid her hand on my chest. Her innocent glance pierced my eyes and reached my heart. Her gaze, wounded … her voice, aching, trembling, she whispered, '*Deva* … in future … I'll never do this again.'

I sighed deeply, feeling a heavy load being lifted from my heart. It was quite late, and yet, I was not sleepy. A sense of tranquillity pervaded my mind.

Chennamma yawned.

'Chenna, go and sleep now,' I said, using that as an excuse. I stood. She got up too. I walked up to the door with her and opened it. I held her hand and turned her towards me, and saying, 'Chenna, Chenna, I swear in God's name that I'm not angry with you,' I held her face in both my hands and kissed her on her forehead.

Chennamma walked away.

6

I woke up suddenly, with a start. Kariyappa was in the room. It was he who had called out to me, rousing me. But how could he have come inside? I had not bolted the door, perhaps.

'What's it, yajamaanare?' I said, rubbing my eyes and sitting up.

'Ayyoyyo! What can I say, swami? Ayyo! My child, my Chenna!' He fell down and rolled about in agony. Some strange fear seemed to rip my heart in two, releasing a sudden gush of blood. Just then, someone else came in saying, 'Swami, Chennamma fell into the well …'

I could not wait until he finished whatever he was saying. I got up from my bed and rushed towards the well like a madman. I could see a crowd of some ten to twelve people.

Will she be alive? Ayyo, what a vain hope! She may have fallen in last night. Will she be alive until now?

In despair, I went and stood with them. They made way for me. I stepped closer and looked in. Ayyo, bhagavantha! What do I see? I felt my blood gushing to my eyes ... and darkness covering me.

That is all I remember. When I came to again, I saw some of the men sprinkling water on my face and head. Blood was dripping from my nose. Not bothering about myself, I darted towards the dead body and stared at it, hoping for any sign of life. Ayyo! What a delusion! 'You're a fool,' I said to myself. The pure speck of life that had been cloistered in her had flown away already. Her punya had separated her from her sinful life. Her immortal spirit had been drained away leaving only the dregs behind.

I could not stand there much longer. I walked back to my room. Slowly.

7

I left the village that very evening. Before leaving, I left Chennamma's photo in their house. But what comfort would they get from it, after losing such a daughter?

I was pensive all the way back. The police had recorded her death as suicide. But in truth, I felt I had killed her. I could not shake away the conviction, however much I tried. Everything I had said to her must have convinced her that her way of life was not worth living; that it was better to die. Now I felt her heart

The Girl I Killed

was filled with the thought of death even as I sent her away from my room. This very thought ripped my heart and poured hot lead into it. If only I had kept her back at that time of night, would her decision to die have wavered? Would she have lived? I was the one who had made her feel she should give up her life. There was no doubt about that. But what right did I have? Who am I to judge whether their age-old practice was dharma or adharma?[13] Every word that I had spoken must have pushed her towards the well, step by step. And, finally, they would have shoved her in.

Ayyo! I ... I have killed her with my own hands! I will have to explain myself to God someday. What will I say?

There is no way to halt my thoughts.

I shall be reaching my hometown tomorrow. I wonder what my Lakshmi will have to say when I narrate my story.

---

13 Unrighteousness

NANAJANGUDU THIRUMALAMBA

The Child, A Teacher

Long, long ago, there was a group of people who were not aware that they were human. They lived like animals in jungles, in caves, in hills and on mountains. They may be there even now. They were known as the Halakki tribe. They cooed and twittered to one another, like birds, and wandered about eating whatever they could find. They were meat-eaters, cannibals. They would lie in wait and pounce on anyone who came their way and kill them to eat them raw. They did not even know the difference between humans and animals. There was no room for any awareness of pain or loss. They would also venture towards the edge of the forests sometimes. But they did not stay longer than a day or two anywhere.

Subba was their leader. Everyone had to listen to him. Once, they were near a small village. Each man walked down a different pathway shouting, 'Halak … Halak'. One of the paths led right to the edge of a village. The man walked about and found himself

---

Originally published as 'Magu Kalisida Paata'.

amid a row of huts. In one of them, he saw a young girl with a baby at her breast. The baby was sleeping. Soon, the girl laid her baby in a cloth-swing-like cradle and went inside. The Halak who had been watching her stealthily, came forward and walked away with the baby, still asleep in its wrap. The mother came outside, saw the cradle swaying a little and went inside, presuming her baby was still in it.

In the jungle outside the village, the leader of the tribe awaited his men. Most of them returned empty-handed. Only one of them offered him a bundle. When the leader opened it, he was in for a delicious surprise. Inside the wrap was a tender baby. Their joy knew no bounds. Here was a celebratory meal.

'What a festive meal!' they said, thumping the man on the back.

The leader had to take the first bite, of course, be it the ear or nose or palm of a hand. The rest could take their turn only after him. And so, he took the little bundle of a baby and stared at it. The baby was cute. It was slowly waking to his touch. It opened its eyes. They were wide, blue-black and sparkling. He was fascinated; he kept staring at the chubby face. The baby too stared at his, all painted and scary. And the baby gurgled, instead of screaming in fright. The old man was astonished; this was so very different from the responses of his previous prey.

'Hey! What is this?' he murmured as he felt an unusual attraction.

The baby kept staring at him and laughed again, loudly this time. The man felt a strange kind of pain, a concern for another he had never ever felt before. He wanted to keep staring at the creature in his hands. He could not get enough of those clear, dazzling eyes, that bud of a nose and the laughing mouth. He had not only forgotten what he was supposed to be doing; he had even forgotten himself. Hardly aware of what he was doing, the man touched the baby's chin, slowly, gingerly. He felt a strange delight, a thrill coursing through his veins. The baby felt tickled; it laughed louder. That laughter seemed to be telling him something.

'What's this?' said Subba, unable to understand; unable to control a grief welling up. 'I'm feeling strange. *Abah*! What an infant! It's sharing so many mysteries through its laughter. *Abbabbah*! I can't! I'll be ruined if I eat it.' And turning towards the man who had brought the baby, he asked, '*Le*, from where did you bring this?'

'From one of those huts,' he responded.

'Was the baby alone?'

'No, the mother had just fed the baby. When she laid it in the cradle and went inside, I carried it away.'

The leader began to weep. 'The mother must be weeping for her baby. No wonder, I'm crying too. Ayya, go and put the baby right back where it was lying,' he said. And he touched the baby's chin with trembling fingers, saying, 'Go … go back to your mother.' Wrapping the baby in its swaddling cloth, he handed it over.

As the man neared the house with the bundle, he saw quite a crowd milling around. Creeping stealthily, he laid it carefully on a ledge and disappeared. The baby, who had been laughing all that while, began to bawl now. Everyone rushed towards the sound and they were surprised to see it. The mother hugged her baby and wept tears of joy.

After watching the scene stealthily, the man returned to his people and told them what he had seen. Subba, their leader, was trembling. So was his voice. He got his people to sit before him and he began to speak. His face had an unusual glow and also an indescribable pain as if some kind of a fear had gripped him. The others wondered while listening to him: Why was their leader trembling? What could have happened to him?

'Have we ever trembled? Have we ever known water to flow unbidden from our eyes?' Subba asked them.

'Never! Never!'

'Look, there was a time when you brought an old man. You haven't forgotten him, have you?'

'We remember! He had a string hanging from a shoulder.'

'Ayyo! Whatever he told us that day has come true. "Can you do *this*? Being human?" he had said. And then he had moaned, "Oh God! Where's your compassion?" How I wish our hands had become limp that day! That our eyes had dimmed! But see what we've been doing … all that we shouldn't be doing! I could hear every word he said in the laughter of that child. As if the child was amused, as if it had whispered, "*Le*, you're human, are you?"'

'Yes, my people, we've done wrong; a great wrong. That day, when that old man called out to Him, God didn't come. But today, He came to us in the form of this baby. Now we know that we must have fear. And also, fellow feeling. We too are human. Can we eat our own kind? No, not anymore. Enough of this way of life! From now on, let's not take another life. Let's eat what we can get; let's starve when we don't. Only, let's not kill anyone for food any more. You can go anywhere you please. If you want to be with me, you'll have to be like me.' And the leader walked away.

Everyone walked behind him, in silence.

SRINIVASA KULAKARNI

A New Tongue

MOST MEN ARE strict with their wives; fearing that they may lose their hold on them if they were indulged. Some are even worse. They are short-tempered. They stop talking to them. They pick up a fight for any or no reason. Some even beat them up as they would thrash their cattle. How unfair! Don't they have a heart? Are they human?

I don't speak roughly to my wife. I treat her like a flower, placing her on my head. What a slender body, tender mind, pleasing face and such wide innocent eyes that can be forgiven any fault! She is like the image of a goddess. How can I bring myself to beat her? This pair of human hands can never descend to that. This is what I used to keep telling myself.

But the other day, I asked her about something. She replied indifferently. I stiffened. She made a face. And then we argued a little. No, not a little; quite a bit. I even resorted to the ritual of wife-beating. We stopped talking. Now, if I stop at this, you may

---

First published as 'Hosabaayi' in *Sampige*, in 1933.

not get the whole picture. You may not be able to guess the real reasons or the person to be blamed. And so, I shall describe what transpired. I would like you to gauge the situation with a clear mind and an unbiased heart and pronounce your impartial judgement.

We were sitting together after dinner the other day, my wife and I, chatting about this and that; about nothing important, actually. We lived in a city many miles away from our hometown; just the two of us. None of our neighbours knew Kannada. And she did not know Marathi. And so, if she recalled anything about her family, she had to tell me; she had no one else. And so, she started, as usual, 'Pachi was like this, but Gundi was different. Chinni was good ...' I had heard it all, many times. How could I be interested in her incessant chatter? But I was happy that she was talking so freely. And so, I kept nodding. The talk veered, somehow, towards women and their singing. Then I said, 'Women have such melodious voices. But I've never heard you. Why don't you sing for me?'

'How can everyone's voice be musical? I don't know how to sing.'

'But you sang when we were made to play just after our wedding; tossing flowers at each other.'

'Amma had taught me those two lines and I sang them. And how? Hardly any tune, hardly any style! They made me sing, and so I sang.'

'Whatever you sang, it was music to my ears. Why don't you sing now because you have to sing it again for me?'

'I don't even remember it! It's been nearly four or five years.'

She did not seem willing to sing and so I said, 'Fine. Don't sing. Tell me my name, at least once.'

'I've told you your name, not once, but many times when I had to.'

'You said it then, of course. Who said you didn't? But both of us were too shy then—you to utter my name and I to hear it clearly. We don't have that problem now! Just say my name. What is it?

'Why're you pestering me like this? Have you forgotten your name? Or is it because you think I've forgotten it?'

'Why can't you just say it because I *want* you to?' I sounded irritated. But I don't think she noticed.

'I'll say it when the time comes again. I can't tell your name like this, without any reason.'

'Why're you making such a fuss? Will you tell me my name now or not?' I think I raised my voice a bit.

That is my nature. If I want something; I have to have it. So, I demanded it now. She may have been willing too. But perhaps because she wanted me to persuade her a little more, or because she thought she might be able to get away without granting my wish, or because she felt it was not proper to say her husband's name without reason, or because she thought I might laugh when she uttered my name, or because she wanted to be stubborn too, like me ... I'm not quite sure what was on her mind, but she just said, 'No,' firmly. This was the first time she had ever been so brusque with me. I felt uneasy; disgusted, angry. I got up, went to my room and sat on my chair with a book. This is how we spent some ten or fifteen minutes; I, here, on my chair with a book and she, there, on the floor with the oil lamp. And then, she came to me.

A New Tongue

'The clock just struck ten. Aren't you sleepy yet?' she asked, as if she had forgotten everything that had happened between us. I pretended to be engrossed in the book.

'Aren't you going to sleep at all?'

I did not respond.

'Have you decided not to talk to me?'

Still no response from me.

'If you act like a child for such a small thing, what am I to do?'

I felt like saying, 'Oh, yes! I'm acting like a spoilt child. And you? You're the lady of the house, I suppose.'

But I held my tongue.

'The fault is mine; as always. I'll say your name. Won't you turn this way?' She sounded penitent.

'Fine! Tell me,' I wanted to say. But I wanted to see how much farther I could push her. It was all I could do to control myself.

She stood there, staring at me, waiting to see if I'd relent.

'Fine! You'll have to read this way, then,' she said, turning off the light. She sounded mischievous. After a moment or two, she turned it on. She was about to smile with the glint of love in her eyes but she straightened her expression when she saw me sitting still, stern-faced.

'So, shall I go? Won't you talk to me, ever?' I turned my eyes towards her. She seemed to have no intention to leave. Instead, she came towards me saying, 'I'll tell you your name. Can't you talk to me even after I've accepted that I'm wrong?' The tassels on the edge of her sari touched the chair on which I was seated. She trembled suddenly, saying, 'Where's that blessed puppy?' It was sleeping on the table, right behind the book in my hand.

'*Thu*, that disgusting dog,' she said. I could not help laughing.

'I don't know how you can laugh. Now, I'm unclean, I'll have to bathe again. But what shall I do? I don't have another sari to change into. I've asked you for a thin sari, countless times. But … Now, what shall I wear?' She sounded worried, anxious.

'Enough, enough! You don't have to blame it on madi[1] to ask for another sari. All those rituals of clean and unclean are for the elderly. You'll be only sixteen the next full-moon day.'

'I should've been an outcaste. Then, it wouldn't have mattered.'

'The dog was on the table. If the edge of your sari touches the chair on which I'm sitting, how can you become unclean?'

'But you're resting your legs on the table, aren't you?'

A dog could be dirty, true. Who knows where it may stray and what it may eat? It could also be home to countless fleas. But our puppy is not even a month old. It has barely weaned and we are giving it only milk. And besides, I had just given it a bath that morning. It looked white and fluffy, adorable. Looking at it, I felt a gush of love, like towards a newborn. It was dozing towards one edge of the table while I had my feet on a strip of wood just below the tabletop. And the edge of her sari touched the chair I was sitting on. Could she be polluted? Could pollution zip through from the 'unclean' puppy to my 'clean' wife? Is it electricity? No, it must be something stronger; electricity cannot pass through wood.

I tried telling her but it did not work; she argued that she was unclean.

'Fine. You're going to have a bath and change your sari tomorrow, anyway.'

---

1   Ritual purity

A New Tongue

'No, I must have a bath now,' she insisted. I let her be. Wrapping the puppy and placing it in its corner of the room, I stretched out on the bed with my book. She came close to me after a while. The edge of her sari was wet!

I sat up and stared at her, wide-eyed, furious. It was the monsoon season with its non-stop rain. She was quite delicate, always sniffling with a cold or heavy with a headache. She had been coughing for the past week. Not a casual clearing of the throat; it was the hacking kind that ended in throwing up. Added to that, she was also with child; three months pregnant. We lived in a distant city, just the two of us; away from family, among strangers, with none to call our own. And now, with her crazy obsession with madi, she was going to sleep through the night in that damp sari.

As I had said before, I was furious. I raised my hand. I intended to slap her gently. But whether it was because she turned her head at that very moment or whether I put more power into my hand than I intended or whether my hand had more power than I realised, the slap left five deep red finger-marks on her cheek. Now, I don't have to tell you that her tears flowed like water from the overflowing Kannambadi Dam across the river Kaveri, near Mysore. It took me the whole night to pacify her.

So, this is what happened. I have put the case before you without taking sides. Even if you were to take a statement from my opponent, I am sure it would not be anything different. I just wanted to hear her uttering my name, and so, I asked her. If only she had gone with the flow of the mood of that moment, would it have led to this? Our first fight?

You be the judge.

Vishu is my nephew, my elder brother's son. He is a little over a year old and we are getting him used to semi-solids.

'How was the porridge, Vishu?' I asked him.

'*Seeee*,'[2] he babbled.

'And how was the chutney I gave you with it?'

'*Seeeee* ...' he gurgled.

That does not mean that everything tastes sweet; that I add jaggery to the chutney instead of a green chilli or two. But that is the way of children. To them, everything is sweet. Truly, babies are naive yogis. Their liberated souls possess an inner harmony, as yet untouched by earthly strife. Everything in life is pleasurable for them.

I must have lost that grace, like anyone else. I too must have longed for it, like anyone else. Amma used to say that I had a craving for jaggery; that wherever else I may have been playing about, I would be home right when she pulled out those balls of jaggery from the tin. It was quite a job for her to find ways of keeping it out of my reach. With my longing for sweet dishes, I would keep pestering her, 'When are we celebrating Navarathri,[3] amma?'

If I say I have not changed much even now, you may laugh at me. In those days, I used to ask for sweetness. Now, I long for it in my heart, secretly. I still have a weakness for jaggery. The stuff I buy for a week gets over within two or three days. It is impossible to be without it. And it is also difficult to afford to buy it more

---

2 Sweet
3 Annual nine-day festival to honour the Goddess Durga

frequently. And so, I have decided to buy only one small block of jaggery per day.

Then, though I have such a sweet tooth, why is it that I cannot eat more than two or three of those steamed sweet pastries, stuffed with jaggery and scraped coconut? I have to peck at some savoury pickle or, at least, chew a bite of green chillies or drink some spicy rasam before I can savour a few more. Then, I can enjoy some four to six more.

Similarly ... My wife and I had lived in harmony, taking our love for granted. We had never quarrelled. Until now, that is. Now, that peace was shattered. I was scared that we had lost each other. But thank God, that was not what happened.

... 'Guess now who holds thee?'—'Death,' I said. But there, The silver answer rang ... 'Not Death, but Love.'

So writes Shrimathi Elizabeth Barrett Browning at the end of a sonnet. So it was with us. The misunderstanding that had come between us like an enemy tearing us asunder, actually soothed us, giving us a new tongue, a new voice to heal the rift.

Since then, I feel a strange tenderness welling up every time I see her. Is it a new kind of attraction? A new love? A new desire? I don't know. But every moment without her seems like an age. You may dump that feeling as poetic exaggeration. But I know it isn't.

The very next day after our quarrel, I bought her the thin voile sari she had been asking for. I also bought a brocade material for a blouse and got it stitched. She wore them as soon as I handed her the parcel.

'*Le*, you didn't keep the new clothes in front of God's image. You didn't even smear a pinch of kumkuma[4] on them. But you've worn them already!' I was stunned.

'I've worn my new clothes, yes. Now I'll offer them to God,' she said. She had me mystified.

I just kept staring at her, in a daze ... at her blossoming body, preparing to bring a new life into the world, at the sparkling gold ornaments that adorned her like a goddess, at the innocent flush of contentment on her face, at the new rose-tinted sari and the gold blouse that barely fitted her.

She stood awhile and then, smiled. I giggled like an idiot. She ran towards me and fell into my arms.

'My offering to my God,' she said.

---

4   Vermilion powder

KADENGODLU SHANKARABHATTA

My Alarm Clock

You know an alarm clock, don't you? You have only to set the needles to the time when you want it to ring, and wind it, and it will go off on the dot, waking your every nerve with its jangle. If every home had an alarm clock, we would not need to depend on the sun and the moon. Whether they rise or set, whether cyclic time spins or it does not; the alarm clock will keep us going!

The alarm clock that I am talking about is not sold in stores. One gets it only as the fruit of punya from many births. And only a few can achieve such merit, can't they? Though the metal clock has the amazing strength to make such noise, it can do it only at our will—we are in control. But there is another that can go off any time it pleases. It is called a wife! A wife like my Venkamma. How many such women can there be in this world?

Published first in 1934 as 'Hodeyuva Gadiyaara'. From the anthology *Hindhina Kathegalu*, U.R. Shenoy and Sons, Mangaluru.

When we were just married, I used to wonder, at times, if God had given her the gift of speech at all. She was still a young girl and I would take advantage of those fleeting moments when we could be on our own, caress her chin and in a voice oozing with love, murmur, 'What? Won't you talk to me ever?' And she would turn away like a dumb animal.

Then as the children came, her ability to speak rose. As their numbers grew, so did the sound of her voice. As they grew up, she did all the talking. And I became dumb. It became quite a problem to listen to her constantly and yet preserve my ability to hear. Sometimes, when Venkamma was furious, even the cows in the barn would become restless. Every created being seemed to want to run away from her hollering. But I was not an independent being. So, how could I run away from her? And where could I run to? I would feel disgusted, persecuted, or at times, even furious. But I had not the courage to voice my fury. Even if I could, it is not in my nature to lose my temper. I practice ahimsa[1] in thought, word and deed. And so, I resorted to humour; I retaliated by calling her an alarm clock.

It is natural for you to wonder: What reason would she have to flare up when I went about the house like an ascetic, observing silence? Those who know her ways would know. If I wake up early in the morning, here is her loving command: 'How crazy! It's misty and cold. Can't you stay in bed longer, nice and cosy?' Or, if I am still in bed: 'The sun is up and you are not! Are you Kumbakarna?'[2] Please note the insulting comparison. If I sit

---

1   Non-violence
2   Younger brother of Ravana, cursed by Brahma to sleep for six consecutive months in the year

quietly: 'Look at you! Staring like an owl!' Or if I walk into the kitchen offering help: 'Oho, your wife can't do anything on her own. This is your trick to boast later that you've got to see to everything, isn't it?' If I sit silently, sipping coffee: 'What? Is it too sweet? Or bitter?' If I do say that it is a bit too sweet or too light—'Oho, so your wife doesn't know how to make even coffee. Why don't you marry another?' I could keep on describing Venkamma's prattle but these few examples will do for this story. I was a deer caught in her net.

Venkamma has a fixation about observing the rituals of madi and mailige. Groceries from the store can enter the house only after a purificatory bath since they might have been touched by outcastes; or, at least, they have to be purified by sprinkling water and dried in the sun. And I, of course, being even more invaluable, cannot enter the house without a bath. And even then, I have to stand at quite a distance from the kitchen. And every month, after the three days of being defiled, when she enters the house after her bath on the fourth day, she virtually wages a war with every item in the house. Why? Because a person like me, who does not care much for the rules of rituals, may have 'polluted' them during those three days. She sweeps and swabs every nook and corner, even the storeroom and attic, scaring away bugs and cockroaches. I have even heard other women ridiculing my Venkamma, that she is crazy; going a bit too far. Whether she seems crazy or not to others, am I not blessed to see her living her beliefs? I can easily focus on her devotion to duty and overlook her idiosyncrasies, can't I? That is how I live with her; as one privileged.

There is an unspoken rule concerning domestic duties; there is one who gives orders and one who obeys. As a result of a cruel tradition among us Hindus, the husband gives orders and the wife follows them. And if they are unwilling to obey, chaos follows. But I have not allowed that to happen in my home. We have interchanged our responsibilities. She lays down the law and I follow them; this domestic rule helps me to survive. I eat the food she serves; and wear the clothes she puts out for the day. I am hungry when she decides; if she decides. If she decides that I am not; I am not. However volatile her temperament may be, I cannot deny that it has given me a large measure of self-control. As soon as I step out of the house, I go straight to the office. I have a great time with my friends. I enjoy my work. I do what pleases me. I am a free man; my own master, until, in the evening, I turn into the street leading to my house. By the time I step inside my home, I have total self-control. Isn't it my Venkamma who has taught me to balance these two natures so contradictory to each other? How strange! God has provided me with air and light to breathe and to grow, day by day, only to be able to earn a living. The rest is only through Venkamma's bounty. I believe that I must be devoted to her, laying my earnings at her feet to be blessed. If I do just that, I will not go hungry, ever. And if one can solve the problem of hunger, what other problems can there be?

Through God's grace, my Venkamma has always been healthy. I am proud that my alarm clock has a hundred-year guarantee. If ever the children are ill, they get well soon with her medication. Even those illnesses that planned to bother them might have run away, seeing her on the warpath. If I ever say, 'Narayana had a headache. The doctor has given him this medicine and has asked us not to give him a bath for two days,' she pours the medicine into the drain, gives him a bath and makes him drink a kashaya,[3] a concoction of some roots she boiled together.

'We should never fear illnesses,' is her belief. 'If we starve like cowards, won't the body become weak? Then, won't the illness step up its power to fight?' is her contention. She has no faith in doctors. If people do not fall ill, and if they do not buy medicines, how will doctors survive? So, doctors have to create patients by starving them, to weaken them to stay ill long enough for the doctors to make money. Since that is their profession, will they go against their professional etiquette? How could people like me argue against her theory?

Once, one of the ailments that persisted among the children tried its hand at their mother. One morning, as I was leaving for work, Venkamma said, 'I've got a headache.' I guessed that her head must be splitting if she herself had to tell me about it. The headache that could not be controlled with her medication of boiled pepper and ginger was possibly defeating her.

'Shall I get you some medicine from the doctor?'

'Medicine? Isn't it better to die in ritual purity than to drink some concoction made from meat and liquor?' she countered. Her expression seemed sympathetic towards the countless who had died, polluted by medication.

When I returned home that evening, there was no sound from my alarm clock. I trembled to see Venkamma stretched out on a mat.

---

3   Traditional medicine

'Don't barge in like that! Remove your clothes. Have a bath and then step inside. If you bring in all that dirt from outside, won't the God of the house be polluted?' she roared. Relieved at her command, I had a wash and stepped inside. When I touched her, she was burning.

'I'm going to the doctor. You have a fever.'

'His medicine won't help my fever. The other day, when Narayana had a fever, I had vowed to do a Satyanarayana puje. I haven't fulfilled that vow. It looks as though God is angry with me. Get that puje done. How else can God remind us to be faithful to Him?' said Venkamma.

When Venkamma believes that God heals us after enjoying our offerings of naivedya[4] and pocketing our money as dakshine,[5] who am I to question her faith? Perhaps God gives us ailments when He desires to eat. I could do this with spending about a quarter of the money towards the expenses than I would have spent on her treatment. Then, there would be relief in knowing that she was well and also benefit from the punya of having performed the puje.

The very next day, I arranged for the Satyanarayana puje. Mahalinga Sastry came home with a bunch of kusha[6] grass under his arm. He was eager to respect the wishes of an ardent devotee like Venkamma. It was around midnight by the time the puje concluded with the distribution of the prasada.[7] Venkamma sat right through the rituals, listening to the purohit while casting an

---

4 Offerings of eatables to a deity
5 Offerings of money to a deity
6 Sacred grass used in sacrificial rites
7 Consecrated food offered to God and then to devotees

eye on the food, now and then. Will he listen to me if I ask him not to give her any of the prasada? Would she? I thought I would try. The pujari may take pity on me and oblige, I thought.

'Sastrigale!' I said, with great respect, 'She has a high fever. She has also been delirious. Can she eat such rich food?'

'In which vedasashtra[8] is it written that we are not to eat the prasada? Haven't you performed this puje just so that she may be healed? How, then, can we receive its benefits if we don't eat the food blessed by God? You're a mature person and yet, you're talking like a non-believer. Let her eat just a mouthful, all her ailments will flee.'

My wife backed the purohit: 'He's crazy, Sastrigale! He just wants to drain all his hard-earned earnings towards the doctor. Everyone in town praises that Dr Vishweshwaraaya. And yet, when his son's throat was swollen so badly that he couldn't swallow even a sip of water, was it his medicine or the vow to go on a pilgrimage to Dharmastala that healed him?' There was nothing else I could do.

Venkamma ate the prasada, praying, 'Narayana ... Satyanarayana ... the omnipresent saviour of the world ... heal me by tomorrow.' She slurped a whole handful of panchamrutha[9] and lay down right there. I trembled. Even if I could grant that this medication was more effective, I felt such a generous dosage of milk, curds, ghee, honey and sugar was a bit too rich. But who would say so?

---

8   Scriptures ordained by the Vedas
9   A mixture of five ingredients, blessed and eaten

The next morning, I felt Venkamma's pulse as soon as I woke up. Not that I know much about the pulse, yet I could make out that it was beating faster. This meant that her fever was worse; her blood was racing faster. She was so feverish that if I had placed some grains of paddy on her palm, they would have popped. I was scared.

'How're you?' I said, shaking her gently.

'I'll get well. It'll take time. Sastry said that we won't see any difference for four days. Why should we doubt him?' But her voice was hardly a whisper.

'Don't be stubborn, Venkamma; at least not now. Don't they say children and sick people are alike? Just listen to me. I'll get the doctor.'

'What madness! Is your doctor better than Satyanarayana?'

'We've fulfilled our vow to God. But there's no improvement.'

'There's a time for everything. If God grants our wishes as soon as we fulfil our vows, won't He become a puppet in our hands? How will we value Him? If this doesn't work, we'll send an offering to Dharmastala, or ... to Thirupathi ...' She had already planned on appealing to the higher courts of God to curb not just her illness, but the pride of the doctors as well. Her faith was unquestionable, of course. Let that be. But I felt there was nothing wrong in sending for our doctor as well. Of course, he was not Satyanarayana, just plain Narayanaraya. He might not feed her tasty delicacies. But he could at least give her a small pill. He might not be able to give her a palmful of panchamrutha. Yet, he could give her a spoonful of some tonic. I would be satisfied with that. After the meal that Satynarayana had provided, it was impossible to attend the office. So, I went into my room to write a leave letter, leaving Venkamma alone in the hall.

My Alarm Clock

I had barely finished writing the letter and was stuffing it into an envelope when I heard an anguished scream, 'Appa, Appa! Amma has got up and is trying to run.'

I rushed in. Venkamma looked scary. She was standing wide-eyed, biting her lower lip ... shouting, 'Satyanarayana! Jagadeeshwara! You are my saviour ... my only friend ... I'll survive only with your prasada. Give it to me! Give me tons of it ... give me gallons of it! Sastrigale, please come here. Give me the prasada from Satyanarayana. If you don't, I will knock off all your thirty-two teeth.' She clenched her fist. Generally, I have no problem with her beliefs. But this was something totally different—difficult to describe. She was rolling her eyes while blinking. How was I to protect my Venkamma while protecting her illusions? My companion of twenty years? I felt helpless, weepy.

I had no illusions about the seriousness of her illness.

'Take care of Amma for a while ...' I said to my son, 'I'll be back soon. I'll take her into the room and bolt it. Be careful ... Don't let her out ... Sit here until I return.' And wiping my tears, I stepped out on to the street.

I returned with the doctor. I could hear her roaring even as we entered the veranda. Earlier, only the Sastri's teeth were in danger. Now, even Satyanarayana's seemed to be—if He has any. I opened the door and we stepped inside.

'Who's this?'

'No one else ... Only your husband, Venkamma ...'

'The stranger?'

'He's the doctor ...'

'Doctor? What's *he* doing here?'

'He's come to give some medicines ...'

'To whom?'

'To you, Venkamma ...'

'Is this monkey going to give medicines to Venkamma? Ha, ha, ha ... This monkey! My doctor is there.' She laughed at the doctor, smartly dressed in a suit. Even the doctor laughed. He had not removed his hat yet. So he may have looked like an actor in a street play, dressed as a monkey.

'Amma, you're not well ... You have fever. I'll have to examine you ... I'm a doctor. Please give me your wrist.'

'Idiot! Have you come here to touch a strange woman?' screamed my faithful wife. I felt tears streaming down my face. 'I've given my hand only to him,' she said, looking at me. 'Try to touch me if your teeth are strong enough.'

Even as she was talking, she dashed to the door suddenly. I stood in her way.

'Venkamma ... Venkamma ... listen to me. The doctor has come to give you medicines ... to save you.'

'He's one of those outcastes, a Holeya, a meat-eater. Why did you bring him in? Won't Satyanarayana run out of this house? Let Him run. I'll run behind Him and fall into the well to die, clean.' Her fixation with ritual purity seemed to assert itself over her physical weakness.

'Krishnayya, there's no need for me to examine her,' said the doctor, smiling. 'I can see that this is a sure case of delirium. It has reached her head. It cannot be healed until the fever comes down. I can give her some medicines to bring it down. But will she take them? You'll have to take care of her; see that she doesn't get up from her bed. Is that at all possible here? Take her to a hospital.

My Alarm Clock

You can never be sure with this type of an illness. Some have even survived after the pulse has stopped ... and some have gone after they seemed to have recovered.'

I wept like a child. Since my childhood, that was the only day ...

Venkamma's fury reached newer heights. She became violent; she seemed unhinged. By the time I could fetch the car to take her to the hospital, she was semi-conscious. I could hardly make sense of what she was muttering, 'Time ... Kaliyuga[10] ... ritual purity ... pollution ... God ... dharma ... right conduct ...' I could only presume that this pure being was mourning the pollution in the world in this corrupted Kaliyuga.

The doctor in the hospital examined her thoroughly before giving his verdict, 'What do you think would be the state of a wheel with a flat tyre? Her state is much like that. Her condition has been brought on by an imbalanced diet. And it is now a fire raging up a dry tree. Who can do anything now, Krishnarayare?'

I did not need anyone to advise me further. Venkamma's faith in her dharma was unwavering. In her bid to live up to it, she had never faltered in facing any opposition from this physical world and overcoming it. Though her ways were old-fashioned, her yogic detachment provided them with a righteous dignity. What didn't she do to assert her rule in our home? She fought with everyone, even me, her husband. Even when she opposed me, it was only because of her sense of righteous living, not to belittle me. How many women are there in the world with this kind of commitment?

---

10 The fourth, the worst and final stage of the world—according to Hindu Cosmology

Until this moment, I had been confused, like a demon without a fixed purpose. But now I decided to live like her, facing the world fearlessly even unto death. I did not want her to feel polluted with those doctors and nurses and ayahs touching her. I brought her home that very night. I cleaned the whole house, bathed and tied a madidhothi[11] around my waist. I spread a madi silk sheet on the bed and laid her on it gently.

Until then, she did not seem aware of anything around her. Suddenly, she seemed alert. She turned towards me and stared as if she had gone a long way from this polluted world ... disgusted with its ignorance about madi[12] and mailige ...[13] about being faithful to the diktats of religion. Something must have stirred in the depth of her being to see me bare-bodied, except for the silk dhothi. She may have been satisfied to see that I had followed her rituals of purity at least during the last moments of her fleeting life.

'Are you here?' she said, softly.

'Yes ...'

'Have you had a bath?'

'Yes ...'

'I'll be going. Give me some water from Ganga ...'

'Where're you going, Venkamma?' I began to weep.

'There ... to my God ...'

'Isn't the husband the wife's God, Venkamma?'

---

11   A length of silk cloth worn around the hips to cover the legs, after being made ritually clean
12   Ritual purity
13   Ritual pollution

My Alarm Clock

'True ... But which woman respects that? Which husband lives like one? It's easy to say such things ... But hard to live up to it ...'

True. We do speak of many beliefs but how many do we keep? As for my Venkamma ... she was different. Her deeds matched her words. She lived as my companion for twenty years and so, I know. How could she live in a world she could not tolerate?

'Someone's coming ...' She began muttering again, 'He's wearing only a madi-wrap around his waist. He's smeared the caste mark on his forehead ... the paste of rice flour and sandalwood with turmeric ... some spirits from heaven are calling me ... I must go ... Narayana ... is seven. See to his upanayana[14] ... Teach him the evening rituals ... the sandhyavandhane.'[15] Even her last words were instructions regarding our son's thread ceremony.

'I'll see to *every* single thing ...' I could barely speak, I was sobbing.

'Be ... safe ...' She gasped and breathed one last time heavily before becoming still.

'Venkamma! Venkamma! Where did you go, leaving me behind?' I wailed.

There was no response. My alarm clock did not go off; it was silent, the mechanism inside had snapped. As for me, I felt as if my whole world had suffered a heart attack.

Just a few days ago, I had this alarm clock ticking away. The house was a home in her presence with signs of life in every room. And everything went on like clockwork; smoothly, in an orderly manner. But now ... there is a silence, an emptiness.

---

14 Ceremony to initiate a Brahmin boy into spiritual responsibilities
15 Mandated morning and evening prayers

As soon as I return from work and step into the house, who is there to roar, *Get into the bathroom ... have a bath and come for tea?* Who will keep a watch over me with those commands, even if I yearn for them? There is not a creature who will care to talk to me that way. This house is empty; my mind is empty.

An emptiness talking to an emptiness.

KORADKAL SRINIVASARAO

The Master's Satyanarayana

H<small>E WAS BARELY</small> six years old. He was tired of walking over the village sheep-track strewn with stones and thorny plants. On his head was a banana shoot with its roots and all intact; a burden too heavy for him to carry. Whenever his neck hurt with the weight of his burden, he shifted it to his right shoulder and then on to his left shoulder and then under his right arm and then his left arm, holding it firmly. And then back again on his head. But the boy in a ragged shirt and loin cloth walked with determination towards his home as a poor man would if he had found a pot of coins. He was still about an hour's walk away and he was already exhausted. His forehead, neck and chest were bathed in sweat; his face was red and hot. And yet he could not bring himself to toss the sapling by the wayside. Not just that. He carried it carefully lest he should crush the delicate stalk by holding it too tight or drop and bend it

---

Published originally as 'Dhaniyara Satyanarayana' in 1938 in *Nandadeepa*, Kiriyara Prapancha, Udipi.

by holding it too loose. Would even a mother carry her new-born with such care?

'When will we reach home if you keep lagging behind this way?' His mother scolded him as she walked ahead. 'Can't you see the sun setting? I told you not to bring it. What karma are you fulfilling? Throw it away and walk ahead of me or else I'll drag it from you and toss it away, you wait and see.'

Couldn't she carry the load for him? She had enough of her own. The three-year-old in the crook of her left arm was old enough to be heavy but young enough to be carried. Her right arm felt as if wrenched from its socket with the weight of the bag, loaded with the things her mother had given her: four stale cucumbers, some other vegetables and some kesavu[1] tubers. She had gone to her poverty-stricken maternal home for a whole month of festivities and was returning to the poor man's home that was her own.

Fearing that Amma might carry out her threat, his four-year-old sister in a torn skirt and with thick kaajal blackening her eyelids stopped trailing behind her mother, took the sapling from Anna and carried it as he had done; on her head, then shoulders and then under her arms. She managed to soldier on for quite a distance before Anna took over, feeling better for the respite. And so, between them, the brother and sister somehow carried the banana shoot to the doorstep of their hut.

It was the shoot of the rasabaale variety of bananas. One of the plants in their Ajji's house had put forth a bunch, and she had stored it to ripen in time for her grandchildren's visit. But it had ripened a few days before her daughter could bring her children.

---

1   Stemless plant with edible tubers

The Master's Satyanarayana

It was after all, rasabaale, wasn't it? The bananas drop from the bunch as they ripen. Her son's children would not listen to her; they ate most of the fruit. And yet she had somehow managed to save four of them, hiding them in a pot. She even managed to give them all to her daughter's children; her son's children had eaten enough and more anyway. These children had only seen bunches of bananas hung in shops at fairs. They had never eaten any. All they got to eat at fairs were some savoury snacks like chakkuli and mandakki; their father, Thauda, could not afford to buy them anything else. And so, eating the slightly overripe bananas was like tasting amritha.[2] They sat beside their Ajji and asked her to tell them the story of the bananas.

'Last year, your maava[3] brought a sapling and planted it here,' she said, 'And this year it yielded a bunch. The bunch ripened a bit too soon; you were late in coming. Now that plant has sprouted four shoots. They will have a bunch each by next year. I'll send you one; a whole bunch of bananas.'

The brother and sister thought for a while.

'Why shouldn't we take a shoot and plant it in front of our house where we wash our faces?'

They were caught up with the idea for the next few days. Can anyone describe their joy when at last their maava was willing to give them a sapling to take home? And then we know what happened, don't we?

Boodha and Thukri reached home at last that night. They woke up early the next morning and pleaded with their father to plant

---

2   Nectar
3   Mother's brother

the sapling. Thauda was very poor; he was a daily-wage labourer on a farm. He lived with his family on the edge of Kotemane Nagappa's coconut plantation, in a thatched hut. His master had demanded a rent of six rupees before Thauda could even erect the walls and roof of that shack. And, of course, there were also the countless times when he had to toil without pay, to compensate for his master's bounty of letting him live on the land. If he had tried to grow any vegetable, they would have provided a feast for the wandering cattle belonging to the other wealthy families of his master. Could poor Thauda have the courage to say that the cattle should not be allowed to wander about that way? Or to drive them away, for that matter? He had to slog for those families to earn the two seers of rice to provide for his family, didn't he? And besides, could he ever survive under the onslaught of his master's displeasure? And so, Thauda did not plant anything. But now he had to plant the banana sapling because his children pestered him. Once he planted the shoot, he had to tend it too. Or else, how could he survive their weeping every time he entered his house? And so, he erected a strong fence with the wood scraped and saved for the fire. And only then did the children go in to have their gruel.

From that day onwards, the first thing Boodha and Tukri did even as they rubbed their eyes awake was to go out and see their banana plant. And who could keep count of the number of times they checked on it during the day? They could not sleep if they did not see how it was doing as they came home in the evening. Even as they watched it day by day and stood beneath it to check its height, the sapling grew into a sturdy banana plant. During the summer months, Boodha and Thukri could not fetch enough water from the tank to feed their plant. Who could measure the sweat that poured from their tender frames?

'Ayyo, the wind, the wind! What if our banana plant falls?' Boodha woke up one night and wept bitterly as summer made way with gusty winds for the early rains of the monsoon. Thauda had to go out and firm up the fence with fresh support and show his son that all was well before he could be pacified.

'Anna! Anna!' shouted Thukri as she jumped up and down excitedly beneath the banana plant one day. Boodha ran outside, and what did he see? Why, the tip of the banana flower was peeping out of the stem! As the days went by, the flower emerged, the sepals spread out and the flowers blossomed, row by row by row. Each flower put out a slim finger-like fruit. And each fruit filled out as a raw banana. Together with Boodha and Thukri, their little brother, Dhooma, too watched to see the bananas ripening. They promised to share the fruit with him. It was the plant they had brought from their Ajji's house, the one their father had planted and they had watered and watched over. They would be the ones who would share it among the family; there was a share for their Ajji too.

'Ai Thauda, where's the two rupees you owe me for the rent?' thundered the master, Nagappa, one day. 'Did you think that piece of land belongs to you?'

'Let the rains make way for summer, ayya, and I'll somehow save enough to pay you during the sugarcane season.' Thauda did not dare to raise his head to see his master's face.

'That's been the bane of your life,' grumbled the master, 'It's always, "Not now but later!" whenever I ask you. Fine, I'll wait until summer and see how you'll pay up.' And then, 'I saw the bunch of bananas on your plant when I was coming down that way. We're having a Satyanarayana puje this coming poornima[4] night. If you chop down the bunch tomorrow the bananas will ripen in time for the festivity. Bring it home on the full moon morning. Understand?'

Thauda was thunderstruck. What could he say? He was tongue-tied.

'What, did you hear what I said?' The master sounded ominous.

'The children have fondly watched over it, ayya. Perhaps they could have a few …' Thauda stammered.

'Rasabaale bananas for children!' The master flared up. 'Feed the God; He'll take care of your children. Satyanarayana! Do you want to keep some for your children before offering it to God? No wonder such utter poverty is the bane of your lives!' He became red in the face again.

Thauda came home. He whispered to his wife all that had happened.

'Ayyo, the children have sweated and watered it for a year now, dreaming of eating the fruit …' She broke down, unable to continue. Her throat tightened; she could not speak further.

---

4   Full moon

The Master's Satyanarayana

But what could they do? The bunch of bananas had to reach the master's porch by full-moon day. Thauda cut the cluster from the plant. The children danced with joy.

'Don't keep bothering me. Let's wait and see ...' he said to shut them up when they asked him probing questions. He shut up his own grief too as he wrapped the bunch in an old rag to keep the fruit warm enough to ripen. Every day, many times a day, the children peeped into the wrapped bundle to see if there was any sign of the bananas ripening.

Two days before the full-moon day, Boodha saw a yellowing banana through a tear in the rag. He ran to his father, overjoyed.

'No, it's not yet ready,' Thauda roared. 'If you keep peeping this way, I'll throw it into the garbage pit.' The children trembled at their father's fury and piped down.

On the morning of the full-moon day, the children went where the bunch of bananas was hung. It had disappeared! So had their father! The three children wept their hearts out. Deyyi, their mother, told them stories about a wild cat devouring the fruit. Nothing worked!

'Let that thieving cat die!' Little Dhooma cursed. But Boodha and Thukri were not convinced.

'Appa took it to the master's house,' confessed Deyyi at last. 'He wanted it for their Satyanarayana puje.'

'Does God eat bananas?' That was Boodha.

'Did God want all of them? Couldn't he give us some; at least one each,' Thukri argued.

'Let that be.' Their mother hoped to comfort them. 'Anyway, there are two or three more shoots coming up. One or two of them may soon give us fruits. Those will be all for you.' Deyyi went inside, unable to see their tear-stained faces.

The children sat on the platform in front of their hut, careworn as if a tragedy had befallen them.

After a while, Boodha jumped down with a sense of purpose.

'Thukri, come here,' he called out to his sister as he ran towards the place where the shoots of banana were thriving. Thukri ran after him. Boodha got hold of each sapling, twisting and wrenching it off the ground.

'Nnnnno need to plant these banana plants! Nnnno need for Satnaarana to eat them up!' Destroying every shred of the saplings, Boodha danced in their place to level the ground. Thukri danced with him.

What a frenzy! What a sight!

SARASWATHIBAI RAJAWADE (GIRIBALE)

The Battered Heart

1

Balabrahmachari Bhramananda Yogi has been murdered!

THE NEWS SPREAD like wildfire all around the town. People ran towards the matta[1] of the ascetic, shocked and eager to know how that could have happened. His disciples too were hurrying in the same direction, chanting the name of Hari, sweating with fear that some great calamity was about to fall upon the world. Some of them even wondered if their Guru could be working a miracle by disappearing. No one was convinced that the news was true, though they were rushing to find out the truth.

---

1   Monastery

First published as 'Aahatha Hridaya' in 1938 in *Giribaleyasannakathegalu.*

How well-known he was as a yogi! How could *he* have been murdered? Anyway, true or not true, the matter would be sorted out. And so, the people were hastening towards the monastery.

When they reached the matta, a crowd was already at the door. People who generally folded their umbrellas, stuffed their shawls under their arms and held their slippers in their hands out of respect whenever they passed the vihara, the residential quarters of the monastery; outcastes who would never have been seen in the vicinity and even those who would think twice before driving their cars down that street—all of them were in front of the matta that day, forgetting caste differences; wearing different kinds of clothing. There were also some three or four cars parked right at the entry passage. The people were so caught up in the tension of the moment that they dropped cigarette butts and spat red betel juice right where they were standing, unaware that they were in the precincts of the ashram.

All they wanted to know was: had the Yogi really been murdered? And if he was, they wanted to rush in for a glimpse of the body. They did not mind being caught in the stampede.

2

Suddenly, they heard a loud, commanding voice, 'Make way! Make way! Move!' They turned to look, shocked. The Superintendent of Police was striding in, pushing his way through the crowd.

For a moment, there was pin-drop silence. He ordered his squad of policemen to disperse the crowd around the corpse; both the

The Battered Heart

disciples and the devotees. And then, as he removed the kaavi[2] cloth spread over the Yogi, his hands trembled.

There were some four to six stab wounds on the chest, some of them quite deep. A deep slash marked his right hand. The khadi cloth covering the body was like cardboard, caked with dry blood. The face looked scary, quite disgusting, in fact.

The police officer looked around. Everyone looked nervous. He scribbled something in his notebook, and then, looking up, he said, 'I need some information regarding the administration of this matta.'

'I live here, mahaswami.' The Administrator stepped forward.

'When do you think this could have happened?'

'We got to know of it at seven this morning.'

'Didn't you know of the murder earlier?'

'No, swami.'

'Didn't you look for him? Even when you didn't see him until seven?'

'No. That's because he is used to sleeping beyond seven whenever he was not well.'

'Who got to know about this first?'

'Puttanna Shanbhagaru, Swami. He's right here.'

'Oho, Puttanna Shanbhag[3]! Why did you want to see the Yogi this morning?'

Tears flowed down the Shanbhag's cheeks. He began to tremble.

---

2 Cloth dyed in red-ochre, the traditional Hindu colour signifying renunciation
3 Village Accountant

'Mahaswami, I'm a poor man,' he said hoarsely, 'I know nothing about this. When I went in, as usual, to wake the Guru, he was not in his room. I felt bad. "*Che*, I must be late," I thought, "What a shame! He may have got up and gone outside to relieve himself." I just stood there for a while.'

'Didn't you suspect anything until you saw him this way?'

'I'll swear by the feet of God, mahaswami! I had never thought, not even in my dreams, that such a thing could happen in this matta. In this very matta, where the very seat of the Divine is set! And that too, the murder of the head our Mattaadhipathi. I'm bewildered.'

'Stop the drama! All I need are straight answers to my questions. So, you didn't suspect anything when you didn't find him in his room?'

'Ayyo! I don't suspect anything even now. I still feel this is some kind of a maya. Just an illusion.'

'When you didn't see him in his usual place, what did you do?'

'I told you already that I stood there stunned, didn't I? And then, I ran to the orchard by the stream.'

'And then?'

'He wasn't there. I ran to the tulsi[4] garden. There ...'

'And there you saw. What did you do immediately?'

'*Ayyo*! What a question! All my five senses left me! I couldn't trust my eyes. I stood ... stunned. I felt giddy ... I screamed!'

'And then?'

---

4   Sacred basil, used in worship both at home and in temples

'And then, people from inside the vihara[5] came rushing. And then, we carried the body inside.'

'Describe the body.'

'Just as it is lying here. But the legs were spread out.'

'Show me that spot,' said the Superintendent, moving ahead. He asked a few policemen to follow him and ordered the rest to keep watch over the body.

He went to the grounds, scrutinized the spot and took down notes. He questioned the Shanbhag and others and wrote down something. And then he looked around the grove. Areca, coconut, mango and other trees were abundant in the distance. Closer, in the garden, were a few flowering plants and plenty of tulsi amid lush green grass that had been flattened in spots by footsteps. Puttanna Shanbhag and some others said the body was on the spot where the grass was stained. The Inspector returned to the body once his job was done at the spot and resumed his interrogation.

3

'After moving the body to this place, did you ask around to get any details?'

'We didn't know what to do, Swami. We sent men to the police station. And the news spread all over town. You've seen the crowd and the noise they were making. But no one could make sense of what has happened.'

'Any ... enemies?'

---

5   A temple with living quarters for monks and nuns.

'Swami, what do *you* know about our Yogi? Don't take me amiss. He? Enemies! You can ask these people what they think of our Yogi. People from different faiths, people from different castes, all of them praise him with one voice. *This* ascetic! Enemies?'

'Even so ... Couldn't he have had some secret enemies? Can't there be some paapa with his punya? Some weakness? Can anyone of you say, "It *could* be this way?" Can't you speculate? That would help us with the investigation.'

'We won't be able to suspect him even if we sit for years trying to guess, Swami. He was such a man. He was so compassionate, the very image of dharma. Who would have had the courage to murder him? And why?'

'So, could the Yogi himself have taken his life, in a spirit of detachment?'

'Shanthampaapam![6] Even the common man knows that suicide is a sin. And he was a wellspring of wisdom! An incarnation of God himself! Would he have thoughts of suicide even in his dreams?'

'Impossible! Impossible!' shouted the others.

'Anyway, someone must be responsible. From what I've gathered from all of you, it seems as if the Yogi wasn't murdered.'

'It *is* very strange. We can't figure out anything. More than everything else, how can anyone even enter the matta?'

'Why can't it be one of the inmates?'

Everyone paled as soon as they heard that!

---

6   Literally, 'God forbid!'

'We're Hindus, swami. We don't have any chandalas[7] who would indulge in such guru-dhroha.[8] Who would be so irreverent towards his Guru?' Many voices in the crowd exclaimed.

'Okay, line up all those who were in the matta yesterday.'

There was some commotion among the crowd when they heard the command. Finally, some ten or twenty men struggled forward, whispering prayers to their forefathers.

The police officer questioned each of them, taking down notes. And then, looking a little lost, he sighed, 'A case, indeed, to teach a lesson for a lifetime!'

4

People were still trying to get in, trying to edge past those who were already inside. The police were threatening them, but to no avail. Finally, the Superintendent stood at the threshold and thundered, 'The Yogi has died from stab wounds.' A fresh fount of speculations erupted in their agitated minds.

The whole town was drowned in grief. The poor who had benefitted from his bounty were sad that their benefactor had met with such a gory end. The sorrow of his disciples and other dependants was beyond description. Not just those who had relied on his help, but even those who would come to him to be cured and had been healed, most wondrously. Their sighs warmed the very air.

There was no beginning, and no end to their curses directed at the murderer. They speculated on the gravity of the other crimes he

---

7   Outcaste
8   Treachery against the teacher

must have committed that would have led him to take such a life at last. What an ultimate insult to the yogi who had observed every divine precept religiously, who had nipped the budding shoots of agnosticism and was propagating dharma, not only through his sermons but through his actions as well. All of them were sure of at least one thing: this heinous crime was surely a sign that the end of Kaliyuga[9] was not very far away.

Even children wept, 'Amma, isn't he there? The man who used to give us two spoons of thirtha?'[10] It seemed as if the goddess of joy, who used to traipse about the town, was hiding in some corner.

While the people of the town spent time seeking some sense from their conjectures, the policemen who were patrolling around the corpse and their boss focussed on only one issue: What next?

They felt helpless.

Suddenly, the Superintendent said, 'Without any objection, you'll have to give me permission to check *every* corner of the matta.'

Those in charge obliged; even guided him towards every nook and corner.

And the only place left was the pedestal on which stood the idol.

'Last night, there was the puje to worship the idol, wasn't there?'

'Then? Of course! That's the rule.'

'The jewels on the icon have been left untouched! How strange! I can't see any reason for this murder!'

---

9   The fourth, final and worst age of the world
10 Sanctified water

'There's going to be a huge calamity in the *region*. This is a bad omen, just an indication. But ...'

Suddenly, the sound of a woman's laughter! What a surprise! A shock! No one could believe their ears.

'Catch her!' The Superintendent ordered.

5

She laughed even more. She sounded drunk.

'No need to catch me! If I'd been scared of being caught, I wouldn't've appeared before you. The satisfaction of capturing me is not written on your forehead. Ha, ha, ha!'

The crowd stood stupefied, their grief mingled with curiosity, wondering what would happen now, when the Administrator of the matta darted towards her like an arrow and slapped her.

'You cruel man! I'm heady with the blood of your Guru, the moment has come for me to drink yours as well! Here!'

With that, she pulled out a blood-stained knife from the folds of her clothes. Immediately, someone stood in her way. She was gasping. Her eyes were blood shot.

The police bound the Administrator.

'Are you done, Saheb-sir?' she yelled, 'Have you seen the matta? Are you satisfied? I don't want to trouble you any further. *I'm* the one who killed this godly Balabrahmachari. I! I alone! I, Sita! I confess. Please believe me! I won't run away. I have nowhere to go. But ... wouldn't you want to look into the rooms in the matta?'

'Amma, who are you?' asked the Superintendent, astonished.

The rest stood, dumbfounded.

'I? Come home, I'll tell you. Hm? Why're you staring that way? I'm not crazy, I swear. Come, this way … not far from here. Don't be surprised! Just follow me.' Even as she was talking, she entered the next room. The Superintendent followed with a few policemen. He was worried that he had not bound her.

'What do you see here?' she asked.

'Nothing.'

'Now?' she said, moving aside a wooden cupboard for clothes, set against the wall. She put a key into a keyhole in the wall and pushed it open!

'Without doubt! This woman is a conjurer,' decided some watching her. They were stunned to see the wall open easily, like a door, making an entryway. In some others, flashed a thought, like lighting, 'Could she be a goddess of the matta? Will she vent her fury on us to avenge his death?'

'This is my home,' she announced.

They looked in. They were astounded; it was that well furnished. Surprise on surprise! What a difference! The matta was sparsely equipped … ascetic, but this room looked like Manmatha's[11] bedroom.

'Amma, whoever you may be, you will have to tell us what's behind this secret display of yours.'

'Saheb-sir! I've come well prepared to reveal everything to you. I thought this was the only room, all these days. Only yesterday, I realised that there are many rooms like this in this hellhole.'

'How did you find out this secret? What's your intention, anyway?'

---

11   God of love

'What is so great about me discovering the secret in my own home? But I have a mission: to rescue other ignorant, helpless women.'

She laughed bitterly.

The Superintendent stared at her, wide-eyed, not knowing what to say.

'Listen, sir! Who'll endure this? Yogis are also men of flesh and blood. But those who've renounced the world are expected to live as celibates. Where's the justice in this? Isn't it foolish of people to expect them to give up such a primal urge? Perhaps that's possible in the forest! Even there, there could be apsaras[12] like Rambha or Menaka. And perhaps, there may be one in a thousand who could fulfil his vow of celibacy, like Bhishma. Let that be. Even if that can be forgiven ... what about this? ... A betrayal of trust!'

She burst out laughing again. But the very next moment, her eyes filled with tears. She looked mournful.

No one knew what to say to her ...

After a while, she spoke, in a voice soft with grief.

'For five years I've lived in this hellhole, believing it to be a paradise. What deception! What a scheming sanyasi![13] ... He's been punished rightly! Even if the ignorant weep, I laugh!'

She laughed, softly ... And then, she continued her lament.

'If one hasn't the strength to control his senses, isn't it better that he dies rather than live? ... Live in deception by throwing mud in the eyes of those who trust him? ... What I've done is dharma! ... I've vindicated dharma! ... Truly! I was young, five

---

12   Heavenly nymph
13   Ascetic

years ago. I didn't know the difference between what's worthwhile and what's worthless. Now I do. Not just that ... I'd been taken in by his pretence, I was devoted to him ... I saw him as my God. Only yesterday did I discover that he's a tiger with a cow's face, a gomukhavyaghra[14] ...

'Sahebare! Though I'm happy that I've destroyed this yogi, I loved him as the life of my life ... right until yesterday. Selflessly, truly ... And yet, I didn't have the courage to love him ... until he taught me.'

She stood hugging herself, as if she were crushing her heart. Those around her stood like stone.

6

Recovering, she said:

'This happened some five years ago. We had a practice of washing this Guru's feet to wash away our sins. Only now do I realize what a thick veil blinded us in the form of a belief. But then ... I was washing his feet, when I heard a whisper, "Have you forgotten?" I shuddered ... I looked up. What a divine glow! I must've imagined it. A smile was dancing on his lips. That face! I didn't understand what he had said. Forgotten? Forgotten what? "Tonight," he whispered. I was thrilled. I knew what *that* implied. Or, I may have understood it through his expression.

'I was young then; but old enough to imagine the pleasures of this world. Oh, the way my mind would wander when I was

---

14 Cow-faced tiger

alone! At that moment, I felt as if thousands of steam engines were rushing through my head.

'In whichever body God dwells, he will be mine … But isn't that a sin? *Che*! Being as ignorant as I am, how will I understand such a mystery? I comforted myself. That day seemed long. And that night …

'He was waiting at the door. And again, that same question, in a firm voice. And then …

'"Why're you behaving like a stranger? Why is it that you can't recall even a bit of your previous birth? How long have I wandered about, looking for you! I thought you'd recognize me."

'I stood there, stunned. Why was he talking to me so familiarly? I didn't seem to understand anything. How could that be?

'"I'm sorry, I can't understand what you're saying. Will you … will you please be clearer?" I muttered.

'In response, he clasped my hand, firmly. Aha! What did I consider myself? As blessed! But now …'

She closed her eyes. Her faced reddened. Tears flowed. Wiping them with the edge of her sari, she continued, 'He said that I had been his wife in our previous birth … That he had been a debaucher, cheating on me. And so, he had to be reborn as a sanyasi … He was able to know all this through insight while serving in this vihara!

'I lost myself in his embrace. Our liaison was secret until today. And would've been so in future too … Our intimacy grew so deep from that night, that within a month, I moved in here, into this secret chamber, with no one suspecting a thing. This is my fifth year! And today I have, on my own, made myself a widow! How happy I am!'

SARASWATHIBAI RAJAWADE (GIRIBALE)

She laughed. The Superintendent focused on her; all ears. Whatever she was saying was coming from her heart. He knew all of it would make sense, would fit in as evidence. And so, he did not ask for any explanation.

She began again. 'We have lived as a couple these five years. We were married in front of the deity. And yet, he has become well known as a Balabhramachari, a celibate! Whenever I talked to him about our sin, he would shut me up with some reference or the other to Vedanta. And I served him with all my heart, blissful in this blessing ... until yesterday! Yesterday, the truth was revealed!'

She gritted her teeth in fury.

'God willed it otherwise ... Yes, now I suspect. There, that's a tumbler of milk. I would drink it every night. But yesterday, I didn't! There must be *something* mixed in it! I'd go into deep sleep as soon as I drank it. But it wasn't so yesterday. We sat a long while, chatting and laughing.'

'"Drink the milk and sleep, chinna,"[15] he said, tenderly.

'"I'll drink it a little later," I said, "I'm still feeling full with dinner."

'He was stroking me down, gently. I began to feel drowsy. He gave me the tumbler of milk, saying, "Drink." I thought that was his gesture of love, as usual. I was about to drink it, though I didn't really want it. Just then, there was a hint of someone coming to see him. "I'll be back," he said, hurrying out ... I hid the glass of milk and lay down. I was soon asleep ...

'I don't know why I woke up. The lord of my heart wasn't beside me. I sat up; I waited awhile, expecting him to be back. "What kind

---

15 Term of endearment; literally, gold.

The Battered Heart

of a job is this? There's no rest at any time. Do they have to come to the matta even in the dead of night? Stupid people!" I cursed. I stepped outside, unable to bear the loneliness. I wanted to walk about on the veranda, while waiting for him. As I walked past my room, I found another wall-door, just like this one. I hadn't known that there were any others. I stood wondering why it could be there ... And there was light ... I pressed my ear to the hairline slit ... Oh, what a dreadful sound!'

Her fury returned. She raised the knife! Everyone surrounding her moved a step away. She laughed strangely and continued, 'Yes, the sound was horrible. Why? ... Because it was a woman's voice. Shocking! Because ... because! A thought occurred to me like a flash of lightning. I had been deceived. Ayyo! The grief I endured! Only a woman spurned can understand. I decided. I dashed back to my room. Here, with this very knife I went back and stood in the very same place ...

'In about half an hour, the drama unfolded; like this very door, that one opened. The Balabhramachari walked out after enjoying his child's play.

"'What's *this*?" I asked him, holding his hand.

"'You've no right to ask me about this." The yogi roared like a lion in fury, pushing me aside.

"'I'm your wife; I do have a right," I said. He kicked me.

"'You're a Balabramachari. But you broke your vow of celibacy only to redeem me, didn't you?"

"'Even sages accept Sri Krishna as a Balabrahmachari.[16] Get back to your room."

---

16   A celibate

SARASWATHIBAI RAJAWADE (GIRIBALE)

'And so we argued, on and on. He pinched me, kicked me, slapped me ... I lost my patience; am I not human? He kept shoving me towards the garden as I pondered over my life with him ... Aha! Is this the end to my love for him? My devotion? Have I been deceived like this ... all these years?' He's supposed to be my husband. I wasn't willing to share him with anyone else. That's when I realized what sort of a person he was.

'There were many others who believed in him ... even as I did. I realized only yesterday that they too were imprisoned like me ... to satisfy his lust. We'd been blinded. I'd imagined this place as my Vaikunta[17] ... until last night. Vaikunta! Aha! Isn't this a gory hellhole? ... Can't I save other hapless women from falling into it? Who knows?

'At that moment, I felt a fury I'd never known before. From where did it spring? I raised the knife ... and it landed. Now, I know! My husband is my own!'

She darted out of the room, suddenly.

7

When the Superintendent followed her, he found her seated beside the dead body, weeping like a child, blabbering like a drunkard. He had not the heart to ask his men to arrest her. She was caressing the body, sobbing while talking to it. She was a frightening sight; and sad too. But the disciples could not stand it.

'She's mad,' they said. 'Drive her away.'

---

17   Abode of Mahavishnu

'Yes, I'm mad, aren't I?' she muttered, laughing while weeping. 'And you? I trusted him as my husband; he did not have the dignity of a grihastha.[18] You served him as a Balabrahmachari but he was a Ravana in the guise of a sanyasi. Aren't you crazy too? You and other celibates like you have lived in this matta for generations and yet, all you know are these few rooms. But a mad woman like me has been able to solve the secret of many more. Right now, I can show you yet another mad woman like me, right here, in this very place. But I don't want to. It was for her sake that I had to kill the God of my heart. And I don't know how many more mad women there are in such secret chambers. *Ayyo*, I believed it was possible for men to be faithful to a woman for life. Yes, of course, they can! But *he* was not a man. If he were, would he have cheated me?

'You may be furious with me, my beloved, for I've tarnished your image. I've stained your reputation. You may be cursing me; wherever you are right now. Only *that* is bothering you, isn't it? Then listen, my heart is battered. It is suffering a thousand times more. Thousands of thousands. I killed you just so that I may not be deceived any more ... Yes, I had the guts to do it ... for you are mine. I was your wife in our previous birth, wasn't I? ... Isn't that true? ... What? You want me to come to you? ... I'll come ... But there ... you can't ...'

Even before the others could dart towards her, the knife in her hand had entered her heart. She slumped over the dead body.

The Superintendent asked for a broad sheet and covered the bodies.

---

18   Householder, a married man

'Why did you slap her?' he asked the Administrator of the matta, angrily.

'Can she be false to the hand that had fed her?'

There was no way of knowing who was thinking what.

'Knowing that she was a dependent here, you could've told me, couldn't you? That you suspected her?'

'*Che*! I never ever dreamt a woman would have such guts.'

'Anyway ... In one way or another, all of you are guilty of tarnishing the image of your yogi.'

'We're but servants here, bound by our vow of obedience. It's our duty to obey our Guru's orders.'

'This is an outcome of being compelled to follow the rules of the monastery. The government will have to run this matta until a true ascetic can take over.'

'So, are you saying this matta should fall to ruins? Who knows how long it'll take for such a hermit to be born? How many years? How many ages?'

'Not that it should deteriorate,' clarified the Superintendent. 'Just that it should be what it professes to be; a monastery. The name of whoever started this matta shouldn't be dragged through the mud. It's already a harem. We've seen one embellished bedroom. We learnt from this resident that there's another such ill-fated woman. Let's release the prisoners, at least. Come.'

He ordered his policemen to look for other such doors in the walls. They brought some seven or eight women outside. When they were assured of their safety, each one spilt out her story ... much the same as Sita's ... It was amazing that each of them was under the impression that she was the only woman in the mattaadhipathi's life! They were shocked to hear that their guardian had been murdered. Darkness descended on the lives of these hapless women.

∼

A spirit walked about in the burial grounds, looking for a grave.

'Oh, my husband!' it cried, stopping at a fresh mound. 'Wake up! Wake up! Why're you so lazy?'

'I got tired of waiting, my beloved. Why did you take so long today?'

'Am I late? I was cremated while you were buried. You're a big sadhu, aren't you? Why didn't these people bury us together? I had to come from another graveyard.'

'I don't know why these foolish people give such importance to our bodies … We're one now, anyway. But let that be … You must forgive me.'

'Why?'

'I cheated you. But you showed me the pinnacle of love: constancy. You're one heroic woman, aren't you?! You did a great job. Or else, I would've continued sinning, knowingly. You've saved me from that. That's your punya.'

'It's *that* difficult to preserve celibacy, isn't it?'

'Yes. And in the ambience in which I lived; it was impossible.'

'Whom do we have to fear now?'

'We're free! Free to wander; to wander about until the morning! Come.'

'Your wish is my command!'

married Ramabai, respect it now and get her to consent to my plan. Redeem our ancestors by being a link to the future generations.'

'I'll try again tonight, avva. When I listen to you, I feel there's sense in what you say. But when I listen to her, I feel she's also right. I'm confused.'

Originally published in 1939 as 'Kulaputhraathava Gupthadhaana' in *Jayakarnataka*.

The Scion of the Family or A Secret Gift

'How can she be right? Think about it. Our puranas[1] don't say that niyoga[2] is wrong. Didn't Satyavathi get her son, Vyasamuni to sleep with her widowed daughters-in-law, Ambika and Ambalika? Didn't they beget Dhritarashtra and Pandu? Didn't Satyavathi herself beget Vyasa when she was still unmarried? Didn't he eventually become the sage, Vedavyasa who—'

'Avva, I know ... I know what you're getting at. Let me have my dinner and go to bed.'

'Good. But before you sleep, be smart enough to get her consent to carry out our plan. I'm tired too. I'll have something light: just a glass of buttermilk with a handful of puffed rice, two sweet potatoes and a glass of milk ... and get to bed.'

The Jaghirdar had died, leaving his wife, Gangabai, with their only son, Keshava. Keshava was quite good-looking, true. And his nature? How else would it be when he strutted about flaunting his status as a wealthy landowner; adorning himself with coats embroidered with gold lace, strands of gold chains and bracelets in eye-catching designs and chewing tobacco with paan[3] while shouting orders to the peasants? He did look half-crazy sometimes, rather absent-minded at other times. He could read and write a little, both in Kannada and in English. But ever since his father's death, his mother had been managing the affairs of their lands and houses with the help of a clerk for the past two years.

---

1 Sacred legends
2 Engaging a kinsman to marry the widow to beget a son
3 Betel leaves and areca nuts

Many fathers vied with each other to give their daughters in marriage to Keshava. But was there anyone among them who could offer a dowry to match his earnings? Yes, there was one. A zamindar gave his only daughter, Krishnabai, together with all that he owned. But, unfortunately for Keshava, she was not destined to live long. She seemed to be bothered by a stomach ache from time to time. When she could bear it no longer, she jumped into a well, leaving a note for the police asking them not to embarrass her with a post-mortem. Some six months later, Ramabai, the daughter of another wealthy person, was given in marriage to Keshava. Ramabai was a fairly educated girl, brought up well in a traditional household. She was quite smart and was willing to help her mother-in-law with handling the affairs of the household. But she realized quite early that the old lady expected only grandchildren from her. 'So what?' she thought often, 'That will be done when God wills.' But then …

One day, it occurred to Ramabai to wonder why Keshava's first wife had committed suicide. What led to it … why wasn't her husband more open with her? Wouldn't a husband want to spend time with his bride? Was it possible for a man to be so spiritless, so disinterested when he is alone with a young girl? And also, the mother-in-law seemed anxious to have a grandchild. What might that imply? Had her father tied her to this useless man, impressed by his wealth? The gossip whispered among the womenfolk helped to firm up her suspicion that the previous wife had not died due to a stomach ache. Ramabai became extremely agitated, confused by an eddy of conjectures. And one day, her scary speculations took a tangible form.

The Scion of the Family or A Secret Gift

One day, Shyamachari, a twenty-year-old bachelor who had recently been appointed to serve in the temple, was beaten and coerced by his father and Keshava's mother to sleep in her house. That very night, around ten, when Keshava and Ramabai were in bed, Keshava bemoaned his fate; God had not blessed him with the grace to father a child. His mother shouted through the door, 'Don't give her time. If you do ...'

Keshava shut her up with, 'I'll handle this, avva.'

Shyamachari was a strapping young Brahmin. All he had to do was to perform the daily puje at the temple, eat with the Jaghirdar and roam about. He had never thought of sleeping around, but he was also too naive to think he should be celibate until he got married. And so, everything went as Keshava's mother had planned. Ramabai had screamed in protest. But what else could she do? She was helpless. Her husband was helpless too. Her mother-in-law believed in the stories of the puranas about miraculous births and she was bent on having a grandson. Stuffed with ideas about how the puranas interpreted niyoga, Ramabai became pregnant. And she delivered her baby in due time. But to the old lady's ill luck, Ramabai did not have a son. She had a daughter. They named her Sharadhe and called her Shari.

When Shari was old enough to walk and would toddle up to her father on the front veranda, his friends would pass snide comments, smiling, 'Doesn't our little Sharakka's face look a bit like our Shamaacharya's?' But his loyal farmers would waive them off with, 'How could you say that, ayya? Look at her colour! Just like her father's. She's a rosebud.'

And if ever Gangabai took her granddaughter to the temple when she went to listen to talks on the *Puranas*, the women around her would not fail to pass comments: 'Come, little Sharakka, let's see you weighed down with ornaments! You're very precious to your ajji, aren't you? You almost did not *happen*. And now, she's saddled you with all the jewellery in the house.' And someone else would even have the guts to add, 'That Shyamachari must've cast his shadow on you this morning to bring you such luck.' Gangabai would be seething. And yet, it was below her dignity to pick a quarrel, wasn't it? But she had other ways to settle scores; their husbands would be made to pay extra for the millets they had to buy back from their Jaghirdar.[4]

Shyamachari too benefitted from his secret gift to Gangabai's family. As per her agreement with his father, the old lady gave him a thousand rupees. He took it and ran away to some distant village, married a girl whose father was well versed in the Vedas and lived in his father-in-law's house. Gangabai might need him some two years later. She had not expected such a turn of events, though.

Keshava had given her his word that he would convince his wife that she would have to accept a secret gift from someone, once again. Ramabai was shocked when he spoke to her about it that night. She hardly heard him as he tried to parrot his mother's version of the age-old story of Vyasamuni's gesture that gave birth to the Pandavas and the Kauravas, redeeming the Puru dynasty. Her heart had turned to stone. And yet, she pleaded with him gently. But how could he even dream of seeing her point? Would he then have the guts to face his mother? He suggested Narayanaraya, the clerk who went about their villages with his mother, collecting

---

4 Land-holder

The Scion of the Family or A Secret Gift

tax from the peasants who farmed their lands. He was also the family's accountant.

This was too much. Ramabai stood up, trembling with fury. She gave her husband a mouthful, 'In which birth were you a demon? Is that why you are born as my husband to sully me with such demeaning practice, just to preserve your questionable lineage? I can't do this. You forced me once, and with that Shyamachari's help, we now have Shari. I'm not an idiot to bow my head to all your commands. I too can think for myself. With anyone else, you may have got your way. But I'm your wife according to our dharma. I do understand your plight; I feel for you. Fine, for your sake, I'm prepared to bow to your wishes this once. Because I offered myself to you with the dowry that my father gave you, I had to offer my body to that Shyamachari for your sake, to continue your family line to preserve your property and your standing in this stupid society. But you have to do at least this for me. Send for Shyamachari again. Let him live with his wife in those rooms in the backyard. I'm not saying this because I want it this way. I have no way out. I have to accept my husband's decision though I can suggest an alternative. I have a relative who's very smart. I had suggested that we could adopt him. But what can you do? You have no say in the matter …'

'True, Rama, I have no say,' Keshava stopped her with a sigh, 'I'm a puppet in avva's hands. I don't know why I can't resist her. I have no worldly wisdom. I can't even protect my wife from disgrace. I lost my first wife for this very reason. I can understand what you're going through; I even feel furious enough to want to kill my mother. But I don't have the guts to do it. Everyone knows that God has made me a man in name only. When your parents and my first wife, Krishnabai's parents offered you girls in marriage with large dowries, they were not giving you to me. They gave you to my wealth, my revenue and my prestige as a Jaghirdar. If we adopt the child that you're talking about, avva says that his parents and his relatives may manipulate the situation to drain our resources. People know that I'm like this. Let them also know that I've made you like this. This stupid society may not respect us. But our respect for each other is beyond this, isn't it? If that child is yours, your love for him and his love for you will grow naturally. Not only will it bring us joy; it will also protect our prestige, our property.' They spent the night advising each other, supporting each other, drawing strength from their mutual love. How amazing! The divine grace of the Paramathma!⁵

Finally, Keshava managed to somehow convince his mother to send for Shyamachari. She had been impressed with the priest; he had maintained the secrecy of his previous secret gift. So, she got someone to write him a letter the very next day. He was to come immediately; there was an urgent need for his presence.

Shyamachari was shocked, initially. But he thought over it, 'The Jaghirdarini herself has sent for me. If I don't go, that anxiety will plague me.'

He left home immediately, arrived that very evening and met the old lady. He was happy to see two-year-old Sharadhe—a favourite with everyone in the family—strutting about all over the house.

---

5   Supreme Being

The Scion of the Family or A Secret Gift

'So, where're you working now?' asked Gangabai.

'What work does a pujari have these days, avva? I'm grateful if anyone comes to the temple at all. I'm lucky if they give me enough to buy a meal. I fend for myself somehow. But *she's* very smart. She goes to different houses, offers to help with household chores and brings home some money. If I grumble that she works late into the night on some days, she shows me small pieces of stolen jewellery she has tucked into the fold of her sari at the waist! I was furious.

'"You know it's wrong to steal," I shouted at her, one day.

'"Why don't you earn enough to feed me, then?" she retorted.

'I even tried teaching children to read and write. But people teased me, "Hey, you bell-ringing pujari!⁶ What can *you* teach those little ones? Go ... go about ringing your bell. Or else ... go and teach people like you to ring the bell." I feel bad. So, I let my wife do as she pleases. There's no other way. But even that should last, shouldn't it?

'One day, she had brought home a copper pot from the purohit's house. They suspected her and came home right away to check. They spotted it easily as they had their name engraved on it. She was caught. I signalled to her with my eyes and beat her up in front of them. But now, no one calls her. Even if they do, they don't let her into the house. They get all their washing done in the backyard and send her away.' The pujari had many such stories to tell the old lady but he did not forget to let slip that his wife was four months pregnant.

'Come, let's have lunch. We'll talk later,' said Gangabai, getting up. Much later, she told him why she had sent for him. If he was

---

6   Temple priest

willing once again, she would set him up for life, she promised. They say that even a corpse opens its mouth wide when it comes to money—none of us have seen that happening, of course. But we have seen and heard about the living doing just that, haven't we? Anyway, the pujari was engaged to perform the daily puje in the Jaghirdar's house. Not just that. He got a house to stay. And he and his wife were to have their meals with the family. They also got to ride about with Keshava and Ramabai in their car.

The Jaghirdarini[7] was concerned for the pujari's pregnant wife; a girl from a poor family, a poor man's wife. So, she conducted all the auspicious rituals of seemantha[8] to bless the young mother-to-be and her unborn baby. She even catered to the girl's urge for different kinds of food. At the end of her term, Godhabai delivered a bonny boy. But who cares for a boy in a poor pujari's household? Now, if only he had been born in the Jaghirdar's family, instead of Shari ... Such thoughts drifted through Shyamachari's and Gangabai's minds and through Ramabai's and Keshava's too. And yet, the old lady was caring enough to get a peasant woman to take care of the young mother and baby. Not just that. She also gifted them new clothes as well as anklets for the baby when they named him Gopala.

Eventually, Godhabai sensed the reason behind Gangabai's bounty. But was she an idiot to be upset? When there are countless men who carry on with women of the lower castes, losing what little they had and bringing untold misery to their wives, her husband's connection with the Jaghirdar's family was good enough

---

7   Here, mother of the Jaghirdar
8   A rite performed to bless a pregnant woman

The Scion of the Family or A Secret Gift

to keep them in comfort all their lives. And not just that. It became a matter of prestige to see her husband strut about with dignity. It suited her to keep her knowledge a secret.

Gopala brought luck to the Jaghirdar's family. Ramabai was blessed with a son. Is it ever possible to describe the pomp and show with which the child was welcomed? They distributed peda[9] all over town, gifted clothes and money to Brahmin men and their wives and held a special puje for Hanuman, the local deity. The old lady went about with a bright smile, saying to anyone who was willing to listen to her: 'That little rascal Gopala has brought good fortune to our family.' The baby was named Srinivasa Urfi Rajasaheb. Godhabai took care of the new mother and baby; she considered it her privilege. And as a gift she received a gorgeous silk sari interwoven with gold thread; something she had only dreamt of.

As the years sped by, Gangabai could not contain her joy while watching her grandchildren decked in gold ornaments, playing on the veranda. Now, Shyamachari was not just their family-priest. He was also their accountant, maintaining their financial records. The previous accountant, Narayanaraya was 'suspended', to keep gossip at bay. And now, Shyamachari's son, Gopala accompanied his father to the Jaghirdarini's house to play with her grandchildren. He caught her eye one day and she shouted at him, 'Le, Gopya, why are you jumping on the carpet all the time? You're wearing it out.' Shyamachari's hand that held the pen shook a bit as he looked up. Ramabai looked out of the kitchen and said, 'What difference does it make to a child? A

---

9   A sweet

carpet is much like the muddy ground beneath it. Don't scold him!' Godhabai too had heard the old lady scolding her son and was darting out of her house to comfort him. But when she saw Ramabai giving it to her mother-in-law without mincing words, she retreated, relieved.

Though everyone went back to their jobs, Gangabai could not help musing, 'Gopya is Shyamachari's son. So are Shari and Srini. And yet ... these two are only ours ... and he is only his ...'

The same thought was whirling through Shyamachari's mind too, even as it flashed across Ramabai's and roared through Godhabai's. In fact, it raised such fury in Godhabai that she had rushed out to take it out on the old lady. But Ramabai had inadvertently defused the situation and restored peace.

In the course of time, Godhabai had a daughter. The child was named Susheela and both mother and child received gifts during the usual ceremonies. Ramabai became pregnant a few months later. The old lady's joy knew no bounds as the family had enough and more wealth to burn and yet have enough to spare. And yet ... and yet? She had heard that Godhabai was with child again. Did she have to spend on two births every other year? Wasn't there any way out?

That day was Ekadashi.[10] Gangabai was fasting. She had not eaten anything even the previous night. And so, she was in a corner, resting, instead of wandering about the house, as usual. Just then, Godhabai came to her, moaning, 'Avvaaa, my stomach has been cramping since last night. What should I do? I've completed four months.'

---

10   Eleventh day of the lunar cycle

The Scion of the Family or A Secret Gift

'Wait, I'll get you an amulet from someone,' she said, getting up.

Right by their town was Hakim Allahbhaksh's house. He was known for his black magic and charms and his medicines for women and children. The old lady set out to visit him. On the way, she thought she heard a voice mocking her, 'How crazy can you get? You have three precious children running about in your home, thanks to that man's favour on your barren daughter-in-law. How can you turn against *him*?' Gangabai looked back with a start. There was no one.

'Why is my mind playing tricks with me today?' she wondered. She was still mumbling as she pulled out a note from her pouch on reaching the hakim's house. She looked this way and that, to make sure; no one was wandering about since it was midday. She handed over the money to him, whispering the reason for her visit. How could he refuse her? The lady herself had come on behalf of the patient and thrust a ten-rupee note into his hand. Shouldn't the doctor listen to her and do the needful? He gave her three small packets of a green powder. If the stomach ache became unbearable, she was to give the patient some hot coffee to drink and soothe her stomach with hot fomentation. He also gave her a black string as a charm to be tied around the patient's arm. Ganagabai returned home with a smile.

Godhabai was waiting for her with sago porridge; she knew the old lady would be hungry as she was fasting. Gangabai was touched. A fleeting thought crossed Gangabai's mind, 'Shouldn't I throw away the Hakim's medicine?' But ... but ... by then, Ramabai came inside, tore open a packet and gave the pregnant woman the green powder with water to wash it down, and tied the black string on her left arm.

'Avvaaa, how can I thank you?' moaned Godhabai, 'You went all that way even while you're fasting, to get me this medication from the hakim. What great punya[11] you've earned, avva!'

'Punya or paapa …'[12] the old lady muttered to herself.

By nine-thirty that night, Godhabai had taken all three doses. Her stomach ache was getting worse. Ramabai gave her hot-water fomentation, as advised by the hakim. Godhabai felt bad that the young mistress of the house should be taking care of her so late in the night. So, she went to her room to lie down. Her husband took over the nursing care.

Around midnight, Keshava and Ramabai heard the old lady muttering in a loud voice. They went to her room, anxious. And as they stood watching her, she was shouting, 'Ayyoyyo, don't thrash me, please. I'll never do this again. Ramaa! Keshava! Please come and release me from their clutches. When I went out to get the medicine to extract her foetus, no one had seen me. I'm sure of that … Then how do these scamps know? They're beating me … Come and save me! Ramaaa … Keshavaaa!'

Both of them woke her up and asked her why she was shouting that way. Godhabai confessed to what she had done. Keshava was shocked. He sank to the floor, holding his head. He was bewildered. Ramabai could not tolerate this. Not only would the medication cause a premature delivery but it would also make Godhabai sterile. She was upset that *she* had fed her the three packets of that green

---

11   Spiritual merit
12   Sin

The Scion of the Family or A Secret Gift

powder, the medicine from that hakim. What trickery! And what if it had killed her!

By then, Shyamachari arrived at their door, knocking and calling out to them, 'Rao Saheba! Rao Sahebare! Avvaaa! Avvaaa ...' Keshava opened the door.

'How is she?' he asked.

'You'll have to send for the doctor right away,' said Shyamachari, dazed. Ramabai darted towards his house. Godhabai was in severe pain and was exhausted by the time the doctor arrived. He checked her and gave her an injection, saving her from the brink. Suspecting Gangabai's intention in getting medicines from the hakim, he whispered to her that he could disclose her secret to her family and fleeced another hundred and fifty rupees from her.

It took another four to five months to nurse Godhabai back to health—she had become that weak. Ramabai felt sorry for her and decided never ever to give her any strenuous work around the house.

Thanks to Ramabai's concern, Shyamachari's children too were able to get a good education with the Rao Saheb's children. And one day, Gangabai entered the funeral pyre happy and contented, witnessed and surrounded by her grandchildren.

Now at last, Keshava and Ramabai were in charge of their property. Ramabai was satisfied with the two boys and two girls she had, thanks to the old lady's intervention. And Shyamachari and Godhabai too were able to raise their two children in comfort.

And yet, whenever Keshava and Ramabai saw Godhabai's ashen face as she sat about listlessly, whiling away her time, they could not help feeling a stab of guilt. And whenever she looked at the children, all of them coming on very well in the sight of the world, something troubled Ramabai deep inside her, making her lose weight. And that same something troubled Keshava too ... and Shyamachari ... and Godhabai.

KODAGINA GOWRAMMA

Vani's Confusion

1

WHEN INDU STEPPED out one morning, she noticed that someone seemed to be moving into the house next door; it had been lying vacant for some four or five years. And now, there stood a lorry laden with household items. She could also hear voices from inside. Indu should have been glad to have a neighbour at last. But she felt a distaste. It was not like that familiar saying: *When the ajji in the neighbouring house goes, we can use it as a barn for our calf.* Perhaps, it would not be wrong to say that she was more sad than happy. And she had a reason to feel that way.

Indu had lost her father even before she was born and then her mother at her birth. She had been brought up by a foster family who made her feel like she was a burden. As if that was not enough, she became a widow barely six months after her wedding. Her little cottage of a house was a blessing. When her husband realized that

---

First published in 1939 as 'Vaniya Samasye' in *Kathaasankalana*.

he had not long to live, he willed that cottage to her and left her all the money he had. It was not much, but just enough to help her get by on her own at last; without depending on any of her relatives.

She loved her home. Her only interest in life was to keep it homely. It is not surprising that she loved it so deeply; she had been tired of living with nothing and no one to call her own. If she had found any happiness at all in her life, it had been in that house. It was all she had and all she needed. Even before she could realize that her life would be awful if her husband died, he was gone. She had seen his face only at their wedding—the next time was at his funeral. For that matter, her life became endurable only after his death. Her relatives became fond of her—on seeing the wealth that her husband had left her. But Indu had learnt the hard way that it was best to live on her own.

'It's not proper for a young girl to live alone,' they advised her. But Indu would not budge.

All this had happened some six years earlier. Now Indu was twenty. The house next door had been vacant even when she had moved into hers. She would walk about freely, not only in her backyard but in the neighbouring backyard as well. Even when the fence between the houses had broken down, she did not think it necessary to repair it.

She loved the solitude. She had been a loner all her life; she had never had anyone to call her own. And now that she could be independent, she saw no need to rely on love or friendship. Even if she did feel like reaching out to someone, she was too shy to make the move. So, it was not surprising that she was not excited about her new neighbours. Not that her happiness depended on whoever came to live next door. She knew that, of course. It was just a sinking feeling that the house was taken and that she had lost her privacy.

'Now, I must see to that fence,' Indu thought as she went inside. And she did not come into the garden for the rest of the day.

2

When Indu was repairing the fence the next day, she saw someone at the well in the backyard of that house. She seemed to be around her own age. She too stared at Indu and then, she smiled. That smile reflected on Indu's face too. Well, since then, the work on the fence did not proceed.

After that introductory smile, the acquaintance between Indu and the next-door Vani developed into a deep friendship, all within a week. Indu was surprised at her own concern for Vani; she had never yearned for companionship. As for Vani, she was new to the town. She knew no one. All she saw every morning was her neighbour's face. It was not surprising that they bonded easily. But Indu had never known such deepening connections. She did not know that she could respond to Vani with equal warmth.

Indu's neighbours were Vani and her husband, Ratan. He was a doctor, newly posted to that town. Since he was the only doctor, he barely made time to come home, even for his meals. Vani was bored of being alone. And so, she spent most of her time in Indu's house. Indu too had gone to Vani's house, but just once or twice.

Indu had noticed that the house was always a mess with everything strewn about any old how.

'I haven't had the time yet to sort things out and arrange them,' Vani would say. That would make Indu say to herself, surprised,

'But it's a fortnight since she moved in!' And one day, Indu decided to help Vani set up her house. Though they had started around two in the afternoon, it was quite dark by the time they were done. The house looked more like a home now, clean and welcoming.

Instead of saying that Indu helped Vani to settle in, it would be more honest to say Vani helped Indu. Indu did most of the job. She was the one who arranged and rearranged each item, not just for convenience but also to make the house attractive. Vani helped her lift the heavy furniture and also ran about fetching things for her. Anyway, the house looked pleasing by the time they were done. Vani could not believe the transformation; she was stunned and happy.

Vani was, by nature, not much of a homemaker. She had ways of putting off things that had to be done. Her chores had to keep waiting for the tomorrows that never turned up. And so, naturally, that day, her house looked as beautiful as never before.

That evening, when Ratan came home from work, he was stunned. Vani had gushed that all credit was due to next-door Indu. 'How I wish my Vani too would be as interested in homemaking,' he thought as he sipped his coffee. But he knew it would not be that easy to see his wish come true; he had been married for five years now. But he had not lost hope yet; he did keep thinking, 'If only this …' or, 'If only that …'

At times, when he returned home tired from work, Vani would be in Indu's house, chatting. Then, she would rush home to make him some coffee. And by the time she was done, someone or the other would come to take him to attend to some emergency. Quite often he had rushed back to the hospital without eating anything. Vani would regret later, for sure, 'Ayyo, I should have kept your coffee ready.' But that was only for a while. It was the same story the next day, and the next. Though he had many clothes, Ratan would not be able to find a matching tie when he needed one.

When they were newly-weds, Ratan was not quite aware of Vani's shoddiness. But as the years went by, he could not help thinking, 'Why is my Vani like this?' And yet, when he saw her penitent face with her tearful eyes, he could not help but pet her and comfort her until he could see her smile again and be happy with her. Though he did intend to ask her to not be so careless again; even to be angry to teach her a lesson, he could never get down to scolding her, somehow. He knew she meant well, but …

As the days went by and their friendship grew deeper, Indu could not help but notice Vani's indifference to her household responsibilities as a wife. Vani would also come and talk to Indu about her feelings, every time she felt like unburdening herself. She would scold herself for her stupidity. Indu used to console her, at first. But then, when she realised that Vani was that way by nature, she would muse: 'This Vani has a husband like Ratan! Can't she keep him happy?' And then, with a sigh, 'If only he had been my husband, how well I would've looked after him!' And then, with a clouded smile, 'Thu! Crazy thoughts!'

3

One morning, Vani dropped in at around eleven when Indu was busy cooking. With her, there was no such thing as visiting hours. She was used to skipping back and forth, whenever she pleased, from morning until she went to bed. Usually, she needed no reasonable reason to visit. Even that day, she had just come for a chat while the dhal was cooking over a slow fire in her own kitchen. But that was enough to brew a storm into Indu's placid waters.

Ratan had come home early for lunch that day as he had some special duty later in the afternoon. But Vani was not at home. He called out to her, once or twice. No response. And so, when he stepped onto the backyard, expecting her to be there, he heard her voice from Indu's house. He was furious; she was spending time with her neighbour when she should have been seeing to his lunch.

'Vani,' he called out, quite loudly.

She did not hear him in the excitement of her chatter. And even Indu could not hear him above the noise Vani was making.

'Vani!' Ratan shouted, coming right up to the fence. Both of them got a shock.

'Ayyo, Indu! My cooking is not yet done,' wailed Vani, rushing out of the house. As Indu followed behind her, she saw Ratan at the fence, looking spent.

'How long have you been waiting? D'you have to go back on duty?' Indu heard Vani asking her husband and guessed that he would have to go hungry again.

Though that was quite the norm for Ratan; to Indu, this was the first time. She was upset that she was guilty too, in a way: She had been quite happy having Vani with her, enjoying her ceaseless chatter. As she stared at Ratan's tired face while closing her door, she felt sorry for him. And other feelings came creeping in, unbidden. And following them, a deep sigh. 'Ayyo, devare!' she gasped, wiping the tears welling up, as she saw Ratan and Vani reaching the back porch of their house together.

4

Indu went inside. Just a moment earlier, there had been peace in her life; a sense of tranquillity and happiness that came with contentment. Also, a deep sense of pride in her home, its beauty, its cleanliness. But somehow, all those feelings had vanished even as she came inside. Instead, questions about their value that had never before occurred to Indu, bothered her now: 'Why has God given Vani every blessing in life? Blessings that she doesn't even know how to value ... And why has He filled my life with this emptiness?' Now, this became an overriding question in her life. However much she thought about it, she could not fathom an answer. She sat where she was until Vani came in that evening. Her food, too, was not eaten.

Indu was pleased to see Vani looking sad whereas previously, she would have been concerned. 'Why should God keep aside grief only for me?' she said to herself, 'Let Him give her a taste of it too.' Though she was well aware that she was being self-centred; that Vani was in no way responsible for the tragedies in her life, she felt no compassion for Vani's tear-stained face. When Vani said, 'He had never said anything hurtful, but today, he just walked away, furious.' Indu felt a queer sense of pleasure. But she felt ashamed the very next moment; she had never ever entertained such thoughts. As a penance for her feelings, she comforted Vani and helped her with her chores, as usual.

Indu had just finished helping Vani and was leaving her house when Ratan returned from work. Even he had been upset throughout the afternoon. He had never lost his patience with his wife. But the simmering anger that he had always kept in check had brimmed over due to hunger and tiredness. And now, he felt ashamed of his behaviour. He was worried about having upset Vani and so, had returned home straight from work, without stopping at the Club. But Vani was not in bed in a dark house, as he had expected. His home was bright, thanks to Indu, and his wife was looking forward to his return, as bright and bubbly as ever. Even dinner was ready.

But his surprise and joy were only for a moment. Even as he was eating the food Vani had served him, he guessed that it was Indu's cooking. Instead of thinking, 'How I wish my Vani would cook this way!' he was imagining Indu whom he had never seen—as yet. Everything that Vani was saying to please him seemed to come from a distance. Noting that he seemed preoccupied, Vani was overcome with remorse, 'Poor man, he's slogged since the morning on an empty stomach,' she said to herself, 'I'll *never* let this happen again.' Previously, she used to make such resolutions and break them. But now, thanks to Indu helping her out every morning, she did not find it difficult to stick to it. In fact, it was Indu who kept Vani's resolution.

5

Indu saw to it that she was engrossed in Vani's household chores only to keep away pointless thoughts from bothering her. And so, both their routines were running smoothly. It was not as if Ratan did not notice the changes in his home. And as he watched the improvement, he could not help but appreciate the change in Vani as a homemaker. Yet, he could not help seeing Indu's hand in every touch of sophistication. He could create an image of her in his mind though he had never seen her. The Indu of his imagination was an ideal woman. Together with all the assets of a mistress of the house, she was also endowed with a strange beauty. But the Indu he had created so deftly had no smile; her eyes held no laughter. Perhaps that was because he was so used to seeing his Vani ever bubbling with joy. He may have imagined Indu to be as different from his wife as possible.

This habit of imagining Indu every time he noticed something appreciable became quite an addiction, eventually. Indu would flash across his mind when he was engrossed in his duties. Even he was surprised at the way he remembered her without his bidding. 'This is just an illusion,' he would say, brushing it away. He would be irritated with himself. But then, that lasted only awhile, like his wife's well-meaning resolutions. Ratan was an eminent doctor, capable of healing his distressed patients. But he seemed incapable of curing himself of his obsession with his Indu. Since he could not wipe her image out of his mind, he decided that the only way out was to see her. Surely, the real Indu would not match his fantasy. And that would cure him, perhaps.

Ratan knew that meeting Indu would not be a problem. He knew that she spent most of her time in his home when he was on duty. He knew that he would surely see her if he went home unexpectedly. And so, one day, though he had told Vani he would be late from work, he went home before three. He knew Indu was inside just as he had guessed; he could hear the murmur of conversation. He crept inside, slowly.

On the table in the drawing room was a pile of his clothes. Indu was pressing them, with her back to the door. Vani was sitting on a corner of that very table, swinging her legs, lost in her jabber.

Though he stood at the door for about five minutes, neither of them was aware of his presence. Ratan saw them together; his wife, rapt in whatever she was saying, and Indu adding her bits to the conversation though she was engrossed in what she was doing. Seeing the unbridgeable difference between the two women, Ratan began to rework the Indu of his imagination. And to think he had come home, hoping to wipe it away! Though the real Indu did not match the beauty of his dreams, her diligence compensated a hundredfold. Five, ten, fifteen minutes ticked away, and yet, Ratan did not stir. Vani happened to turn towards the door.

'Oh, how come you're *this* early? Are we going to a movie?' She slipped down from the table. That was when Indu became aware of Ratan's presence. She was baffled. She set the iron down quickly and turned towards him. Good, Ratan was able to correct the picture in his head.

Embarrassed at the way Ratan was staring at her without batting an eye, Indu stopped ironing and slipped away by the backdoor. Vani did not even think of stopping her; she was excited that her husband had sprung a surprise on her, to take her to a movie.

About an hour and a half later, when Vani went to Indu's house to ask her to go with them to the movie, she found her in bed, with a splitting headache. Her persuasion, her cajoling had no effect. Indu had a headache, true. But Vani did not even try to figure out why her friend's head was hurting all of a sudden. Had she thought about it, she would not have asked her husband to check on Indu, dressed and waiting as he was.

Ratan had decided on watching a movie, with the hope that he might get Indu off his mind. But before they could set out,

Vani's Confusion

Vani had rushed off next door saying, 'Let's take Indu with us,' even though Ratan had protested. When his wife returned from her friend's house without her, he felt relieved. But when she said, 'Come and check on Indu; she has a headache,' he lost his temper.

'What's so great about a headache?' he snapped. 'Give her an aspirin and hurry up. We'll be late!' At any other time, he would not have minded seeing the patient. If only she would, after all, be one of the many.

Now, especially when he was trying hard to get her out of his mind, he found Vani's fussing distasteful. But how would Vani understand? She was much too childlike. She stood her ground and, finally, managed to persuade him.

Ratan had never expected to see Indu again, in her own house, that too as a patient, barely a few hours after seeing her for the first time. And for sure, not even in his wildest imagination did he expect to see her weeping. Yes, Indu was weeping; heaving like a child. She knew she was not crying because of her aching head, but then, she did not know why else she was sobbing. She had broken down as soon as she had returned from Vani's house. Her tears flowed unrestrained, knowing fully well that no one cared whether she wept or even died weeping. How was she to expect Vani to come dragging her husband along, when she had thought they were on their way to the cinema?

Both Vani and Ratan put her anguish down to a throbbing head. Indu stopped crying on seeing them. She was most embarrassed to realize they had both seen her sobbing helplessly. He was a doctor, true, but nevertheless, she was upset that Vani had brought her husband inside without asking her if she could let him see her. Even Ratan felt awkward. Seeing Indu weeping like a child, he longed to comfort her as he would comfort a child, forgetting his feelings towards her. But he was saved by his experience as a medical practitioner and also by having his wife by his side. Despite the riot of his feelings, his bearing as a doctor was impeccable as he touched her forehead.

'She has a fever too,' he said, turning towards Vani.

'You give her some medicines and go to the cinema. I'll watch her,' said Vani, pushing aside the quilt and settling down comfortably on the bed.

Ratan saw the movie alone and, if Vani were to ask him that night what the movie was all about, he would have had to say, 'It was about Indu's weeping face.'

6

That day's headache laid the foundation for Ratan and Indu's friendship. Indu was a little reticent at first but soon began to feel comfortable while talking to him. It also became quite a habit for her to go to the movies with them. And that is how Indu's lonesome life changed radically barely six months after the neighbours had moved in. It changed, of course, but it would be wrong to think that she had found greater joy or contentment from this change. The initial security she had felt in the peace of her own home, in her new-found independence and in the confidence that all would be well with her at last, was no longer hers. The more she saw Ratan and Vani making a life together, the more she could feel the emptiness in her own. And what began as a fragile shoot soon sprouted leaves and began to flourish. And perhaps, Ratan was thinking of her often: her mind veered his way on its own.

Vani's Confusion

At this juncture, Vani had to go to her mother's house, unexpectedly. The husband and wife had planned a month-long visit during the summer anyway, but Vani's elder brother came unexpectedly to take her; their mother was ill and needed her. Ratan could not get leave. And so, Vani left with her brother. And that stupid girl had said, 'Indu, Mother's ill. I'll return as soon as she gets well. Take care of my home till I get back,' while Ratan was right there beside them.

'Sure,' said Indu, not knowing what else to say.

She had said, 'Sure,' to Vani, true, but Indu did not step that way, not even once. She was highly principled by nature. She had grown up respecting social norms as if they were divine commandments. She was already scared when she realized that she was beginning to get fond of Ratan. And her fear grew ten-fold after Vani left. How could she nurture emotions that would agitate her placid life into a storm? And yet, Ratan's image was installed in her heart. It was beyond her to control her feelings for Vani's husband. And so, she never went towards their house, for fear that Ratan might sense her improper love for him. She even stopped tending the flowers in her backyard for fear that she might meet him.

And now, the only way she could spend her time was to daydream ... and to weep that her dreams would never come true.

Ratan was used to seeing Indu around when Vani was at home but now he was bored. He also realized how much Indu had invaded his heart only when he could not see her. And though he felt it was good that she was keeping away, his fickle mind yearned to see her.

Once Vani left home, Ratan virtually lived at the Club and ate in a restaurant. He came home only to change and to sleep. He was the last person to leave the Club, then find a place to eat and come home around eleven to crash out. But even then, if he happened to be home during the day, he did not fail to go to the backyard, hoping to find Indu.

There was no indication of Vani returning, though she had been away for two months. One day when Indu was drawing water from the well, Ratan stepped out into the backyard. That was the first time both of them had seen each other since Vani had left. They used to talk to each other freely when Vani was around but now, they felt tongue-tied.

'When is Vani coming back?' asked Indu, fearing that Ratan might become aware of her feelings if she did not make casual conversation.

'Are you well, Indira?' said, Ratan, instead of replying. 'Why haven't I seen you these days?'

That was the very first time she had heard him call her name. Until then, she never knew it could sound so melodious. The change in the very sound of her name changed her sombre expression. Her face bloomed. Her eyes stared at him, laying bare her innermost feelings. Not that Ratan's eyes could hide his emotions. His very look brought Indu down to earth; right down from where her passion was soaring. Forgetting to carry the pot of water, she went into her house. Ratan waited a while, hoping she would come for it. But she did not.

Ratan waited one day, the next day and the next but he did not have Indu's darshan.[1] On the fourth day, Indu received a letter by post. She could make out that it was from Ratan; she was familiar

---

1   A devotee's glimpse of the deity in a shrine

with his handwriting. She sat with it for a long time, without opening it. She had not opened it even when she got up from the chair but had wet it with her tears. She went with it to the kitchen. And within a few moments, it was burnt to ashes in the wood fire.

Vani returned a week later. She went to Indu's house as soon as she arrived. It was locked! Vani was shocked. Where could she have gone, when she had always said she had no one to call her own? She asked the people who lived on the other side of the street. They told her she had gone to the family who had brought her up. Vani was even more perplexed. She could not understand why Indu had gone back to *those* relatives. She had always maintained she would never have anything to do with them, ever. Vani was too naive to guess Indu's reason for moving away. Ultimately, Indu's surprising behaviour was too much for Vani to fathom; she stopped trying. And since Ratan made no move to enlighten her, Vani's confusion stayed with her as a mystery.

MUNDKUR NARASIMHA KAMATH (M.N. KAMATH)

Who's the Thief?

It was the day of the village fair. Since the fair was held only once a year, there was great excitement in the village; naturally. Not just that. This time, the District Collector himself was present. Not with the Revenue Inspector or with any of his retinue, as usual, but alone. And just so that no one may be inconvenienced, he had asked his butler to go ahead of him and buy whatever was needed, for cash. He planned to camp in the village for the next four days.

Had the Collector come on an official visit, the four days would have been a long fatiguing day for the office peon in the village. The Shanbhagh (clerk) would be hiding behind the pages of the government registers and ledgers, checking the accounts and rechecking them. The Patel (village headman) would be parading about, as if he represented the goddess of the village herself—the *gramadevathe* incarnate, protecting the village on her behalf.

First published as 'KaddavaruYaru?' in 1941; in *Andina Aavuru*, Mitramandali, Mangaluru.

Who's the Thief?

But this visit was different. And so, the peon was busy putting up a thatched roof for the cowshed in the Shanbhagh's house. The Shanbhagh himself was engrossed in preparing receipts for rent received from the tenant farmers for land belonging to the Patel, stamping them with his right thumb impression, or was it his left thumb? And the Patel sat on the swing in his veranda, chewing betel leaves and nut while fanning himself with a fan made from areca palm.

No one knew exactly why the Collector had come to the town; not the clerks nor the peons in his office, not even the police officers. Or else, they would have whispered juicy bits of information to the Patel or the Shanbhagh, as if they were the only ones entrusted with the secret; smiling knowingly or affecting a serious expression while receiving favours in the form of tobacco or balls of incense from the storehouse. But now, the entire retinue of the Collector was only one person, the butler. He visited the village whenever the Collector needed anything. And since he also accompanied his boss on his tour of the districts, the butler knew a smattering of Kannada, Tamil and Telugu. But we who spoke only Tulu could not grasp whatever he was saying, for he mixed up idioms from all those languages. We felt we were listening to the twitter of birds. And so, there was no way we could find out why the Collector was visiting so unexpectedly.

But would our people rest with that? They began to speculate. Rumours floated freely: A wealthy Jain had died with no claimant to his property, and so the Collector had come in person to evaluate it and to claim that the government alone had the right to it; someone, who had taken land on lease, had found a metal pot with gold coins while digging the foundation for a temple for a spirit, and the Collector had got wind of it and had come to investigate; some of the villagers were somehow managing to steal buffaloes in the late evenings from a neighbouring town, and so he had come in person to catch the cattle thieves; anonymous petitions against the Patel had reached the Collector and so he had come to investigate; he had come to improve the status of the village, it would be made the capital of the taluk, it would eventually become a city, everyone would be vaccinated; the Collector was planning to distribute, from here, the equipment and other material for the War ... so the rumours floated, all in whispers. Some of them blended into one another and juicy gossip flourished: some people were rustling cattle and gathering them near the temple dedicated to a spirit to be sent as goods to the War; the Patel had sent anonymous petitions to the Collector that a wealthy man had died without a claimant to his wealth and that he could arrange for a pot of gold to be used towards the expenses incurred due to the War ...

All in whispers, of course, for the Collector was familiar with Tulu, Konkani and Kannada. When a wealthy person had hatched a plot one night to smuggle a log of wood from the forest to be used as a beam for his family temple, the Collector, in disguise, had heard the secret plans. The news was all around the village the next day that he was in the forest in time to apprehend the guilty. He was in the habit of going on solitary walks for some three to four miles every morning and evening. Not just that; even his butler strayed into the village every once in a while. And so, the villagers had to share their news only in whispers.

The Shanbhag was the Patel's writer. The Patel carried on the responsibility of his lineage by learning to put his thumbprint on official documents, just as he did on papers concerning his lands.

Who's the Thief?

He owned nearly half the village; his fate was virtually in the hands of the Shanbhag. Though the Patel was Uggappa Shettar and the Shanbhag was Narayanaraya, the tenant farmers thought that the Patel's name was Narayana Shettar. Such was the friendship and trust between the two of them. Narayanaraya's godown was the place where the tenants brought the Patel's share of their crop. The tenants had also to buy back the extra grain or else their tenancy would not be continued for the next year. After all, the Shanbhag too needed to make money, didn't he? Was it enough for him merely to enjoy the stature of being an important person in the village? Prestige doesn't feed the family, does it? The private transactions in the godown between him and the tenant farmers were thus his secret source of income.

The day of the fair was the third day since the Collector had camped in the village. It also happened to be the day when the Shanbhag had to cook at home. His wife, Nagamma, had gone to the river but she could enter the house and the kitchen only the next day, after her ritual purificatory bath at the end of the three days. And so, the Shanbhag was in a hurry to leave the village office adjacent to the Patel's house, after entering the details of the rental contracts to the tenant farmers in the register.

Just at that moment, returning from her bath in the river, the Patel's wife entered her house.

'Ayyo, my necklace is lost!' she exclaimed. 'I met Nagamma at the river. Both of us chatted for a while and then entered the river together. She was still bathing when I finished and walked back. When I was halfway home, I realized that my neck felt light. A crow crowed over my head, just at that moment. Scared by the bad omen, I touched my neck and my life nearly left me! I couldn't feel my necklace. I ran back to the river for it. Nagamma was returning home after her bath. I went after her. "I know nothing about it. I swear!" she said. But there was no one else who had come to bathe. Even the boys who watch over the cattle weren't there. We have to offer a coconut to the spirit. The necklace has to be found.' The Patel's wife was in tears; complaining, whining.

The bundle of official papers and ledgers that the Shanbhag was tying up in a cloth fell out like they were its guts. The Patel leapt up from the swing with such a start that the seat swung back and hit his head and he toppled on the platform! The tenants could neither laugh nor weep; they were stricken with fear. One of them was sent to fetch Kuppannayya, the priest at the Marigudi temple.

When Kuppannayya heard the reason for the summons from the Patel himself, he noted the omens he saw on his way: a watersnake slithering after a rat and a hawk swooping down to pick up a chick. He washed his feet before climbing the steps to the platform.

Even before he could be told of the reason for sending for him, Kuppannayya opened the panchanga[1] to check the calendar for the conjunction of the planets. Trusting in the good omens he had seen, he assured the Patel that the culprit would be caught within the day, shackled and brought to the platform since the goddess, Mariamma, had already sent her minions after him. He had relieved, to some extent, the Patel's anguish in losing a jewel worth three hundred rupees. He bundled the two seers of rice, two coconuts and a pumpkin that he received as gifts; chewed some betel leaves to respect the hospitality of his host and left with the Shanbhag, as he headed home.

---

1   The Hindu almanac

Who's the Thief?

The Shanbhag was thoroughly shaken. Nagamma was his third wife. It was two years since Narayanaraya had married the orphan. She was from a village; barely fifteen. If he had had a son, he may not have needed to marry her at all. But, of course, you and I could speculate that in case he had had a son by his first wife, Nagamma could easily have been his daughter-in-law. She was virtually a destitute, uneducated. And so, she was gullible, devoid of deceit. She would talk to other women only during those three days in the month when she could do nothing in the house, anyway. She never stepped out beyond the backyard on the other twenty-seven days. There were also the caste-restrictions regarding the people she could talk to. She had to maintain her husband's prestige too. And so, the only days she could enjoy the cool of the village beyond the backyard of her home were those three days when she had her periods, when she could wash her clothes by the river, have her bath and return home to eat the food her grumpy husband put out for her because the strain of cooking fell on him on those days. To her, it tasted like the food for the gods, as she ate it recalling her chatter with the other women by the river.

The Shanbhag was thunderstruck by the insinuations of the Patel's wife. And now, he dropped that thunderbolt on Nagamma.

'Did you have to set fire to the house you've come into? You turned your father's house into a cremation ground. Wasn't that enough?' Nagamani could not make sense of her husband's fury. She looked at the roof, confused. There was no fire, no smoke. What was he so furious about?

'I can step into the house only tomorrow, after my bath.'

The Shanbhag thought she was making fun of him.

'Yes, you can step into the house only tomorrow. That'll be like the never-to-be tomorrow of Ganapathi's wedding.[2] Tomorrow, your body will be bathed in the river and carried straight to the cremation grounds,' he thundered, standing at a distance. His wife saw stars. She could not understand what he was saying and yet, she could sense that he was blaming her for something that had gone terribly wrong. She sat in the yard. The Shanbhag plonked his cane on the platform. Poova, the watchman of the village, also served as the watchman of the granary attached to the Shanbhag's house. He was now repairing the thatched roof over the porch, listening to every word:

'Who else was there when you were bathing in the river?'

'The Patel's wife. There was no other woman, let alone men.'

'Oh, hang the men! What were you doing with the Patel's wife?'

'She told me that she was going to visit her mother on the day of the next village fair. I told her that my mother's home was near hers but that I didn't have parents. She felt sorry for me. I waited until the water was clean again after her bath. And then, I bathed. That's all.'

'Why are you remembering the dead after they're long gone? Is it to blacken their names as well? Were you waiting for clean water to flow down or were you waiting for her to go before you could pick up what she had left behind?'

'What did she leave behind? Oho, yes! She returned as I was walking back home. She asked me if I had seen her necklace by

---

2   Ganapathi or Ganesh found it hard to find a bride because of his elephant head

the river. I told her I hadn't seen it even when it was around her neck. She went her way and I came home.'

'Don't say, "I came home." Say, "I brought it home." Where have you kept it? Give it to me right now. I'm a poor man. This house, this yard, everything belongs to the Patel. I may be the Shanbhag here. But our lives depend on the Patel's goodwill. Never mind that we are poor. Be satisfied with your nose ring and your mangalasutra.[3] Don't covet her necklace. No one knows about it yet. No one suspects you yet. They have prayed to the demon-god. You will be sacrificed at the temple of Mariamma.[4] Give it to me, or else, tell me where you've hidden it. I'll take it to the Patel and convince him that I found it near the river. Come on, give it to me. You're my third wife. I'll be in great trouble if you die. It'll be difficult for me to get married again, difficult for me to be cooking for myself, difficult to die without children to perform the rituals after my death, difficult to have a maid in the house and keep the gossip from flowing. Look at me! Ayyo, if I could've touched you, I would've chopped off your nose like Shurpanakhi's.[5] I'll have to punish you. Give it to me. Or else I'll drop this stone on your head. Give it to me, quick!'

Nagamma was drying her hair in the yard. She was seeing stars. And now the stars had gathered into one mass to become the moon, and that very moon became a grey cloud shedding rain; Nagamma wailed. A mensurating woman is not supposed to drink

---

3   Symbol of marriage that a wife wears on a thread on her neck
4   Goddess, guardian of Indian villages
5   Ravana's sister who was mutilated by Lakshmana for making advances to Lord Rama

even water before bathing and so, she was exhausted, hungry and thirsty. And now, her husband's ranting, his heaving, his rolling eyes, his fearsome expression, his scary threat to chop off her nose and the more immediate threat of dropping a boulder on her head and above all that, his demand that she should give him something—nothing made sense. And even as he screamed, 'Give it to me, *quick*!', she sank to the ground and lay there.

Would the Shanbhag let her be?

'Are you trying to play games with me? Has the devil got into you? Has Mariamma got hold of you?' he kept shouting even as he raised a huge stone as if to drop it on her head. Nagamma did not stir, even then.

Poova had been enjoying every detail of the drama while repairing the thatched roof of the porch. Now, he crept down softly, stood behind the Shanbhag, grabbed the stone and tossed it away. He had saved the Shanbhag from serving a life sentence for murder, probably. A watchman is much like the village policeman, isn't he? Even as the stone was out of his hands, the Shanbhag's fury abated.

'Shanabhagare, shouldn't you bring a pot of water and sprinkle some on Amma's face? She might die if you delay ... Or else, I'll sprinkle some myself.'

Is Poova a Brahmin? What if even a drop of that water touches his wife's lips? Won't she become an outcaste? And so, as the Shanbhag battled with these questions, he ran, in a daze, to get some water and pour it over her with trembling hands. Did he remember then, that he had threatened to wash her dead body in the river before cremation?

The young girl opened her eyes, slowly.

Who's the Thief?

'Amma, get up, get up,' said the watchman. 'It's very hot here. Go to the porch. I've repaired the roof. Go and sit there. Ayya will call you when the food is ready.'

What could anyone say about Narayanaraya's cooking if he had to cook that day? Fortunately, it was Ekadashi.[6] The fruits and milk that went with the fasting were like food for the soul; the penance brought some healing to his spirit.

In the Patel's house, many vows were being made to the many gods for the recovery of the necklace, but not even a single, tiny tinkling bell on it was found. No magician, no pujari,[7] no astrologer could provide a single clue to its whereabouts.

The night too was spent in fasting. Nagamma slept in the courtyard at the back of the house, the Shanbhag on the front porch and Poova, the watchman, slept near at hand to keep watch over them, much like the village policeman that he was.

Narayanaraya could not sleep ... The Patel would believe his wife's story, for sure. Ugrappa Shettar had lost a necklace worth three hundred rupees. Why would he not believe his wife? So, he may get some schoolteacher from the village to replace him as his writer, paying him a paltry measure of rice. Then, he will lose his job as the Shanbhag. The Patel will then ask him to vacate the house saying he would like to use it to store grain; just an excuse so that there may be no ill feelings between them. Then, he will also lose the money he had been making on the side from the tenant farmers. And all because his wife happened to go to the river to bathe, right when the Patel's wife happened to be there. Though

---

6   The eleventh day of every fortnight when Hindus fast
7   Priest

the Patel would naturally suspect Nagamma, he would pretend that he did not until he was able to get a replacement for the Shanbhag, because, after all, he was in charge of the land register. Not just that, he even had the record of the receipts for the money the tenant farmers paid the Patel for buying back the grain. And so, he himself would have to somehow see that Nagamma was proved innocent beyond a doubt ...

Just then, the cock crowed. Narayanaraya woke up Nagamma and sent her to the stream to bathe. He sent the peon too, just in case there were others heading that way and there were room for gossip about the loss. Someone may even try to drown her. In the meantime, he would have to think up ways of getting her to confess her guilt.

That year, the revenue officers had come to fix the land tax as per the Settlement.[8] Just as Vishnu came as Vamana, stepped on Bali's head and retrieved everything that rightfully belonged to Indra, they came to measure the lands owned by zamindars and to fix the tax to be paid by the peasants—which was to be spent on governance.

With the officers came their staff. But quite a few of them did not return with their bosses once their work was done. Instead, they found other ways to make a living here. Perhaps they did not want to step back after putting their foot here. Whatever the reason, they displayed their proficiency in various trades.

---

8   The Permanent Settlement introduced by the East India Company

Some set up shops selling beedi and soda.[9] Some of them were good at making brassware. Some drove jutkas.[10] Some others even became beggars displaying their open sores, begging by the roadside. Some became overseers of building constructions in the summer and during the monsoon, went on a pilgrimage to Gokarna in the red ochre robes of mendicants, thus catering to both their mundane as well as their spiritual needs. Sometimes, pouches lost from other people's pockets at railway stations, fairs and markets were found in theirs. Some of them displayed incredible knowledge of palmistry. They could also interpret omens, both good and bad. But one could hardly make out what they said. Perhaps the gods would weep to hear them speak in Sanskrit. Their Kannada sounded like Tulu; their Tulu like Tamil or Malayalam. The problem was not with just the words but with the accent too. Whatever they spoke sounded like the language of the gods. Perhaps, that is why the elders have the wise saying: *I am the Spoken Word; I am the Written Word.*

And so, among those who stayed behind was a mason-cum-bronzesmith-cum-exorcist. He worked as a bronzesmith only when he could not earn enough from exorcising his clients of demons or the spirits of the dead or from the evil influence of the planets. If even that did not work, he became a stonemason. He had not bought any land; he was that confident in his proficiency as a sorcerer. The diviners from the Veerabhadra temple, who were good only at propitiating the planets to ward off evil, were jealous of his confidence.

---

9   Local cigarettes and soft drinks
10 Horse-cart

The Shanbhag remembered that man that morning. He thought of sending for him when he saw Poova's wife, Rukku, walking towards the house, fresh from a good night's sleep. It was not easy to forget her familiar face. Everyone in the village, man and woman, stopped—at least for a moment—to chat with her. She was well built, like a Kshatriya, walked with a horse's gait, and spoke like a Jamadar.[11] Everyone who saw her said *she* was like the village policeman, more than her husband, Poova. But truly, the best way to describe Rukku was to compare her to her namesake, Rukmini, Krishna's wife.

The Shanbhag smiled.

'Rukku, you have to get that witch-doctor. He has to be here by the time Nagamma returns from the stream after her bath,' he said, briefly giving her the impression that his wife needed to be exorcised. Rukku crept like a cat towards the magician's house. She looked back once or twice. Who knows why? Some said, that was her style. Some others said, she was haughty. Whatever that may be, let it be. How does it matter to us?

When Rukku reached his house, the black magician was smearing sacred ash on his forehead, calling out to Shiva—as if he was waking him up. He guessed why such an important person as the village accountant had sent for him that early in the morning even before Rukku could tell him. After offering her the tambula of betel leaves and nuts, he collected his bag of cowrie shells, a book that looked like the panchanga, the Hindu almanac, a ball of red mud and followed Rukku to the Shanbhag's house.

---

11 Armed official

Who's the Thief?

I am unable to write whatever may have transpired between the two as they walked down the mud track. I would like to, at least for us to become familiar with the blend of Tulu and Kannada that he spoke that sounded like the language of the gods. But there are no letters that can be typeset to bring out the flavour in his pronunciation. Of course, as a bronzesmith, he could create new letters of the alphabet that could be printed but he has not had the right kind of encouragement to pursue the craft … But that is the way it is. Those who can create new jobs are unemployed in the field where their real talent lies. And we engage in august discussions about eradicating unemployment. And so, the bronzesmith had to survive as a magician and we had to lose a way of learning new sounds in a new variety of language that was a blend of two or more tongues.

As soon as the Shanbhag offered him a place to sit, the magician drew, with the ball of clay, a rough sketch of the plan for a newly built house where he had worked as the stonemason. He placed a few cowrie shells in each of the rooms, calling out the names of some four or five gods. And then he began to ask questions. From what we could make out from his muttering, he seemed to be saying what we expected to hear: something of great value is lost. Someone is suspected but the suspect is not guilty. She has hidden it through the power of the river goddess who has entered her and so, she has to be exorcised. As the goddess leaves the woman, she will return the object through the very hands of the woman. To cast out the spirit of the river goddess, the woman must be made to sit in front of a pit with burning coal and made to touch it. The embers must be poured over her as if to bathe her in fire. Then, the goddess of the river will leave her and your purpose will be served.

How amazing! The magician would have hardly had time to glean information from Rukku about the situation. And yet his prescription to rid the woman of the water goddess through embers was not only in accordance with the superstition of the villagers; it also seemed quite scientific. He must have become a popular magician not just by his magical powers; he was also astute enough to gauge the situation to tell his clients what they expected to hear.

Even as Nagamma returned from bathing in the river with her hair dripping water, her husband was convinced that she was, indeed, possessed by the water-spirit. He asked Poova to dig a little pit, fill it with dry leaves and twigs and light a fire. He also added some of the hay left over from thatching the roof. Then he asked the exorcist to proceed with the ritual.

Nagamma was dumbstruck. For every question that her husband and the witch-doctor posed, she had only one response, 'I don't know.' And so, she had to sit in front of the fire on and on. Her sari, which had been damp, was almost crisp. She had let down her hair to dry in the sun. But now, it was dry in the heat and all askew, thanks to a brisk breeze. The tips were getting burnt wherever tongues of fire could lick them. She had not eaten, she had hardly slept; she was sad, bewildered. The smoke rising from the fire made her red eyes redder. Her body sagged. Even as the fire pit was fed with strips of firewood and questions were rained on her, Nagamma swooned over the fire. Narayanaraya dashed towards his wife to rescue her. But the magician lifted her. She had patches of burns on her forehead, face and chest. Her sari was burnt in places.

'Now, the water-spirit will leave her surely,' he said.

Who's the Thief?

'What should we do for the burns?' asked her husband. Someone said, 'Butter'. Someone else said, 'Cow dung'. He got butter. Nagamma would not speak. She was gasping for breath. He was scared for her. And yet he could not stop the ritual.

Right then, some of the tenants came from the Patel's house, looking for the Shanbhag who had not yet reported for duty. The Patel wondered if he had absconded with the necklace and used his absence from work as an excuse to find out. Wouldn't they have guessed what could have happened? Couldn't they have gone back and reported to the Patel? No. They stood about watching, lest they should hinder the ritual.

The witch-doctor continued with his chanting but Nagamma did not regain consciousness.

'This is rahukala.[12] I can't do anything unless this inauspicious phase passes,' he said, and sat a little away.

'She hasn't yet spoken a word! What kind of magic is yours?' The Shanbhag growled, though he was trembling with fear. For a moment, he was worried about the gathering crowd. But he soon took comfort in his mind: *They'll be witness to the trouble I'm taking to find the necklace. Good.*

It was nearly noon. The Collector's butler came to the Shanbhag. He had been to the bronzesmith some two hours earlier. The Collector was returning to the capital that day. He wanted to buy any old bronze idols that the local people worshipped. He had quite a collection and wanted to add to it. The butler heard that the bronzesmith was here and so, had come over.

---

12   Inauspicious time of the day

'I've got a beautiful idol of Panjurlidaiva,[13] the local deity. I could give it to you for four rupees. It's been lying at home for want of buyers since there hasn't been a new temple for it to be installed. At least you can take it. I'll bring it to the bungalow once I'm done with this magic, in about two hours,' said the bronzesmith.

Now, his mind was on getting the four rupees. The Shanbhag was focused on the bronzesmith-magician who had not yet completed the ritual. He became restless. The magician could not leave until he had worked his magic and released the Shanbhag's wife from the clutches of the river goddess. But unless he went, the Collector could not get the idol of the Panjurli spirit. That would be a problem.

The butler came back with an order: the Patel, the Shanbhagh and the village peon were to be at the Collector's bungalow in half an hour. The bronzesmith too was to accompany them. Could they disobey? Even as all of them were preparing to leave, the Collector himself appeared on the scene.

'I had asked all of you to come over. But then, I'm here myself on hearing that you were conducting some religious rituals. I didn't want to mess it up. What's happening here?'

All of them knew that the Collector could understand Tamil, Tulu and Kannada. The sorcerer spoke.

'This is to drive away the goddess of the river. She has entered this woman yesterday while she was bathing in the river and made her hide the necklace belonging to the Patel's wife. Through my magic, I can see that she is the guilty one.'

---

13   A spirit worshipped in Mangalore

THE COLLECTOR (Smiling): Strange magician! What else do you have to do?

THE MAGICIAN: I'll have to make this woman sit on the burning coal. It's not dangerous.

THE COLLECTOR: How do you know that she is the culprit?

THE MAGICIAN: By studying the influence of the planets on her life.

THE COLLECTOR: How strange! Who got you here?

THE MAGICIAN (Pointing to Rukku, the peon's wife): This woman. She knew nothing about the theft.

THE PEON: It's not her fault, deva! She's my wife.

THE COLLECTOR: Who sent her to get him here?

SHANBHAG: I did, devare.[14] My wife said she was bathing alone in the river. That's when the Patel's wife realized that she had lost her necklace. My wife kept insisting that she knew nothing about it, however much I probed. That's why I had to send for the sorcerer. Now, the truth will be out.

The Collector sent for the Patel's wife and questioned her. She repeated her story about losing the necklace … When he asked the Patel, he said that he did not suspect anyone. But that he had vowed to propitiate the gods; he had implicit faith that the jewel would surely be found.

THE COLLECTOR: What if you find the necklace?

THE PATEL: I'll keep it. I don't want my wife to wear it. My wife who's unaware of what's on her. It costs *three hundred rupees*, devare!

---

14 Term of respect; literally, God

THE PATEL'S WIFE: Keep it! Wear it around your neck. You have the armlet, earrings, bangles and other jewellery anyway. You'll look impressive at the gram panchayat[15] meetings.

SHANBHAG: I'm in great trouble, devare. Shouldn't the Patel pay me for my efforts to find the necklace? Or else, why should I be maintaining his records? And an account of his family expenses? I should get to keep my job or at least the house and the granary.

THE PEON'S WIFE: I brought the sorcerer to work his magic. What do *I* get?

THE PEON: I kept watch over the Shanbhag and his wife. Or else, wouldn't there have been one or even two dead bodies here?

At that moment, Nagamma opened her eyes with a groan, '*Hooon*.'

'Shahbas! Give me back my necklace,' roared the magician, leaping towards her with a spine-tingling scream. 'Come on, give it to me, right now. I know you have it. The Collector is here. I have to hand over the Panjurlidaiva to him. Hurry!'

Nagamma did not speak a word. The sorcerer kept screaming at her, making strange faces and staring at her with fearsome eyes.

The Collector pretended to be stunned. Suddenly, he ran his hands all over his body as if he was feeling for something. Then, he pulled out the necklace from his shirt pocket, looking innocent.

'What's this? How did it get into *my* pocket? I thought it was a snake, all curled up,' he said.

Everyone stood stunned; each with his own thoughts. The spirit had shown them compassion through the Collector. She was

---

15   Village government body

Who's the Thief?

indeed a royal *daiva* who worked with royal dignity. The necklace was found, anyway.

The sorcerer was beaming. If he had opened his mouth wider, it would have split in two. The Patel raised his bangled hand, shouting, 'O! O!' His wife began laughing but ended up sobbing. The Shanbhag had been standing. Now he sat down and then stood up again. The peon was swinging his arms about dramatically as if he were measuring the land. And his wife, Rukku, stared at the necklace; it seemed as if she would swallow it with her eyes. All of them assembled there felt their Dore[16] was indeed a just man; the power of his presence had enabled the necklace to manifest itself. Everyone stared at the Collector with reverence. They were about to sing his praises.

'So, now that you've got your jewellery, what do you have to say?' he asked the Patel.

'Now, we'll fulfil all the vows we had made to different goddesses. I'll take personal care to see that it is never lost again. Of course, I'll have to reward the sorcerer for his efforts.'

'This poor girl is full of burns. She's still bewildered. Was the jewel found only through this ritual of witchcraft performed over her? How're you making it up to her?'

'To *her*? I'll see that she gets the traditional plate of fruits and flowers with kumkuma and arshana[17], offered to married women. It's been proved now that it was right to suspect her. Would we

---

16 Referring to a British officer
17 Vermilion powder and turmeric

have got the jewel if all this magic had not been performed on her, Sahebare?'[18]

'What do *you* have to say?' The Collector looked at the Shanbhag.

'What sort of a wife is she to be demon-possessed? To disgrace me? My grief is great, Dore!'

'Since you have such impressive magical powers,' said the Collector to the sorcerer, 'Why should you waste them here in this village? Come, let's go to the capital.'

'As you please, Dore.' The magician brought his palms together. But the Patel, the Shanbhag and the peon pleaded that he should not be transferred.

Then the Collector addressed them:

'Yesterday, I'd gone fishing near that river. While returning, I noticed a handkerchief with a small roll of betel leaves and below that, this necklace. I picked them up, returned to my bungalow and sent a note to the police officers to locate the owner. This morning, I put it in my pocket to take it to the capital with me. And now, who is responsible for forgetting where the jewel was left? Who is responsible for putting the blame squarely on this poor girl? I had heard about the way the Patel and the Shanbhag try to retrieve lost property. Now, I've seen it with my own eyes. The magician would've got all the pertinent information from the person who came for him and manipulated it to convince you. This is, after all, a small village. News will travel easily from house to house. That could be her misfortune. You would say it's the influence of the planets. But there's great injustice done to this poor girl. The

---

18   Term of respect while addressing a British officer

magician is responsible. He has to be transferred to the capital for further investigation.

'He has turned the blind belief of ignorant villagers to his advantage to exploit them. For this crime, he can be sentenced to two years of harsh imprisonment. The Shanbhag and the peon and his wife too will be punished as abettors. Of the three, the Shanbhag's crime would be greater. The Shanbhag and the peon will be disqualified to hold their jobs. But if the Shanbhag is relieved from his post, this poor woman will have to suffer even more at his hands. Their behaviour will be on record. Since the Patel is illiterate and is obliged to the Shanbhag, it seems more sensible to look for an educated person within the Patel's family and give him the position of the Patel.'

And turning towards the peon, he said, 'As a watchman, shouldn't you keep an eye on your wife too?'

The Collector had pronounced his sentence on the guilty persons with such ease. The tenant-farmers moved closer to the sorcerer. He had fleeced them in many ways; and now, they were eager to see him one last time. Rukku was touched by the compassion the Collector showed towards the hapless victim. After all, she was a woman too. She rushed towards Nagamma to take care of her. It never occurred to her that she was, after all, just the peon's wife; that she was not a Brahmin. The Patel took out fifty rupees from his pouch, pulled out some betel leaves and areca nuts from a corner of his wrap and handed the gift to his wife to be handed over to Nagamma. The peon darted across to the bronzesmith-cum-magician's house and brought the bronze image of the Panjurli demon and handed it over to the butler respectfully. And thus, the curtain was drawn on the last act of a great drama.

The Collector handed over the necklace to the Patel. He paid four rupees to the bronzesmith—the price of the idol—and advised him to become a gardener instead of a sorcerer. Then, he took out a small container of balm from his pouch and handed it over to be smeared on Nagamma's burns. And he walked back to his bungalow, smiling to himself.

'People keep complaining that the Collector comes to raise the tax because of the Settlement. But he is a true Dore. Yes, he does come to survey the farmlands to levy the tax, true. But whatever you may say, see how just he was in dealing with our problem. Our idea of magic is no match to the magic of the British sense of justice.' The Patel and the Shanbhag sat chatting amicably, while the tenant-farmers stood about, trying to make sense of the whole experience.

As for Rukku, she would not leave Nagamma, now that the river nymph had left her; she took it upon herself to nurse her bruised body and battered spirit.

The courtyard of the Shanbhag's house is no longer the barn. It is well-swept and decorated with artistic rangoli[19] patterns, for it now houses Rukku and Poova as well. Rukku is now a mother, without the intervention of magic. She has named her child Nagamma and hugs the baby close to her, as if she were her necklace.

---

19 Traditional patterns drawn on the floor with rice flour

S.G. SASTRY

A Gift for the Festival

VENKATARAMANA: KAMALA, DID the Book Post come from the Post Office?

KAMALA: Yes, Anna. It did.

VENKATARAMANA: For how much?

KAMALA: For twenty-three and a half rupees.

VENKATARAMANA: Then it's one and a half rupees less than I expected. Good. Where's the book?

KAMALA: Where else? In the Post Office.

VENKATARAMANA: Didn't you receive the Book Post?

KAMALA: No.

VENKATARAMANA: But why? Hadn't I told ayya that a book would be coming by Book Post? That I would need it for my course?

KAMALA: Yes, you had.

VENKATARAMANA: Then, why didn't he receive the Book Post. Wasn't he home when the postman came?

First published as 'Habbadha Udugoray' in 1946 in *Iddaruu Irabahudu*, Kaavyaalaya, Mysuru.

KAMALA: He was.

VENKATARAMANA: Then …? Why didn't he get the book? What did ayya say? What could be his reason?

KAMALA: What's the point is asking *me*, Anna?

VENKATARAMANA: You know why. You just don't want to tell me. You're not concerned about me at all.

KAMALA: What's the point in getting angry with me, Anna? I am, after all, a woman. What would I know about such things?

VENKATARAMANA: Ayyo, paapa! Just a woman, indeed. Does she know *anything* at all? Nothing. Except to write to her husband faithfully twice a week. That's all! Let your husband's next reply come. I'll open the letter and read it.

KAMALA: I'll tell ayya if you do that.

VENKATARAMANA: Tell me, then. Why didn't ayya receive the book that came in the Book Post?

KAMALA: Why? Why? Why do you keep bothering me when it's obvious? You know why? He didn't have the money.

VENKATARAMANA: I had told him about this some eight days ago. Even before I had ordered the book from Bombay. I sent for the book only after he said, "Send for it. I'll arrange for the money, somehow." Now, what do I do if he has no money! I need that book urgently. Can we get it tomorrow, at least?

KAMALA: Isn't tomorrow a holiday for Gowri?

VENKATARAMANA: Not a Postal holiday.

KAMALA: I don't think ayya will have any money by tomorrow.

VENKATARAMANA: That's my fate! God has been hindering my education in some way or another. I feel bad to see ayya struggling to make ends meet. I haven't the heart to bother him. And yet … if I get through this final exam, none of us will have a problem.

I'll be earning enough and more. I only hope God will provide, somehow, this once.

KAMALA: Don't we all know how hard you've been studying, *Anna*? Both ayya and amma think of you as their treasure-house. Haven't they educated you until now, despite all odds? Last year when ayya had to pay the fees for your BA exams, didn't they sell Amma's eardrops to provide for it? When our neighbour, Komalamma, said, "Ayyo, why did you have to sell your jewellery?" Amma boasted, "What have I lost, Komalamma? Once my son completes his education, he'll get me ten pairs of such eardrops to go with my earrings!" Just wait, ayya will somehow manage to get the money in a few days. Don't worry. Aren't Anna and Amma eager to see you get through the Civil Service exam? Aren't we all?

VENKATARAMANA: Seri, seri, there's no point talking about it. Is there any shopping to be done? Where's ayya?

KAMALA: He's gone to the sari shop. Amma's father has sent twenty-five rupees as his gift to buy her a sari for the Gowri festival. She wants to wear a new Dharmavaram silk sari and go to the temple tomorrow for the Gowri puje.[1] She has been longing for a Dharamavaram sari for the last four or five years. When Thatha visited us last month, she had told him about it. And so, he has sent the money and ayya has gone to buy it.

VENTAKARAMANA: Is there anything I have to get from the market?

---

1 A significant festival in Karnataka when Lord Ganesha's mother and wife of Lord Shiva is worshipped as the primal female power

KAMALA: Yes. We need to buy flowers. We've bought everything else. Here's two annas.

VENKATARAMANA: How can two annas worth of flowers be enough for tomorrow? You need some to take to the temple. You'll have to offer some to married women who come home. Tomorrow's also our Upakarma.[2] We men will have to change our sacred thread. So, we'll need some for our puje. And you and *Amma* will need some to wear in your hair. However can two annas worth of flowers be enough on a festive day?

KAMALA: Then get as many as you can for the two annas from the market. Here, take these four annas. Get some good strands of flowers for us to wear from the flower vendors' street.

VENKATARAMANA: You have some of my money with you, don't you? Give me one anna from that.

KAMALA: Why d'you want to waste money, Anna? You may have passed your BA, but you don't yet know the value of money.

VENKATARAMANA: Oh, yes, of course, of course! My little teenage sister knows how to handle money. But I—a nearly-twenty-year-old graduate—don't! No wonder you've got a stingy husband, just right for you. All this pointless talk is only because I asked for *my* money.

KAMALA: If you want your money, take it all back. But don't say a word against your bava[3]. Here, take this anna. Why d'you want it? Tell me.

---

2   Annual ceremony when Brahmins change their sacred thread
3   Brother-in-law

VENKATARAMANA: These women want to know everything! I want to buy some palmyra flowers for Amma.

KAMALA: Then buy them from my money. Buy two sweet-smelling bunches.

VENKATARAMANA: No, I want to buy it for her from *my* money ... I'm off to the market now.

KAMALA: *Anna, Anna*!

VENKATARAMANA: (Returning) What now?

KAMALA: I called you to say I have only a rupee and five annas of yours. Keep a tab on the accounts.

Sitting inside, Lakshmidevamma had heard every word of the dialogue between her children on the verandah.

After a while, Venkatasubba Sastry came home with some four or five pure silk saris. He called out to his wife, '*Le*, come here. Look at the saris I've brought from the shop. Choose whichever you like. I'll return the rest.'

Kamala rushed inside and gushed, 'Oh! What gorgeous saris! Every one of them looks beautiful. Take this, Amma. It feels heavy. It'll drape well on you.'

LAKSHMIDEVAMMA: I don't need a new sari right now.

Kamala and her father were stunned.

KAMALA: What're you saying, Amma? You've been longing for a pure silk Dharmavaram sari all these days. And now, with such a fine choice in front of you, you're refusing to choose one. Tomorrow's the Gowri festival. Thatha has sent the money so that his beloved daughter might wear a new sari. Even you had accepted it. You aren't making any sense, Amma! Just take one of these and wear it to the temple tomorrow for the Gowri puje. There's no need for any further discussion.

LAKSHMIDEVAMMA: I don't want a sari *now*. If I'm alive next year, I'll get a sari through Gowramma's grace. But this year, I want only the money; not the sari, definitely. Please return all the saris.

SASTRY: Why're you talking like this?

LAKSHMIDEVAMMA: I don't want the sari now. That's it. Please don't pester me.

SASTRY: You've got something on your mind … Hadn't you been looking forward to a new Dharamvaram sari ever since your father sent you the money for it?

LAKSHMINDEVAMMA: Yes, I've got a reason. I'll tell you tomorrow. Don't bother me now … please.

And she walked away. Her husband returned the saris, crestfallen, and came home.

The next day was festive. The family had to celebrate two feasts on the same day. The women, of course, had the Gowri puje. And because they belonged to the Saamaveda[4] tradition, the men had to observe the Saamaveda Upakarma by changing the sacred thread. Sometimes, with the Ganesha puje falling on the same day, there would be three feasts to be celebrated. This year at least, the Ganesha festival was on the next day.

Venkataramana and his father finished their bath and sandhyavandhane[5] and left for the large water tank to perform the rituals for Upakarma. Kamala wore a grand silk sari and left for the temple with the purohit, Rangabhatta's wife. Lakshmidevamma finished cooking a festive meal and sat making her delectable

---

4 Compiled during 1200-1000 BCE, a compilation of chants meant for ceremonies

5 Morning and evening prayers

obbattu[6] for the first course. It was around eleven when someone called at the door, '*Avvaa … Ammaa …*'

'Who's that?'

'It's me, Amma. Bora. I've brought sweetmeats distributed from the Palace for Gowri.'

Lakshmidevamma opened the door, received the winnowing fan with sweets, flowers and the tambula[7] with betel leaves and areca nuts, offered Bora a coconut with tambula and sent him off. Right then, the postman brought the book-post. Lakshmidevamma took twenty-three rupees and eight annas from the bowl with sanctified red rice near the idol of Gowri, handed it to the postman and took delivery of the packet. She took it to Venkataramana's room and hid it in his trunk. She bathed again to purify herself ritually, changed into another clean sari and sat down to continue making the obbattu.

It was around twelve by the time the father and son returned after the rituals of changing the sacred thread for Upakarma. Even Kamala arrived around the same time. Sastry called out to his wife, 'Go and finish your Gowri puje now.' And as she stepped out of the kitchen, he said, 'What's this, Lakshmidevi? Why're you wearing this old silk sari?'

'This is the sari your father, that's my father-in-law, sent me for the first Gowri puje after we got married. Do I need any other to wear for my Gowri puje? If all of you can come for lunch, I could serve you and then go and do my puje leisurely.'

---

6   Sweet-stuffed roti, festive food
7   An offering of betel leaves with areca nuts

Sastry and his children sat down to lunch. Lakshmidevamma served them. After that was done, she collected the items for the puje and was about to leave when Venkataramana said, 'Amma, you've forgotten to take the fruit tray.'

LAKSHMIDEVAMMA: I'll first leave these trays in front of Gowri in Rama Sastri's house. Rangabhatta is the purohit officiating at the puje today. I'll come again and take the rest of the trays.

VENKATARAMANA: I'll bring these. Why should you come again for them?

Lakshmidevamma participated in every phase of the ritual with great fervour. And when Rangabhatta chanted, *manasodhishtaprarthanamsamarpayami*, and announced, 'Now, you can make your petitions to Gowramma', Lakshmidevamma stood before the goddess with some palmyra flowers, repeated a prayer to Gowri that she had learnt in her mother's house, and prayed silently for her husband's long life, 'Amba! Gowri! Protect my mangalya!'[8] And then she added, 'Bless the task my son has undertaken.' Completing her puje, she prostrated before the goddess with a namaskara.[9] As soon as she stood up, one of the flowers that she had offered to Gowri, slipped from her right side.

'Did you see that, Amma?' said Rangabhatta, shocked, 'Devi has answered your prayers. The palmyra flower you offered fell from her right side. That's a sure sign!' And taking that flower, the

---

8 Symbol of marriage worn by the wife
9 Salutation with palms brought together

purohit offered it to Lakshmidevamma, together with some of the red rice, consecrated for manthraakshathe.[10]

When she returned home, Venkataramana said, 'Amma, now sit down for lunch. I'll wear my silk dhothi[11] and serve you. It's a festive occasion, after all.' Lakshmidevamma was happy. She sat down.

While she was eating, he said, 'Amma, if I get through the Civil Service exam this year—I'm studying hard for it—I'll get you a gold-laced Dharmavaram silk sari. You won't have to worry about anything. You'll see then how much I worship you.'

LAKSHMIDEVAMMA: Don't worry ... God is with us.

VENKATARAMA: I'll serve you another obbattu.

LASHMIDEVAMMA: No, no! Don't! *Ei*, why did you serve me when I asked you *not* to?

And both of them burst out laughing, staring at each other.

LAKSHMIDEVAMMA: Now, you better go. I'll get Kamalu to serve me some buttermilk.

Venkatarama went to his room and opened his trunk. And the book-post caught his eye. He was thrilled. He held it aloft and came out shouting, 'Ayya, who received the book-post? From where did you get the money?'

SASTRI: (Bewildered) I know nothing about it.

VENKATARAMANA: Kamlu, who paid for the book-post?

KAMALA: I don't know, Anna.

VENTAKARAMANA: Amma, did you...?

---

10 Consecrated rice for blessing
11 A length of cloth worn by men around the waist to cover the lower part of the body

LAKSHMIDEVAMMA: Hm.

VENKATARAMANA: Is that why you refused to buy a sari?

LAKSHMIDEVAMMA: Hm.

Venkataramana was tongue-tied. He went towards his mother and held her hands, with tears streaming down his cheeks. He just could not control himself. He sat there for a while and walked away to his room wondering how ever he could repay this runa.[12] He lay down, realizing that such debts to a mother can never be repaid. And he slept like a baby.

---

12 Obligation

DR MASTI VENKATESHA IYENGAR (SRINIVASA)

The Story of Jogi Anjappa's Hen

JOGI ANJAPPA IS one of the elderly men in our town. Whenever he has to narrate an incident, he always begins with, 'When I was about fifteen …' No one is yet alive who has seen any such events. He was supposed to have been a lad during the time of the Sepoy Mutiny. If anyone asks him how old he is, he says, 'A hundred, maybe.' He has been a hundred for about the last ten years. More relevant than that is the authority he has gained to advise anyone in any situation. Others may have doubts about his privilege, but, surely, not Anjappa.

If he said, 'Do this,' or 'Do that,' to anyone, Anjappa got furious with those who did not obey.

'Ayya, my beard was greying when your father was yet a child. Does *my* advice mean nothing to you?' he would fume.

Originally published as 'Jogyora Anjappana Koli Kathe'.

DR MASTI VENKATESHA IYENGAR (SRINIVASA)

Probably due to his vast experience, his counsel would surely be worthwhile. Anjappa was as old as Jambavantha and as wise as Hanumantha.

Anjappa had visited Rangappa some three days ago. Rangappa had received an order recently, appointing him as the Bench Magistrate in our taluk. Everyone in our village was very happy, since our Shanbhag now had the authority to punish. The power to punish is considered a great prestige among our villagers. They feel that such a person should be equal to, at least, a subedar.[1] Previously, only subedars and people with higher ranks in the army had such authority. And so, a Bench Magistrate was deemed slightly superior to a subedar. As an esteemed elder of the village, Anjappa visited our Rangappa, the Shanbhag, on hearing the news; to greet him and, of course, to proffer advice.

'Come in, Anjappa. Sit down,' said Rangappa.

ANJAPPA: Rangappa, I heard you've got the magistrate's post. I'm happy for you.

RANGAPPA: Yes, that's good, no doubt. But what's the use, Anjappa? I'll have to slog for nothing. No salary; no money.

ANJAPPA: No money? But why?

RANGAPPA: The Bench Magistrate's post is one of honour, that's all. The government doesn't give a salary.

ANJAPPA: You may not get a salary, ayya. But why won't you get money? Aren't there people who use their salary only as pocket money? The salary is only one source; there can be ten others.

RANGAPPA: That was in those days, Anjappa. Now, we can't take bribes and get away.

---

1 Junior Commissioned Officer in the Army

The Story of Jogi Anjappa's Hen

ANJAPPA: It can still work for those who can wangle it. But let that be. Can't you impose a fine on a subedar when you're angry with him?

RANGAPPA: That worked in your days, Anjappa. If you were a magistrate, perhaps you could've done that. Now, everything has to be recorded. As a Shanbhag, if I fine a subedar, I'll have to enter the details in a ledger. If I don't, I'll lose my job.

'Oh, I see,' said Anjappa, opening his pouch and picking out a betel leaf and nut from it.

Most of the leaves and nuts were, most probably, as old as he. Though he chewed quite often, he had a habit of picking out only the faded leaves; he did not have the heart to throw them away. By the time he finished with all the dried ones, the fresh ones would be wilting. And even if there were a few fresh ones, he always picked out the dried ones, anyway. Even the betel nuts in his pouch were well known. Only those who do not know any better believe that nuts are meant to be chewed and swallowed with the leaves. Anjappa believed that nuts were meant to make his mouth water. After they soaked in the drool long enough, they would become pasty and blend smoothly with the leaves. The whole process had to take time. If it were a quick job, how could anyone afford the leaves and nuts to be chewed every other moment? So now, Anjappa pulled out a dried betel leaf, smeared some quicklime on the leaf and stuffed it into his mouth with a nut.

'Let that be,' he said, 'I came here to tell you something.'

RANGAPPA: Tell me, Anjappa. You're an experienced person. You'll have a hundred things that we should know about.

ANJAPPA: That's exactly why I came. You're a magistrate. When criminals are brought to you, you should be able to make out who's honest and who isn't. You shouldn't depend on the reports from policemen or lawyers to punish them. That's what I came to tell you.

RANGAPPA: What you say sounds right, Anjappa. But one can make out if a person is a criminal or not only through the proofs provided. What else can a Magistrate do?

ANJAPPA: A Magistrate *should* be able to sense the truth in a situation. He should question the culprit too.

RANGAPPA: Don't get angry, Anjappa. I want to ask you a question.

ANJAPPA: Ask me. Why should I be offended?

RANGAPPA: Was there ... has there ever been a complaint against *you*?

ANJAPPA: Fine! That's what I came to talk about. There was a complaint that I had stolen a hen. "I didn't," said I. "He did," said they. "We'll leave you if you'll pay a fine of twenty rupees, or else, you'll be sent to jail," was the verdict. I paid the fine and came out, respectably.

RANGAPPA: How did they say you had stolen the hen? Did they see you with it?

ANJAPPA: Yes, it was with me, that stupid fowl. Isn't that why I got caught?

RANGAPPA: Then, doesn't it prove that you had stolen it?

ANJAPPA: That's exactly what I'm trying to tell you, Rangappa. The hen was with me, true. But not because I stole it.

RANGAPPA: Then, tell me what really happened. I'd like to hear the whole story.

And so Anjappa began.

The Story of Jogi Anjappa's Hen

This may have happened some forty years ago when Anjappa may have been middle-aged. In those days, Anjappa would wander from village to village. He was a jogi,[2] and like other mendicants, he dressed in attractive colours, and with a cloth sling on his left shoulder for grains collected as alms. With a single-stringed kinnari[3] that he strummed, hanging from his right shoulder, he went about begging, singing songs from his forefathers' times. His ancestors too were mendicants; not tillers of the soil. Of course, times have gone bad. Now, even the community of jogis farm land. Anjappa describes the trend as, 'Just as Brahmins have set up shoe shops these days.'

We may consider such begging as disgraceful. But not Anjappa. 'What? Is it easy to become a jogi?' he would say, 'Is it easy to learn the profession that involves walking with the father or the uncle, carrying the kinnari, and singing with them? Any idiot can till the land. All he has to do is to stand behind the ox, twist its tail and say, "*Cho, Cho*". But don't we need the tongue to sing songs? And the intelligence to get the words right? Can everyone say, "Lakshmi"? Ask them. They will say, "*ksmi, ksmi,*" as if they're sneezing. Is it easy to move the mouth to say, "Draupadi devi?" I was around twenty-five by the time I learnt my trade. That was when my father said, "Now you're good enough to go on your own."' He implied that it is as difficult to become a jogi as it is for us to earn a BA degree.

Anjappa may have wandered around to some sixty or seventy villages around here. A jogi could not just walk out of his house every morning, like a beggar. Much like an actor doing the role of

---

2   Wandering minstrel
3   Lute

a king in a play, he had to paint his brows, cheeks, moustache and lips suitably, as per his tradition. A jogi is neither a Shaivite nor a Vaishnavite. And not a Shudra. Yet, he was a blend of all three. So, smeared with turmeric, kumkum and ash, his face was a blend of yellow, red and grey. A jogi's eyes looked cruel. And more so, if he were singing songs as Bhima or Hanumantha; people could faint at the ferocious sight. And so, he softened his expression by lining the eyelids with the black of kankappu.[4] Even his clothes had to be suitable, much like his face. The turban had to be in three colours at least, made from strips of cloth. Anjappa must have been quite good-looking with a great voice when he was younger. Women and children crowded around him whenever he came singing into a village. The women would lead him towards the yard in front of the headman's house and after a satisfactory session, send him on his way, suitably honoured.

'I've sung many songs and pleased many people,' says Anjappa, from time to time. His profession was in great demand some forty years ago. And he would have been a hot favourite.

Kalapura was one of the villages he visited. This is an imaginary place—if there is a Kalapura, one must understand that I am not referring to it. It was a fairly large village. Anjappa stayed there for two or three days whenever he happened to visit it. I told you that Anjappa was good-looking, didn't I? Well ... remember that. Because when he went to villages all decked up, it was natural for the women to fall for him as any woman would fall for actors in movies. And if they were older women, Anjappa did not hesitate to stop and chat with them since no one would scold him for talking

---

4   Eye black; kohl; kaajal

to them. He was reserved with younger women, of course, for fear that the men of the household would take him to task, 'Ayya, Jogi! You've come here to beg. Why are you fooling with the women instead of going your way once you've got something? Buzz off!' Even strangers might pass snide remarks and giggle, 'Oho, Jogappa! Not bad!' For a person living as a vagrant beggar, even such casual remarks can be damaging.

Once, when he had visited Kalapura, the wife of the headman made him sit in their yard and sing. She too sat and listened to his singing. She was the Gowda's third wife. After the singing session, she offered him some betel leaves and nuts. He sat on, chewing them. The Gowda was furious. Usually, Anjappa never retorted. But that day, he lost his cool because the elder had used some unspeakable expressions.

'You cannot speak to me that way, Gowdare,' he said, 'What do you think of your wife? If you're a decent person, talk to your wife. Why d'you scold me?'

'Be careful, Jogi,' thundered the headman, 'I can get you into trouble.'

Anjappa said something rude in response and walked off.

After that incident, Anjappa rarely visited Kalapura. Once or twice when he did go, nothing untoward happened. On his third visit, he happened to be sitting on a ledge in one of the lanes, singing, while a young girl stood at the door of her house, listening. He was about to walk away when the girl stopped him and gave him some alms. He went the next day and began to sing from the same place when the girl asked him to sit in front of her house and sing. Then, she offered him alms. It was quite a prominent house in the village. Anjappa found out some details about the family and about the girl. She lived with her husband and her mother-in-law. The husband was wayward. Not that the girl was very good. But Anjappa did not know about it at that time. They reared fowls and sold them for a living. When he visited Kalapura much later, he went towards their house. The girl was attractive, no doubt. But not that Anjappa had any evil intentions. He only wanted to sing for her since she enjoyed his singing; he was eager to please her. When the villagers had gone their way after listening to him for a while, Anjappa stayed on, munching his betel leaves and nut.

In a while, the girl appeared at her door.

'Jogappa, come this way when you're leaving this village,' she said.

'Why, Amma? I'm leaving right away.'

'I've enjoyed your singing. I'd like to give you something. But you'll have to walk away with it immediately. If my mother-in-law gets to know, she'll create a ruckus.'

Anjappa was scared to accept her gift. And yet, he did not have the heart to disappoint her. Before he could say anything further, the girl went inside and called him, softly, 'Jogappa, come here.' He stepped into a small courtyard. She picked up a hen and put it into his sling pouch.

'Get away! Get away!' she hurried him out. Anjappa stepped out before he could realize what he was doing. His heart was thudding.

'Be careful, Jogappa,' whispered the girl, 'Don't let anyone know that I gave it to you.'

Anjappa walked away without a word. He walked without stopping until he reached a well about half a mile away from that village. There he sat under a tree, chewing his betel leaves while musing on what he had just been through.

The Story of Jogi Anjappa's Hen

He strongly felt this should not have happened. Nothing like it had ever happened before. A hen, of course, was a treat! Who would ever give *that* as a gift? But the girl had given him what she thought he deserved. There was nothing wrong with that. Only, she had given it to him stealthily. That was not proper; that was cheating. Anjappa was impressed with the girl. She was good-looking too, like a ripe lemon. Why was her husband wayward when he had such an attractive wife? That is the way with these men, he decided; if they're wealthy, they squander their money on other women.

Anjappa sat ruminating, quite forgetting that it was dangerous for him to be sitting there, so close to the village. After a while, someone walking down the lane came towards him and stopped.

'What, Anjappa? How is it that you're sitting here?'

'I'm just resting awhile, ayya.'

'Were you able to fill your jolige?'[5]

'As usual.'

'What's this? Ragi?' said the villager, peeping into the sling-pouch. What did he see? A hen!

'What's this, Anjappa? You've got a hen!' Anjappa shuddered.

'Yes, ayya. Someone gave it to me.' Anjappa could hardly get the words out. He stood up to leave, fearing that things could take a nasty turn if he stayed on. Right at that moment, he saw an elderly woman and a young man from the village, walking towards them in a hurry. And trailing way behind them was the girl who had gifted him the fowl. Anjappa felt his knees buckling. He could not take a single step forward. He sensed, somehow, that he was in trouble.

---

5 Sling-bag

As he stood staring at them, the girl signalled to him desperately; he was not to disclose that she had given the hen to him.

'Is this the jogi?' The woman asked the man as they reached Anjappa. He was the watchman of the town.

'Yes.'

'Jogappa, did you, by any chance, see one of our hens?'

'A hen has got into my jolige, somehow,' mumbled Anjappa. 'I'd never noticed it. This person showed it to me just now.'

'But *you* told me that someone had given it to you!' said the other man.

'Ayyo, it's hard to spare even a handful of rice for a jogi. Can anyone gift a hen, ayya?' asked Anajappa.

The watchman looked into the sling. The hen was snoozing in there.

'Not bad!' said the old woman, 'We let him sit about because he sings well. And he exploits that familiarity to steal from us. Come on! Let's go to the Gowda. As the headman, he'll sort this out for us. So much for your singing!'

'Amma, I did not steal your hen. If it's yours, take it. Please don't bother me.'

'Ayya, do you really think you can get away by sounding respectable? How did the hen get into your bag if you didn't put it there?'

And turning to her daughter-in-law, she asked, 'Is this our fowl?'

'I ... I'm not sure. It looks like ours and yet, it doesn't look like ours. Jogappa may have bought it from elsewhere,' stuttered the girl.

'What's the point in all this discussion?' said the watchman. 'Let's go to the Gowda. Both of you can tell him everything. Let him be the judge.'

The Story of Jogi Anjappa's Hen

Anjappa could think of no way out. He knew the Gowda was against him. He knew his fate was sealed as he walked back to the village with them.

There is no point in narrating all that happened there. The villagers who had lost fowls and those who hadn't, all gathered to complain that they remembered losing a hen on a day the Jogi had visited. The Gowda arrived. 'Jogi,' he said, 'Whatever you were singing all these days were not songs. We'll put you in a lockup now. There you'll sing real songs.' The police station was not very far away. He was sent there with a report from the Gowda. After being questioned by the police inspector and promising to attend a court summons, Anjappa was able to go home.

What was there to investigate in the court? It was true that the old woman had lost a hen on the day the Jogi was at her house singing for alms. It was true that it was found with the Jogi; the woman had recognised it. And three others had seen it in his sling-bag.

'What do you have to say, Anjappa?' asked the magistrate.

ANJAPPA: I don't know, buddhi. The hen may have settled down for warmth in my cloth-pouch while I was singing. I did not notice it when I walked away with my sling.

MAGISTRATE: What kind of a story are you spinning? Will any hen just walk towards a man and sit in his bag? Tell me the truth.

ANJAPPA: Mahaswami, I'll tell you the truth swearing on any God you'd want me to swear. I did not steal that fowl.

MAGISTRATE: Let's accept that you didn't steal the hen. Surely, it couldn't have walked into your bag. Did anyone give it to you?

It was on the tip of Anjappa's tongue to admit that the girl had gifted it to him. But he remembered that at her home, she had requested him not to tell anyone. She had also signalled to him desperately on the street. Poor girl, she had given it to him because she had enjoyed his singing. How could he betray her now? And so, Anjappa was silent.

MAGISTRATE: What d'you have to say, Anjappa?

ANJAPPA: What can I say, buddhi? God alone must show you the truth. I did not steal the hen.

MAGISTRATE: Do you have any witnesses?

ANJAPPA: Ayyo, Mahaswami! God alone is my witness.

'See how well he speaks to defend himself despite being a thief,' said the magistrate, but he could not be convinced. He fined Anjappa twenty rupees or if he was unable to pay it, imprisonment for fifteen days.

Anjappa paid the fine and walked out, sad-faced.

As I had told you earlier, this happened some forty years ago.

And so, Anjappa advised Rangappa, now that he had become a magistrate, 'What's the big deal in becoming a magistrate, Rangappa? Punishing the wrong-doers and protecting honest people rests with God. When such a responsibility is given to man, he should be like God Himself. He should always be in fear that he could be wrong. Or else, he'll be like that person who punished an innocent man in the guise of justice.'

RANGAPPA: What you say does make sense, Anjappa. But how could that Magistrate make out the truth when you didn't tell him?

ANJAPPA: Why would we need magistrates like you if we can be truthful with one another? It's your duty to find out the truth; you should be able to sense it.

The Story of Jogi Anjappa's Hen

RANGAPPA: So, you paid a fine to save that girl? Good!

ANJAPPA: *Ayyo*, listen to this. That girl had been friendly with another man. She used to gift him a fowl from time to time. Whenever her mother-in-law questioned her about the missing fowl, she would maintain that she did not know. But the elderly woman could not believe her. And so, the girl decided to save herself by making me a suspect. This I came to know only much later.

RANGAPPA: What?! Did the girl give you the hen and then foist the theft on you?

ANJAPPA: Yes, it was something like that. The mother-in-law asked about the missing fowl. The daughter-in-law replied that she did not know. "What could've happened?" wondered the old lady, "Someone's stolen it, perhaps … Had anyone come here?" "I'm not sure …" answered the girl. But after a moment, she added, "Oh, yes, some Jogappa had come singing." And the neighbours said, "Yes, yes, we saw him walk away in a hurry." And I was caught.

RANGAPPA: Didn't you go again and ask the girl if what she had done was right, Anjappa?

ANJAPPA: You are still a youngster, Rangappa. Why would you be interested in me or what I did about it … I did go … I did speak to her … But that's another story.

No one asked him what had happened. They did not feel like pestering the old man.

'Let that be,' said Rangappa, 'If anyone brings you to me as a criminal, I'll ferret out the truth from you and set you free.'

'Rangappa, my days of standing before any earthly judge are over. Soon, that Thirupathi Venkataswami will be my magistrate. I'll have to stand before him. When he recognises me, I'll have to fall at his feet and say, "I have sinned." He will save me.'

We sat silent. Anjappa too.

'Ayya, Rangappa,' said Anjappa, after a while. 'Where's your treat on becoming a Magistrate? Some betel leaves and nuts …?' Rangappa sent someone to buy the leaves and nuts and handed them to Anjappa.

'Remember what I've told you, Rangappa,' said the Jogi as he went on his way.

YARMUNJA RAMACHANDRA

The Idol That Chennappa Destroyed

First of all, I'll have to clarify something. People from our town had rarely heard about Sri E.V. Ramaswamy's Dravida Kazhagam movement. Their recent mass protest was to destroy idols of gods and goddesses; something we could never ever imagine. But then, these are the times of news broadcasts and newspapers, you see. Even an ant cannot miss their spotlight, wherever on earth it may be crawling. One such news headline caught our Shivaswami's enthusiasm.

Just as the poor find it a problem to survive, the wealthy have their own worry; how they can make use of the healthy bodies God has bestowed them while enjoying the wealth their ancestors left them. Shivaswami's plight too is similar. He is thirty now. He has built a fine body, thanks to the food at home. But he has no way

---

Originally published as 'Chennappa Odeda Murthy' in 1953.

of putting it to use. And so, is it a surprise if he often wondered how he could be active to keep himself fit?

Somehow, from somewhere, he heard about the campaign to destroy idols. He was fired. He felt inspired. He wanted to give it wide publicity. Shivaswami was not particularly religious. He had quarrelled with their family purohit over something trivial. And so, the swami had not visited his house for over a month. From that day to this, his family gods had been starving but that had not bothered him.

It is true that Shivaswami *had* wondered why he should not sacrifice his own household gods as the first step to his role in the agitation. His mother had sensed his plans and had hidden them away. Even if he had found them, he would not have enjoyed destroying them. They were made of silver, after all, and one even had a tiny golden crown. And so, he gave up that idea and sent for Chinnappa, who made clay models of gods and goddesses.

'I want ten idols,' he said, 'And I want them in ten days from now. I don't want you to make them as impressive as you always do. Don't try to fleece me. They'll be good enough if they look like figures of gods and goddesses.'

Chennappa was surprised; he was also tickled. 'But the festival of Ganesha is still four months away, ayya' he murmured.

'That's different and this is different. And look, all the ten should not be of Vinayaka only. I want idols of different gods.'

Chinnappa did not argue further. Generally, he could sell his idols only twice a year, once during Ganesha Chaturthi and once again, during Dhanalakshmi puje. Through the rest of the year, he could earn only by farming. Not that he earned much even then,

The Idol That Chennappa Destroyed

when market prices had a way of rising day by day. And so, this was an unusual windfall.

'But where will I get the clay from?' he worried.

Shivaswami had said the idols need not be attractive. But then, could he spoil his reputation by making substandard images? And so, Chennappa sent his youngest son, Venka, to Kelur, four miles away. Venka returned that very evening carrying a huge basket of clay on his head.

The next morning, Chennappa woke up even before the rooster crowed, bowed before the smoky picture of a god on the wall and began to knead the clay to get it to the right texture. Had it been around the time of Ganesha Chaturthi, he would have been excited. He would have felt pepped up with at least ten to twenty children in the front yard of his house, crowding around him, watching his dexterous hands intently. But today, no one knew what he was up to. Also, the clay had dried and was not yielding to his touch. By the afternoon, Chennappa was sick and tired of the effort. He had smoked the stock of beedis he had, including the butts he had tossed about. He had reached the sorry state of having to send Venka for yet another packet. But by the evening, the situation changed. The strenuous first phase of getting the clay to the right consistency was done; it became pliable in his hands. As he began the delicate job of shaping an idol, he felt his old, familiar enthusiasm creeping into him. Also, as the afternoon made way for the evening, schoolchildren, with their shoulders sagging with bags of books, stopped and crowded around him, watching him mesmerised.

'How many more days to Ganesha Chaturthi, Chennappa?' asked Gowri, the purohit's little daughter, kneeling beside him and watching his hands keenly.

'Around three or four months yet, maybe?'
'Then, why're you making these *now*?'
'That Shivaswamianna wants them.'
'Are they going to worship Ganesha right now?'
'Why not? Do we need a time and place to worship?'

Late in the evening, the children walked away. Chenappa, too, stopped working, lit a beedi and sat smoking on the veranda.

Many more children came to watch him the next day. Word had got around pretty quickly. Chennappa had finished working on an image of Ganesha and had started on the next one.

'When will you paint that Ganesha, Chennappa?' asked a little boy.

'Let me finish making all of them. Then we can paint them, all together.'

'Why does this one look delicate?' asked another.

'She is Saraswathi.'

'Really? Not Ganesha?'

'No.'

'Do you make Saraswathi's idols too?'

The children saw this as something new. Even Chennappa felt strange as he tried to bring it to shape. He did not like the image in his hands; he was not used to making Saraswathi. But there were many more idols to be made. He wanted to be done with this phase of his job to get on to painting his first Ganesha.

When the elders heard from the children about Chennappa's idols, they were surprised. They could not understand why Shivaswami had suddenly become so pious. One or two of them came in person to see Chennappa at work. Some others went to Shivaswami's house. It did not take long for the news to spread.

'He has lost his head. Have *you* lost yours too?' The purohit of the town came the next day and shouted at Chennappa.

Chennappa was shocked. He could not understand the furore.

'What have I done, swami?' he asked.

'Aren't you dancing according to that idiot's wishes? It would've been better if you were begging, instead.'

Chennappa was stunned.

'Do you know he wants to destroy idols?'

'*God*'s idols? Is he going to *break* them?'

'Yes, the idols of all the gods. He plans to take all these images and break them. You're an idiot, an utter fool. He's got heady with his money. That infidel! Even you're in this plan, aren't you?'

'I know nothing, swami. He said he wanted these idols. That's all I know,' Chennappa stammered.

The purohit described—in colourful detail—the hell that awaited him and left.

Chennappa ran to Shivaswami's house. He could not believe what he had heard.

'Is it true, anna?' he asked.

'What?'

'The purohit was saying something about …'

'Oho, the purohit! You got scared, I guess.'

'He said …'

'Yes. *I'll* do what I want. How does it matter to *you* or to *him*? You wait and see. That purohit will go to hell dragging his believers with him.' Shivaswami guffawed.

Chennappa did not utter a word. He turned to walk away, quietly.

'How many idols have you finished, Chennappa?' Shivaswami shouted after him.

'They're all getting done, anna ...'

Chennappa was not very happy about the money he would be making.

The next day, there were fewer children standing about watching him.

'Don't go to Chennappa's house. Take care!' Their parents had warned them. And yet, the few who came were curious to see him at work. They stood at the door silent, scared. Only one or two entered the veranda.

Chennappa had made quite a few idols. But none of them seemed to represent any particular deity. He had not painted them yet. To him, they were only lumps of mud. He could not give any particular shape to the clump of clay in his hands, though he tried many times. He tossed it aside. His heart was not in his work. He was feeling unsettled. Finally, he brought out the Ganesha idol he had made a few days earlier and tried to draw a green border on the yellow cloth draped on its shoulder.

'Can we break idols, Chennappa?' asked a little girl sitting close to him.

'Which idol?'

'What d'you mean by which idol? Why? Vinayaka's, Shiva's, Krishna's ...'

'No, we should never break them.'

'But then you ...'

'I?'

'No ... I heard that Shivaswamiayya is going to break idols.'

'Oh, that! Yes, he wants to break idols. But how does it matter to us? What does it matter if he breaks these lumps of mud.' Chennappa tried hard to laugh.

'But didn't you always say that Vinayaka is short-tempered?'

'No one can do anything to God, mari.[1] This is just an idol, made of mud. And anyway, *I'm* not breaking them, am I?'

'But ...' the child stopped him but she did not know what else to say.

Chennappa too felt troubled. He felt he could not accept the excuse he had given her. And yet his hands kept painting the Ganesha in his hands. He had completed the green border on the strip of cloth over the shoulder and was now painting the face red.

The children went their way later in the evening. Chennappa lit a kerosene lamp and kept on painting in its dusky light. But his mind was not on his work; it had been caught up in a secret turmoil ever since his meeting with Shivaswami: 'What if I don't deliver the idols he had ordered?' it protested. 'But I would be giving up the money that's come my way without my efforts,' it cautioned, reminding him of the situation at home. 'After all,' it tried to pacify him, 'These idols are but mud. What if *he* wants to destroy them? Why should that bother *me*? God won't let down anyone who trusts in him. I haven't wished Him ill. I have no evil intentions. I'm not sinning in any way now ...' But when he recalled Shivaswami's expression and what he said, a doubt raised its head, somehow. 'Even *I* have a role in it, don't I?'

'What if we don't deliver the idols, Appa?' Venka asked. But Chennappa's mind was elsewhere. He pretended not to hear and went on painting Ganesha's face a deeper red.

'Appa, we won't deliver the idols.'

'Why?'

---

1   Child

'Let's not. The people are talking.'

'So? What can we do? Don't we have to fill our bellies?'

Venka had nothing to say to that. He had no reply to this question. He had not the experience to retort that there were other ways of earning a living. But he was scared of what could happen to them now, in the present situation.

'Appa, they're saying that if you give the idols to Shivaswamiayya, the sin will surely be upon us. Our home will be destroyed. Our family will be destroyed. We won't be able to endure God's curse ...' As he spoke, tears filled Venka's wide eyes and ran down his cheeks.

'Sin! The curse of God! Then living as we do is also God's curse, isn't it? With all his greatness, is *this* the way he lets us live? Wonder where this God is? I don't think he has ever seen this world. He's not anywhere here. Not just ten; even if we break a thousand idols, God won't appear. All lies! A bundle of lies! We should break every idol in every home ...'

'*Appaaaa* ...' screamed Venka, in fear and anguish.

But Chennappa had reached the end of his tether. He raised the very idol he was working on to throw it at his son. But as he raised his hand, his eye caught the deep red of Ganesha's face. His hand trembled. He sighed, placed the idol on the floor and kept staring at its face. But he could not gaze at it for long, even in the faint light of the oil lamp. He put off the light and stretched out on a mat.

Though Chennappa was half asleep, his mind could not rest. It was filled with a thousand doubts, anxieties and fears. He began to think that he could no longer make idols. Blurred visions danced before him—visions of Venka's tear-filled face, the look of uncertainty on the faces of the children standing around him.

And together with these, the angry red face of the Ganesha he had just painted.

Chennappa got up and went outside. He plucked two flowers from a creeper and brought them in. He straightened the idol of Ganesha lying on the floor and stuck the flowers in its crown. He then took the other idols, yet to be painted, crushed them beyond recognition and mixed them with the unused clay. Finally, he took up the painted Ganesha. But the red of its face, the green of the border on the yellow cloth on its shoulder and the sheen from its tin-foil crown caught his eye and stopped him. He did not know what else to do. He paused for a moment. Then, placing the idol on the ground, he picked up the flowers that had fallen and stuck them back on the crown. Then, he went to the veranda, lay down and slept.

When his children woke up the next morning, they could not see any of the idols, except one. They had seen their father's fury the previous evening and so they dared not ask him anything. But, Chennappa was already sitting beside the lone Vinayaka idol, even before lighting his first beedi of the day. He had tried to break the legs of this Ganesha but failed. It had been the very first idol he had made and so it had become hard. He sat helpless and dazed, wondering what else he should do. When the children were not around, he brought a hammer. But Vinayaka's expression stopped him. Today, he did not see anger, only peace. He saw the red on the face enhancing its serene dignity. He took the hammer back into the house, brought a small pot of water and dipping his fingers into it, wiped the feet of the idol. Some of the colour rubbed off on his fingers. By then, he heard the sound of children coming in. Quickly, he wiped his fingers and pretended to be colouring the idol.

No one knew what happened to Shivaswami's protest against idol worship. But that night when everyone was asleep, Chennappa took the lone idol of Vinayaka to the stream beyond the rice fields. And he spent the whole night kneading it in running water until he could break it down completely.

'Did they break the idols, Chennappa?' asked the little girl the next day.

'No, I didn't give them any. I destroyed *all* of them.'

'*That's* a lie,' said the child.

H.V. SAVITHRAMMA

An Episode

Darkness was descending.

'We'll have a white Christmas this year. It's already started snowing,' said Grace, staring out of the window. Maadhu stopped packing his books; he came to stand behind her with his hands on her shoulders and looked outside.

Grace caressed his hands. Tears slipped down her lips. They were salty.

'What's this, Grace? Tears? Didn't you say you wouldn't cry?' Maadhu lifted her chin gently.

'No, I won't,' said Grace, patting her face with a handkerchief.

This moment was not unexpected. Right from the time she had moved in with Maadhu the previous year, neither had hidden their past from each other. She was an orphan, having lost her family

---

First published in Saridha Beralu as 'Ondhu Prakarana' in 1965.

in the dreadful war. Maadhu was alone right now, since he had come to England for further training. Though their friendship had blossomed and firmed up into a deeper attachment, Grace had known that Maadhu would be in England for just a year and that he had left his wife behind. But in the daze of their new-found love, the year had seemed like an eternity to her and Hindustan, a land beyond her world. Even though she knew this unreal world of bliss would make way for the harsh realities of life, that thought was as hazy as a dream.

Now, Maadhu had to leave London the very next evening. She had to face her life alone, all over again. Grace shuddered. Even when Maadhu was around, she had not depended on him for her expenses. She was earning enough as a stenographer. But life had not been dreary until now. Around the time she returned from work, Maadhu too would be returning from the factory where he was training. They would go out for a walk in the evening or to a movie. Home was really a haven of refuge, of love. Maadhu was fun-loving, living contentedly in the moment with no thought for the morrow. He would faithfully write a letter to his wife every week, without fail. Grace had to remind him to add a few details. Their letter made his wife, Lalitha, happy.

'Shall I write to Lalitha about you?' Maadhu asked Grace one day, just to tease her.

'Her heart might stop. Poor girl!' said Grace, smiling, 'Why should we inflict unnecessary pain on her? She hasn't lost anything through our friendship. You had to be away from her, anyway. You'll have each other for the rest of your lives. What's wrong if this one year that isn't hers, is meant to be mine? And yet, if she gets to

An Episode

know about it, the rest of her life will be mixed with poison. Why should that sin be mine?'

'Women like you are rare, Grace,' said Maadhu, caressing her chin.

'Oh, don't say that! I'm a woman too. I can be jealous and cruel, like any other. It's just that I'm scared of the fires of hell.' Grace had laughed.

And now, on their last night together, Grace remembered everything she had said in fun. She had never thought their parting would be so very painful. Tomorrow! Tomorrow, Maadhu would be leaving. She would become a lonely person in the town of her birth, London ... all over again. When she returned home from work, the next day, 'home' would have no meaning. Grace sighed.

'Let's go and watch a movie, Grace,' said Maadhu, who had his arms around her shoulders. 'If you're going to be sighing like this, I'll send a cable to Father that I'm not coming home.'

'Don't be crazy! Come, let's go for a walk. Not a movie,' she said, moving away to get ready.

That last day had been busy. Grace had had no time for tears. Maadhu had been pestering her for over a week to go to Dover with him to see him off. But she had been adamant. The friendship that had blossomed in London had to end in London, she had persisted.

'Does our friendship have to end, Grace?'

'Then?'

'Keep writing. We may meet again. Distance has no meaning these days.'

'What do you mean by, "no meaning"? When you go away tomorrow, it will be like drawing a screen permanently over a chapter in my life.'

'So? Won't you even *write* to me?'

'There'll be unnecessary complications, Maadhu. Better snap the cords once and for all.'

'You're very hard-hearted, Grace.'

'Yes!' Grace nodded with a smile, trying to hide her breaking heart.

Future! What future did *she* have? An important job awaited Madhu in his country. His wife, Lalitha, must be a very trustful person. How naive her letters were! How amusing! Full of fun! They will have children and be a happy family. Why was she thinking about *their* future, anyway? She would have to wake up every morning to slog for her daily bread. She did not have a single relative to feel for her. Now that she had known bliss with Maadhu for a year, she was not sure if she wanted to get married. But she did not regret what she had done, not even for a moment. She had been truly alive every moment during that one year. Maadhu had made every minute precious with his friendship, with his love. Grace knew, for sure, that even if Time were to step back a year and she had to decide afresh, she would still choose to live with Maadhu.

Grace returned from the station ... she stepped into the bedroom. She tossed aside her handbag and lay on the bed and stared vacantly at the emptiness beyond the window. She had no tears to shed. Empty! Wasn't that how her life would be from now on? Desolate?

Why had fate included that chapter in the story of her life? How would it help? She was barely twenty-six. For how long could

An Episode

she rely on her memories? She recalled Maadhu's smiling face as he stuck his head out of a window, waving his handkerchief. 'May his life be full of smiles!' she sighed, as she put a hand under the pillow and pulled out a little book. Maadhu's diary. She flipped through the pages. Every entry had her name in it; she had a role in every incident. She pressed the book to her chest. A photograph slipped from its pages. It was her picture. He had been keen to take the diary with him but had forgotten in the hurry and bustle of last-minute preparations. Just as well. It would have aroused his wife's suspicion. Would she be large-hearted enough to forgive Maadhu? She would have lived a sheltered life within the four walls of her father's home, after all. Grace turned over. She could still smell the fragrance of Maadhu's hair oil. She stroked the pillow, gently. Her tears flowed without restraint; she wept as if her heart would break.

As the boat sailed away and England went out of sight, the reality of his situation hit Maadhu. A chapter in his life had closed. Grace was right. Lives had to fade out even as each chapter ended. On that first night when he had met Grace in the moonlight, he had never imagined she would be tugging at his heartstrings this way. He was feeling lonely and unsettled in a foreign land, far away from his people, and Grace had seemed an anchor; she had brought him a warm sense of security. She had given her all to him, unstintingly. And had expected nothing in return. The whole year was indeed astonishing. He had hardly spent anything on her, except for an inexpensive pair of earrings for her birthday and a hair clip for Christmas. Those were all the gifts he had given her. But what could he have ever given her for the trust she had reposed in him? He would not have found anything *that* worthwhile, even if he had searched the whole of London.

How selfish he had been! He had taken all that she had offered with both his hands and now, he was abandoning her. What would happen to her? Will she slog all her life barely to survive and then, lie in a churchyard? He had suggested that he would like to take her back with him to his country. She had laughed at the idea. But he had not persuaded her strongly enough. He should have. After all, whom did she have to call her own? She was beautiful. She was mature. If fate had not brought them together, she too would have got married and lived happily with some young man. True. But he should have tried harder to persuade her to accompany him. He had not; he did not have the courage to confront his family. And so, he had accepted her decision. Grace had learnt about his situation at home during the one year they had lived together. And so, she had never ever talked about their future together. She had already decided that their relationship would end with the year, with their parting.

Grace! What a fine person she was! So like her name; gentle, self-effacing. What if he had not been married, wondered Maadhu. Even then, there would have been hurdles, insurmountable. He would not have been able to estrange himself from his aged parents. They had no one else; he was their only son. Forget about them accepting Grace as their daughter-in-law. In such a situation, they would not have accepted even him as their son. As Grace had said, it was best to draw a curtain over that chapter of their lives. And yet, as he dwelt on her selfless love, Maadhu shuddered.

An Episode

Maadhu was in an easy chair with an open book on his chest, staring at the sky. He could hear some wedding excitement in the distance; snatches of film songs wafted in the breeze.

'Lalitha!' he called out.

'Coming,' came her voice from inside; she did not appear.

Just one scene crossed his mind and drifted away. He was being eaten up by his memory. Grace! What a companion! Her moods vibed with every mood of his. She would never be bored. Maadhu had not been aware of that whole year passing by. Every incident, every occasion vibrated with Grace's presence. He could not remember a moment throughout that year when he was not aware of her. And yet, how strange! Now, he had not a thing to remind him of her. He had left behind in London even the photograph he had hidden away from her. A thick black curtain had indeed been drawn over that chapter; just as Grace had said. Maadhu sighed. What would she be doing now? He wondered. Making tea, perhaps, after returning home from work. Would she have been alone these six months? She would have met another person, someone like himself, perhaps. Or she may be happily married. *Che*! Grace was not *that* kind of a person. She had not looked at anyone else that whole year through.

And yet ... what was wrong with that? Wasn't he making a life with Lalitha? Forgetting her? Suddenly he felt an urge to get in touch with her, to know how she was getting along. He decided he would write to Grace, come what may; whether she responded or not.

He shuddered as Lalitha placed a hand on his shoulder gently.

'Looks as if you were in your dreamworld? I've been here the last ten minutes,' she said softly.

Forget about living in a dreamworld! His very life seemed to be a dream. But if he shared the thoughts going through his head with her, would Lalitha continue to laugh softly and ruffle his hair, as she was doing right then? Each person had a role to play in the drama of life. And each one had to enact his role as well as he could and exit behind the curtain.

'Shall we go to the cinema this evening, Lalitha?'

'But I have to go to Sundari's house for the arathi.[1] Also, amma isn't well. I'd like to check in on her as well.'

Maadhu was quiet. Grace had nowhere else to go but to him. No friends to invite her, no relatives to claim her responsibility. She was all for him; and he, for her. A sigh slipped out again, unawares. Lalitha heard that.

'Come, let's go, if you want.'

'No, no. You go. I'll head out for a stroll,' he said.

He had not stirred from the easy chair even when Lalitha stepped out in a new sari.

'I'll visit Sundari tomorrow. Let's go to a movie today,' she said.

Maadhu got up suddenly, as if roused from sleep. 'No, even I had to meet some people. I'll go out,' he said and went inside.

It was dark when Lalitha returned. Maadhu had not left the house. Hearing her stepping inside, he hid the pages of a letter he had been writing under a stack of books. The sun had barely set and night had just begun to swallow the world. Lalitha felt sorry.

'Why? Didn't you go out? Why're you sitting in the dark!'

'It's only beginning to get dark.'

'But you said you wanted to go somewhere.'

---

[1] A special worship ceremony to which women are invited

'I didn't. I felt bored.'

'Let that be. Get up! Let's go out for a stroll.'

Maadhu got up from the chair. Can a curtain be drawn over memories, just as they can be over incidents? Grace! He had not cheated on her. Right from the time he had got to know her, he had shared with her every detail of his life. She knew that he had a wife waiting for him as soon as he returned home. That was why she had sent him back in good faith, with the generosity of spirit that came so naturally to her. And yet! Wasn't she sad too? Would she not be bored while going out for a walk without him?

Lalitha was talking away. 'Sundari's daughter is two now. You can't imagine how much she talks! She didn't stop even for a minute. When Grace came in a skirt …'

'Grace?' Maadhu was shocked.

'That Grace, the midwife. Even you've met her at the hospital.' Lalitha stared at him, worried. Maadhu's forehead was beaded with sweat.

'Let's go home,' he whispered. 'I don't feel well.' Lalitha reached for his hand. It was cold.

'Yes, let's go. You may be running a temperature,' she said, scared.

Maadhu had no fever. He felt better once he had mailed the letter. He hoped to be at peace once he heard that she was doing well. Had he been aware of the fire he was stretching his hands into when he had begun his romance? During those lonely days in an alien land, where he had no one to call his own; Grace's unconditional love and concern were vital for his very survival. And what love! Even a child's love would not be so selfless. If only he could see her delicate cheeks and enticing eyes … just once!

No, he too had snapped that connection when he bid her goodbye. That was the understanding between them. After all, whom did she have to call her own? She would have come with him, perhaps, had he forced her. He had been a coward to do what he did. Understanding his plight, she had taken matters into her own hands and severed her ties with him. Instead of letting their love be crushed under worldly values, she had preserved it as an oasis, evergreen in their memory. He had not had the courage then, and now ... he had written to her. Would she have contempt for him?

And now he had a fear. What if Grace's reply reached home when he was away? What if Lalitha should see it? Read it? What if Grace replied to say she was coming? If, tired of being single, she was willing to back out of their decision? Maadhu broke out in sweat. But, the very next moment, he was ashamed of his gutlessness. He had received, with both hands, all the happiness she had given him unstintingly and now, how could he shrink back when it came to fighting the opposition for her sake?

And yet, what had happened had happened. He need not have written to her at all. She would not have expected a letter from him. She would not have found fault with him if he had not written. And yet ... it had been more than a week since he had written. And there had been no reply from her. She may not reply, perhaps. Maadhu felt better.

A few days later, he received a letter at work. Maadhu's hands trembled as he received the mail. He felt like a convict before a judge. It was from Grace, in her well-rounded hand, with the stamp

An Episode

of a post office in London. Maadhu put the letter in his pocket. He was not aware of how he had got on with his work.

That evening, he walked to the park on his way home, sat under a tree and tore open the envelope. A photograph fell out. Was he relieved? Jealous? Or unhappy? He was not sure. In front of a cottage door stood a young man with a baby. And beside him, stood Grace, with her familiar smile. Maadhu's heart was filled to overflowing, as he stared at her. How could he forget that smile, however many blinds he had drawn over it? As he stared at the picture, every precious memory of their year together floated across.

Collecting himself with a start, he read her letter. *'Don't worry about me. I'm fine,'* it said, *'Please don't write again.'* Just that. But what a finale! Maadhu shredded the letter and walked home.

Maadhu did not know that Grace had sobbed her heart out as she read his letter amid the lengthening evening shadows. She had just returned from work, as usual. He did not know that Grace's new neighbour had taken that picture of her while she happened to be standing with the neighbour's husband and her baby.

Neither then, nor ever, did he learn the truth.

TRIVENI
(ANASUYA SHANKAR)

Two Ways of Living

THE MAIDAN WAS lush with fresh grass as far as the eye could see. My heart leapt right up to the skies at the sight. It had been ages since I had seen such a rich pasture. I pranced about as I pleased. The gentle feel of the greenery around my feet brought my sweetheart to mind, my Heera. If only she were here! How happy we could have been! Her tender body was softer than this grass. We had surrendered ourselves to each other the very first time we had met. When I unlocked my heart to her, Heera had come to me shyly, placed her head on my neck and offered herself to me. I had been thrilled by her touch. Abah! Her twinkling eyes!

'Jagre![1] ... Shaitan... Jagre!' Usman, my master, whipped me to wake me up. I stared at him, wide-eyed, shocked. My friends were

---

1   Wake up!

Published as 'Eradu Jeeva' in *Aydha Kathegalu* in 2012, ed. Dr B.N. Sumithrabai.

still lost in sleep, all the other horses and mares. The rich green fields and my Heera vanished with my dream.

'Have you woken up, beta? You were in deep sleep, weren't you?' he said, noting the sleep in my eyes as he stroked me. 'It's already six. I have yet to massage you and then feed you and give you water. When will we get going?'

He gave me a good rub-down and brought me a pile of hay. I turned away from it, disappointed. But I knew I would not get the fresh grass I loved. But from where will I get the energy to draw the jutka[2] if I did not stuff my tummy at least with this dry stuff? I thought of the sunny day ahead and the sting of Usman's whip on my back, and trembled. There is no creature as heartless as Man; everyone else has to grow weary satisfying his self-interests …

'Arre, if you're not going to eat that, I'll put it away and harness you to the cart. You can go hungry,' he said arrogantly. He may do just that; he is more heartless than a tiger. And so, I began to gobble up the mouldy hay.

'See! That's the way to handle you,' he murmured, lighting a beedi.

'Usman bhaiya, how is it you're up before me today,' said Rahim, ambling towards my master. 'What else to do, Rahim? My daughter, Noor, has been pestering me for a new lehenga since yesterday. And so, I've come early, hoping to earn a little more,' he sighed, pulling out the beedi from his mouth and blowing out the smoke through his nostrils.

I stopped eating and stared at him. My blood was boiling. Just because his Noor wanted a lehenga, I had to be out in the chill

---

2   Horse-cart

this early in the morning and sweat it out in the blazing afternoon sun. How fair was that?

Rahim whipped Sonia, lost in her dreams. I felt sorry for her as she opened her eyes and looked about, bewildered. I even felt like laughing.

'Are you awake, Sonia?'

Sonia turned towards me, pathetically. Her eyes were filled with pain. She was still a colt, with the allure of a promising body. Her restless eyes could entice anyone. I fell in love with her on the very first day that I laid my eyes on her. But from a few glances at her tender face, I could make out that she was much younger. Also, Raja, who was around her age was crazy about Sonia. Seeing this, I had moved away, making way for the young lovers. Much later, I met Heera and offered myself to her; body and spirit.

'Yes, I am,' fumed Sonia. 'Rahim doesn't let me sleep peacefully. That idiot!'

'I know. But what can we do? We're their slaves. Our bodies have to wear out serving them. It's an hour since *I've* been up. Did you see Raja yesterday?'

Sonia's eyes brightened on hearing Raja's name. She lowered her head a bit, feeling shy.

'Yes, I saw him in front of the Olympia Talkies. But I couldn't stare at him to my heart's content. We stood for a moment, lost in each other. And then, whiplashes brought us back to reality; to our duty. Not even once could we …'

She had stopped mid-sentence, overwhelmed. I completed it for her.

'Fondle each other?'

'Yes! Raja was staring at me with such desire. These men! *Bah*!'

'Get up! Get up!' shouted Rahim, whipping her.

'*A-a-ah*,' screamed Sonia. I stared at Rahim as if I was going to gobble him up. But there was no way I could help the slender Sonia.

I had barely finished the hay when a bucket of water stood in its place. I drank to my heart's content.

'Sonia, my child, bye!' I said as Usman brought me outside the stable, 'We'll meet again tonight … If I happen to meet Raja, I'll tell him that you asked about him.'

'Okay, I'll tell Heera if I see her. Yesterday, she …' Sonia was still talking. I stood stubbornly still, eager to hear about my heartthrob. But Usman whipped me twice, dragged me outside and hitched me to the jutka.

'Come on, bhai, let's go,' he said and I moved on slowly, dragging the cart.

'Hey, gaadi, gaadi!' A strapping young man stood under a tree, waving at us. He looked tall enough to be chopped into four men; was he an old man to hail us?

'We have to go near the elephant stables. How much?' asked his mother, who appeared beside him.

'One rupee.'

'We can come only if you'll charge us twelve annas.'

'Make it fourteen annas, amma. Please.'

'Never! Come on Chandu, let's look for another jutka,' she said, turning towards her son.

'Come, thaayi,'[3] said Usman, meekly.

---

3   Term of respect; literally, mother

I was mesmerized by the way Chandu was all dressed up. He went right by me to get into the cart and I felt heady with the mingled scent of his cream and talc and aftershave. The mother and son got in.

'Just a moment, Maharaj. I'll be back,' said Usman, getting down.

'Amma, how's the girl?' There was eagerness in the man's voice.

'She's beautiful! One will have to wash his hands to touch her. She has finished high school. She plays the veena. You're lucky!'

'But will they have a grand wedding?' Chandu sounded doubtful.

'Sheela is their only daughter. They'll spend lavishly, I'm sure. Anyway, I've already told them that they'll have to gift you a radio, a watch, a cycle and three suits.'

'Who is she like, amma?'

'Why the hurry, maga?'[4] I could hear her giggle. 'Hold on for just a few minutes. You're going to see her, anyway.'

Usman came back and leapt into the cart.

We stopped in front of an imposing building. The mother and son got down and the man came over to Usman, 'Saab, we'll be here for about half an hour. Take us back home after that,' he said. Usman nodded and lit a beedi. An elderly couple came outside, welcomed them and took them in.

Half an hour later, the mother and son came out of the house with the elderly man. I stared at Chandu's face, curious. It had bloomed like a flower. He was walking with a light step. The mother and son got into the jutka.

---

4   Son; also, a term of endearment

'We'll get the wedding invitations ready by next week,' said the elderly man, 'I'll come and see you anyway, regarding the arrangements.' And then, to his servant, 'Bohra, get that basket of fruits into the cart.'

Chandu's mother looked quite arrogant while replying to him. Bohra placed the basket in the jutka.

Though my eyes were on the street, my ears were listening to the conversation between the mother and son.

'How's the girl, Chandu?'

'Just as you'd said, amma; an ivory doll.'

'Do you like her?'

Chandu mumbled something. Both of them laughed aloud.

'I just want *you* to be happy, maga,' said the mother, stopping her laughter.

Usman pulled on the bit in my mouth to stop the cart in front of their house. When Chandu paid him, his mind seemed elsewhere.

About a month and a half later, Sonia and I were munching grass and chatting in front of Gayathri Talkies. Usman had gone to a teashop nearby. A couple got into my *jutka* after the morning show.

'Sheela, my precious …'

I recognized the voice.

'What if someone hears you? This is not our home, it's a street.' Sheela was pretending to be angry.

'Who's here now? There's only this horse. We can say what we please in front of it.'

'Horses too have ears.'

'So what? What can I do? I go crazy just looking at you. Why're so beautiful?'

'Stop it, please. And sit just a little away from me. I feel nervy when you're so close ... Where did that jutkawallah[5] go?'

'Let him take his time. Why're you in such a hurry to go home?'

'*Hunh*, what else can I do when you behave this way?'

'Wonder what spell you've cast on me, Sheela! Wonder why there're so many walking about?'

A jangle from the jerk of a hand with a load of bangles and then a voice, 'Ayyo,[6] let go, *please*! My hand is hurting.'

'Guess I've got to be satisfied with just this much, right now.'

'How long are we to sit here, waiting for him? Let's get another jutka.'

Usman stepped out of the teashop and seeing customers in our *gaadi*, he hurried towards us.

'Salam,[7] maharaj!'[8] Usman said, recognizing Chandu.

I was happy to see Chandu and Sheela so blissfully happy but I was envious too; Heera and I had not spent even a single day this way.

Some six or seven months later, Usman had barely hitched me up to the cart ...

'Saab[9], saab!' A voice mingled with fear called out desperately. Chandu was running towards us, his hair all askew, his eyes red with tears.

'What happened, maharaj?'

---

5   Horse-cart driver
6   Cry of pain
7   A greeting
8   Term of respect; literally, king
9   Urdu term of address

'Come home and take us to the hospital, saab. I'll give you as much as you ask.'

'Which hospital?'

'Cheluvamba Hospital.'

Usman tugged at my bit and stopped the cart in front of the house. Chandu brought his wife outside, holding her by the hand. I saw Sheela; my heart broke. Her rosy cheeks were pale today. Her hair was messed up and her sari, all askew. Her face in pain looked crushed, like sugarcane in those crushers.

'Can you climb in, Sheela?' Chandu asked.

'No, I can't …' I heard Sheela's moan.

'Shall I lift you in?'

'Here! On the street?'

'Why be shy at *this* moment?' I felt Chandu helping Sheela into the cart, gently.

'Sheela, take courage! Don't lose heart,' said Chandu.

'Isn't there any elder with you, maharaj?' Usman sighed.

'No, saab, there's no one at home. Amma is out of town. My wife's mother has gone to Hasan, to her son's house. Sheela has started her pains. Please hurry.'

My eyes welled up to see Sheela in that condition. I galloped to reach the hospital as fast as I could. Then, I heard her moan; I slowed down to a gentler trot.

I was heartbroken when I saw Sheela being taken on a stretcher into the hospital. We waited for two hours in the compound for Chandu. I kept looking at the hospital from time to time, while munching my hay. And then he appeared.

'How is amma, maharaj?'

'It's all over.' Usman's small brain could not make sense of it.

'Where's the sweet?' he said.

Chandu's eyes filled with tears.

'Where's Sheela? She's left me. Let's go towards the post office, saab. I've got to send mother a telegram.' Chandu got in. I could hear him sobbing. I was weighed down with his grief, I slowed down.

'Hurry up, Shaitan,' shouted Usman, whipping me. We sent the telegram and returned to the hospital. Chandu brought the wrapped-up body of his dear wife and placed it gently in the jutka and then, he settled in.

'*Che*,' I moaned, 'God shouldn't test us so much. But Chandu has grit. Had my Heera died, I would've died with her. This beauty will soon become a handful of ashes. *Che*,' I grieved. I could not eat any hay or even drink water that day.

Some six months later, Sonia and I were chatting at the jutka stand. She was praising Raja.

'Come, let's take a jutka,' I heard a woman saying.

'Why? Are you so tired with walking?' My sharp ears caught that familiar voice. I turned. There was Chandu with his new bride, walking towards the cinema for the first show.

'Jaya ... my precious!'

'Thu, don't talk that way *here*.'

'Why can't I pet my girl wherever I please?'

'Enough! Go and get that jutkawallah now.'

Chandu pressed the horn of our cart, reluctantly. Usman was chatting with a friend; he came running.

'*You*, maharaj?' Usman looked at Chandu's new wife for just a moment. Then, stuffing my handful of hay under his seat, he got on to the jutka.

A whirlwind rose inside me. 'How artificial can these creatures be!' I wondered. 'No one can be so inhuman, so heartless. My Heera is so much better than this person. When Samsher was hankering after her, she told him about us. When he was still adamant, she kicked him and sent him on his way. Even I can't love anyone else in this world except Heera. If she were to die before me ... O, God forbid! I can never love anyone else. If I were to die, Heera has told me she will give up water and hay. She's crazy! But human love isn't like ours ...'

I felt the whip on my back. Usman had noted my being distracted and had struck me.

A fire of hatred for these creatures rose within me. My mind became clouded with its smoke of contempt for them. I heard Chandu and his wife laughing. Their laughter unhinged my mind. I raced crazily ahead, not aware of what I was doing.

'Beta, latif,'[10] Usman tugged the reins, petting me gently. But some demonic strength had got hold of me.

'Ai, shaitan! Wait!' There was a rain of whiplashes on my back.

'O, *shaitaaaan*!'

I dashed head-first against the tree in my way. The cart toppled. Half an hour later, I slowly became aware of what was happening around me. People were settling Usman, Chandu and Jaya in a large van. I could hear them groaning.

---

10 Gentleness

I was foaming. My eyes were closing. I could see splashes of blood around me. I tried to roll over and get on my feet. Abah! What agony! A front leg was broken. I looked around helplessly.

'Thank goodness, no one is hurt,' said someone standing beside the police inspector. 'They must've got up at an auspicious moment this morning. Only the horse is badly disabled. The people inside are saved. Their karma has befallen this creature. Usman said the horse may have gone crazy. It has also broken its leg.'

'Then will it be of any use at all, sir?'

'How can it? We've just got to shoot it. I've told Abdullah. He's gone to get the pistol …'

Froth mingled with blood gushed out of my mouth.

'Hee … raaa!' I murmured my prayer and closed my eyes.

'*Oooo*! Abudullah came!' shouted the gathering crowd, eager to watch a thrilling display.

SHANKAR MOKASHI PUNEKAR

Bilas Khan

SOME FIFTEEN YEARS had already gone by since Miyan Tansen had left his native village, Athrauli. Besides his agricultural land and house, he had left behind his aged mother, his wife, Hamida Banu and their year-old son, Bilas Khan.

Barely two years after Tansen moved to Delhi, the Badshah had heard of his mesmerizing voice and he had become a court musician. And now he had three wives in Delhi—the three of them lived in three different houses. And each of these houses had a hall for public recitals fully furnished with divans, bolsters, cushions and musical instruments: the thamburi, the sarangi and the tabla, all by courtesy of the Badshah's court. Only one of the wives in Delhi was of his choice; of the other two, one had been from among the Badshah's harem and the other was a gift from the Badshah himself. She was one of the presents he had given Tansen in appreciation for the lyric that he had composed in the

---

Originally, also published as 'Bilal Khan'.

raga Darbari Kanada and sung at the concert held in honour of Prince Salim's wedding.

From his first wife, Hamida Banu, whom he had left behind in the village, Tansen had only one son, Bilas Khan. And from the wives in Delhi, he had three children from the first; three from the second and two from the third. Perhaps as a mark of the masculinity of his art, most of Mian Tansen's children were boys. Only the first child of the last wife was a girl. Tansen loved his daughter dearly and because of her, her mother happened to be his favourite wife. He visited her often, mainly to be with his daughter but Sakina Begum exploited the situation fully to her advantage. She would ask her daughter to persuade him to stay on for dinner; she would tell him that the daughter would go to sleep only if she listened to Malkauns and get him to sing the raga for her. Of course, it is also true that children do go to sleep while listening to raga Malkauns. As Tansen tuned the thamburi and started on the aalapana with his daughter seated in front of him, Sakina Begum would softly stir the window curtain and peep out, to see if the elder wife, Ganga Rani's spy, Kashinath or the other wife, Sharanadasi's spy, Rahim, were active. After the child was asleep, she would put off all the lamps but the one in her bedroom. She would invite Tansen for the night, look out of the window once more and then put off the lamp. The news would travel immediately to the other two wives that Tansen had not come out of Sakina Begum's house; he had stayed the night. Seeing Tansen fast asleep after their lovemaking, she would peep out of the window once again to make sure the spies had disappeared. And then, with a deep sigh of satisfaction, she would doze off imagining the other wives wringing their hands in frustration and envy.

Bilas Khan

Nevertheless, it cannot be said that Tansen was partial to any of these wives. He scheduled a visit to each of them once a week or at least twice a fortnight. And even the other wives knew his fondness for his daughter and pleaded with him to bless them also with daughters. 'Bhagavan kare', was all he said to them and God's will for him was only a progeny of sons!

The only one who was out of this family squabble was Hamida Banu of Athrauli.

She got news of everything happening in Delhi in about a month or two. At first, she grieved. That was during the first one or two years when Tansen used to visit his wife, son and mother twice a year. And soon after he became a court musician, he saw them only once a year. This went on for about two years and then he stopped visiting altogether. But he would write to his mother and ask about his wife and son. For the last six years, the letters had petered down to one a year. Not just that. Someone else was writing them for him; only the signature was Miyan Saheb's. Tansen's accompanist who played the tabla for him was Miyan Rahmath Khan Pakwaaji. He too was from Athrauli; Tansen had taken him to Delhi. He was the one who wrote the letters for Miyan Saheb. He visited Athrauli once every two months. He had a wife there and a wife in Delhi. And since he played the tabla also for the dancers at the court, he was familiar with the courtesans. He was well built and the women drifted towards him naturally. Nevertheless, he loved his wife from the village very much. He had two sons by her. Bilas Khan grew up playing with them.

This time Rahmath Khan had come to take his wife and sons to Delhi; he had bought a small house and set it up for them. Bilas Khan insisted that he too would go with them.

And so, his grandmother and mother had to send him to Delhi with Rahmath Khan.

There had been a vague, unreasonable, ongoing animosity between the Crown Prince, Shehezade Salim and Miyan Tansen. Salim was as arrogant as he was handsome. He liked to believe that every girl in Delhi was after him. He did not have any bit of the religious tolerance his father had. And just because all Muslim girls were in ghosha, he thought every Hindu girl in the alley had fallen for him. It is true that some good-looking women had tried to attract his attention; he had spurned their advances. But he liked to believe that every Hindu husband was a eunuch and every Hindu wife was vying for his attention. Thus grew his contempt for the Hindus. He had not given much thought to what was becoming to his stature as Crown Prince.

Miyan Tansen belonged to the original syncretic culture of Awadh, to the Nath–Avadhutha[1] tradition. His father had accepted Islam but had not given up his Hindu way of life. The people of the Avadhutha tradition were liberated in their outlook. They called themselves the panchamaashramis. They could enter anyone's house and would be welcomed with warm hospitality. They respected every religion. They were not aware that one religion was different from another and that each religion had its own distinctive nature.

---

1   A detached person; a total renunciate

Tansen had long hair. He wore a dhothi round his waist, a garland of tulsi[2] beads around his neck and jasmine flowers in his ears. He smeared his forehead with sandalwood paste on the holy and festive days of the Hindu calendar and with vibhoothi for Shivarathri. He conducted the bhajane[3] as a disciple of Swami Haridas and on every Friday, he did namaz and read the kalma.[4] Though he ate meat on other days, he fasted on ekadashi. He had endeared himself to people of all faiths. But Salim did not like the way Tansen practised his dual religion. He ridiculed him in public, insulting him in the presence of the dignitaries of the court. 'Well, such is the fate of every Shehezade,' was all that Tansen said, with infinite patience.

One day the news spread that the Badshah had gifted lands to the Gorakh Mutt—in Haryana and the Nath-Avadhutha-Khan Ghat in Gorakhpur. Salim believed that Tansen had manipulated his father to be generous to the Mutts.

It is true that Tansen had great regard for these Mutts. But the suggestion to give them lands had come from the Badshah's trusted minister, Abul Fazl. Abul Fazl was proficient in Urdu, Hindi and Sanskrit. He had noted that the only diligent followers of Akbari, the religion Badshah Akbar had established, were the yogis at Nath-Avadhutha-Khan Ghat and had advised him to donate lands to them. Pandit Abul Fazl knew that many of the yogis from these Mutts had accepted Islam when the religion had first come to India and that Baba Haji Ratan was one of them. And so, he did not

---

2   Basil, venerated by Hindus
3   Devotional music
4   Declaration of Muslim faith

hesitate to proffer such advice. At Badshah Akbar's coronation, this same yogi, Baba Haji Ratan, had composed a poem in the Vedic metre and named it 'Allopanishad'. He had recited it during the coronation while blessing the Badshah. And Devi Chauda Rani, the principal queen and beloved of the Badshah, had chanted it like a mantra as she performed the tulsi puja and prayed for her husband's wellbeing. Abul Fazl, who had read *Hatayoga Pradeepika*, a book by the same ascetic, had told the Badshah that someone called Allama Prabhu, who belonged to the same tradition, lived in South India. The Badshah had increased the gift of land to all the Mutts in his kingdom and these two were close to Delhi. Salim was irritated that they had been given lands. He decided to complain to the Badshah about Tansen.

There were many things he could have complained about but he focused on the one thing that might stain the reputation of the court.

'Miyan Tansen receives lands as the court musician,' he murmured, sitting at his father's feet one day after dinner, 'but he also sings at the concerts in the houses of prostitutes. And because of this, the value of the court has become five seers per paisa.'

Badshah Akbar was shrewd. He had heard about Salim ridiculing Tansen often in public. But he pretended to be interested only in the issue at hand.

'Is he the only court musician who sings at the concerts at the homes of the prostitutes? No others?'

'I don't know about the others. But I don't like it one bit that this person who's reputed to be better than all of them is a street singer.'

'Which street?'

Salim mentioned a few streets where the prostitutes lived.

'Who are these prostitutes?'

Salim named three who were held in high respect. All three were Hindus. They were known to be very religious people. Among them, they used to hold weekly bhajanes. Tansen, the pious man that he was, would participate in these prayer-meetings sometimes on Mondays, after duly informing the Nawab of the court. These prostitutes were very beautiful. They were dancers of great repute. The entrance fee to their mehfil[5] was exorbitant. They entertained only one guest at a time. The Badshah knew all this. And besides, he had given strict orders that none of the princes should visit the homes of prostitutes. They could invite them to their own homes if need be.

Now the Badshah stared at Salim and came straight to the point, 'How did *you* get to know this?'

Salim was caught off guard. He broke out in a sweat. 'My friends told me—' he stammered.

'They couldn't have told you the names of the lanes in which the prostitutes lived. You must've gone there. Go and sleep now. And don't go wandering about the streets anymore.'

Salim's complaint against Tansen had backfired. The Badshah sent for his commanders, Man Singh, Jai Singh, Diller Khan and Afzal Khan and told them that within the next three days, Prince Salim would be considered eligible for marriage and they were to find him a suitable bride. And at a lavish wedding celebration, the prince was married to an attractive Rajput girl selected by Man Singh. In the month that followed, Salim did not look at the beauty

---

5   Cultural performance

even once. After all, she had come to the palace as a token of his father's retaliation against his plan to get Tansen into trouble.

Tansen Maharaj was a great vocalist, no doubt. But he could not be considered a composer. He did not know how to compose a lyric to fit within the range of a raga. He had got Man Singh to write down many of the drupads[6] and dhamars[7] that he had learnt. He had also given him an inventory of the cheez[8] and unknown ragas that other singers could have in their repertoire. But he did not have even one composition to his credit.

The day before Salim's wedding, the Badshah had sent for Tansen and said to him, 'I'd like you to compose a congratulatory cheez for Salim and sing it to felicitate him at his wedding. I'm tired of listening to the same old Awadhi classical music. Showcase your genius well enough to bring credit to you.'

'I will sing. It rests with the Huzoor to find it pleasing,' said Tansen and left the place in a hurry.

'Now I'm in a tight corner,' he thought, 'Though I've been known in all corners of the kingdom as the best singer in the court, the Badshah doesn't know that I haven't composed a single lyric. By God's grace, he hasn't asked me to compose a new raga. That's my good fortune. The Badshah has asked me to compose only the words for a song.' He was a worried man when he went to see Rahmath Khan. With some effort, the two of them put together

---

6   Solemn music
7   Joyous music
8   Lyric

the very expressions the Badshah had used and made up a song. And Tansen set it to raga Darbari, the raga he had been practicing for a week to sing at the wedding. They set the words to the beats of the taal without focusing much on meaning; they were more concerned with introducing the raga, elaborating the finer nuances of its scale and bringing it to a resounding conclusion.

Today, it is a famous cheez:

> *Sau sau mubarakbaadiyaa!*
> *Aisi shaadi ho! Lakhon hazaara!*
> *Sau sau mubarak!*
> (Hundreds of good wishes at your wedding!
> May you have lakhs of thousands more!)

A composition suitable for a wedding, no doubt, but the meaning was open to interpretation. Did 'lakhs of thousands more' refer to good wishes or to weddings?

On the day of the wedding, the moulvi[9] read the Koran, the purohit[10] read from the Vedas. But Salim sat unconcerned. He did not even look at his bride. His mind was on the banquet that was to follow. That morning, he had sent for the chef and asked him which of the dishes would not change colour if mixed with sindoor and had told him to add a pinch of the red powder to those dishes and serve them only to Tansen. And so, some jalebis, curries and

---

9   Muslim priest
10 Chief priest of a temple

biryani were cooked separately with a dash of sindoor in each of them. 'Miyan Saheb is singing tonight. Hence the special dishes for him,' was the excuse given when Tansen was served on a separate leaf. But as the leaf was laid, Salim had whispered to the chef, '*Zara sambalke*! Be careful!' and disappeared.

As he walked among the guests during the banquet, Salim looked at Tansen's leaf with the sweet dish untouched as yet and asked, '*Kyoon, Pandit Maharaj, jalebi ko haath nahin lagaye?*

'*Dekhiye Shehezade, mooh mitha kiya,*' said Tansen as he put a bit of jalebi into his mouth; a bit that was not as reddish as the rest. By the time Salim came round again, all of Tansen Saheb's jalebis and jahangirs had disappeared under his leaf. Salim wondered how he could have eaten his sweets so quickly and hatched another plan.

After the meal, Tansen's paan was handed to him with a little sindoor added to it. And Tansen ate it, munching on it happily! The sindoor did its job. During rehearsal at Rahmath Khan's that evening, Tansen found it impossible to match the pitch of his voice with that of the instruments. That is the effect sindoor on a singer's throat.

What else could he do? He spent the next four hours somehow, meditating on Allah, Sri Hari and his guru. 'Whatever may happen, may Sri Hari's grace be on me,' was his only means of preparing for his recital.

Whether it was Sri Hari's grace or courage from Allah, that night the Darbari Kanada that began with a low flat note rose to heights of mellifluous excellence.

Bilas Khan

A scale with a jaded pitch is best suited to the Darbari Kanada raga. Most musicians usually think that all ragas have the same scale of notes. This is wrong. Bharathamuni had said that each raga has its unique scale. Though in the tradition that developed later, there grew a belief that the scale was stable. But the pitch of the notes does vary in a scale depending on the raga.

Even Tansen did not know this. He sang shaking his head helplessly thinking his notes were false. But thanks to the flat notes, the Darbari raga shaped up mysteriously. What had begun as an unsatisfactory evening turned out to be a joyous experience for him and the audience in the darbar. Moment by moment, the raga moved through a mind-numbing cluster of notes here, an unexpected twist and turn there, suffering one moment, shining another and thriving on the whole on an unworldly dignity. The audience ejaculated: *'Wah! Wah! 'Sabash!'* or *'Kya baat hai!'* or *'Kamaal kiya!'* And when the raga concluded with tihai, the darbar resounded with applause. The Badshah came down from the throne, embraced Tansen and placed a beeda[11] in his mouth.

Two people seated in the darbar showed a special appreciation of Tansen Maharaj.

Rampyari Bhai was so moved by his singing that she kept wiping away tears of joy. All through the performance, Tansen had been looking at her sitting among thousands of women and Salim had not liked this at all; it fired his jealousy all the more. Rampyari was 'pyari' to Salim only. She was a beauty. She deliberately sat where the light fell, facing Miyan Tansen. She did not have the courage to look at him. She looked down every time he turned

---

11 Various sweetmeats and nuts wrapped in a betel leaf

towards her. But her tears flowed unrestrained. And so Tansen sang to her receptive ears, staring at her boldly as a fellow artiste.

It was not as if he had known her only since yesterday. He had attended the bhajane at her place on many Mondays. He had also sung during those prayer meetings. Neelakanta Bhatta, a Brahmin from Kashi was her family purohit and a dependent. Not just that, he was her obedient servant too. Monday was Lord Shiva's day. On that day, lunch at her place was at four followed by the bhajane. That night, Rampyari abstained from sex as part of a vow. She had followed this ritual for as long as she could remember. She had been in Salim's favour for the past year. But Mondays were rest days, even from Salim. Only twice had Rampyari broken her vow. Once when a Brahmin from Kashi who had given her Gangajal[12] had to return the very next day, he had begged her for sexual alms. And again, when a Nathapanchamashrami had come from Nasik; he was under a vow that he would never stay in a place beyond a day.

'Who knows? Why shouldn't Shiva himself have come to me this way?' she had thought; such was her religious fervour.

Today was Salim's wedding; she would be rid of his patronage! She would get her freedom. With this thought in mind, she had shed tears of joy mingled with those of sorrow. Twice she had sent Neelakanta Bhat to Tansen Saheb specifically to indicate her present position to him. On the third visit, Neelakanta Bhat had gone even a step further, 'What kind of an ascetic are you, Miyan Saab?' he had mocked, 'Why should we call you detached when you can't redeem a woman who's falling at your feet? What did your

---

12 Water from the Ganga, considered holy

Gorakhnath do in a similar situation? A woman from the weaver community had pleaded with him. He advised her as much as he could; she wouldn't listen to reason. He satisfied her sexual need and through it, didn't he make her an immaculate Mahashakthi? You're not detached at all.' Then Tansen had let Neelakanta Bhat into his secret. 'Rampyari is Salim's beloved. As it is, he resents me for some unknown reasons. If I do go to her now, my very life will be in danger. Please explain this to her,' he had said.

Rampyari had been nervous for the same reason. *'Mubarakbaadiya ye Shaadiya!'* So had sung Tansen. 'May this wedding bring good fortune to Salim, to me and to Miyan Saab too,' she had sighed. She did not have the courage to look at him directly, eye to eye. She lifted her face and saw him only when his eyes were wandering and she felt tremulous. Hasn't Kalidasa said, *Athi sneho paapa shanthi?*[13]

During the performance, a boy with a beatific smile sat close to Pakwaji Rahmath Khan. He was nodding his head, mesmerized by Tansen's singing. Rahmath Khan's two sons were sitting somewhere among the crowd but this boy had the courage to sit right beside the accompanist, almost facing Tansen. Tansen felt a tenderness rising in him for this boy; perhaps it was the sparkle of joy in his eyes. The face looked around fifteen but the body was that of a twelve-year-old; still spare, still tender, like that of an undernourished stripling. Slowly, some hidden charisma of the boy embraced Tansen and struck a chord deep inside him. He felt an urgency to ask the boy who he was, right after the performance. Who is who to anyone in such a large gathering or in the wider

---

13 Love too deep ruins the peace of mind.

expanse of this universe? But even then, he vaguely knew he had seen the boy before; only, he could not place him.

Poor Tansen! How was he to know?

Before Bilas Khan had left Athrauli, his grandmother and mother had cautioned him, 'Be careful! Don't ever tell Miyan Saab who you are. He has disowned us now; he's forgotten us. He may not respect you. If he happens to ask you, tell him you're Rahmath Khan's relative. Listen to him, learn to sing from him if you want but don't ever tell him who you are.'

As soon as Bilas Khan arrived in Delhi, his training in music began; but only through listening. No one asked to teach him, no one taught him the notes, *sa, re, ga, ma* ... Every day Miyan Saheb sat in front of Rahmath Khan for riyaaz to sing at the concert for Salim's wedding. Rahmath Khan Pakwaji would sit with him to accompany him during practice. And day after day, Miyan practised the scale for raga Darbari Kanada. Only on the last day did he sing the words he had composed for the song, *Mubarakbadiyaa* ... Call it discipline, masochism or plain humility but Bilas Khan would sit behind the door and listen to his father singing while Rahmath Khan's sons would go out to play. He would disappear just as Miyan Saheb came out of the room. But on the day of the concert, he had a daring surge of courage; he sat right beside Rahmath Khan, face to face with his father, and heard him singing. He captivated his father with his charismatic energy. But he did not divulge his secret. He did not once call him *Baba*. And the opportunity passed him by.

Even as the Badshah rose from the throne and came down to hug Tansen, rows and rows of ministers, commanders of the army and other dignitaries of the court rushed forward and crowded around the Badshah and Tansen. Rahmath Khan felt slighted. Where was he to go when so many of the elite had gathered on stage? At that moment, his two sons came and hugged his legs. But Bilas Khan was deprived of such a sense of belonging. Though his father was right there, there was a distance between them. He looked around and stood beside Rahmath Khan. Rahmath Khan stood waiting, hoping someone would talk to him. But all the admirers had their back towards him. No one turned to look at him. Disappointed, he said, *'Aavo bete'*, held his children by the hand and walked away. Bilas Khan's heart told him his father would surely talk to him. He stood rooted right there. Perhaps Rahmath Khan was not aware that Bilas Khan was not with him. The boy stared at Rahmath Khan, trying to keep him in sight as he mingled with the crowd. But how could he? Every other man looked like Rahmath Khan.

During all the festive celebrations the only person who sat fuming was Prince Salim. Every one of his plans had gone askew. Along with that, he now had an unwanted wife dangling like a millstone from his neck.

There is an evocative term for meaning in Urdu, *'matlab'*. It could define the literal meaning of words or point to the connotative nuances of words in context. It could also hint at a hidden significance in an utterance.

Salim interpreted the clichéd couplet that Tansen had composed at the Badshah's bidding as a satire.

Sau sau mubarak badiyaa! E shaadiya!
Aisi shaadi ho! Lakhon hazaara!

He could sense the sarcasm and bitter irony. He was sure Tansen was taunting him with: *'Aisi shaadi ho!'* Serves you right! I've seen hundreds of weddings of this kind. Mend your ways, now that you're married.

∼

Chauda Rani, the Badshah's chief wife who shouldered all the responsibilities of his household, consulted an astrologer and set an auspicious date for Salim's shobana. The nuptials had to be held three months later, avoiding inauspicious times like the Pushya masa and Rahukala. Within two days after the wedding, the bride sensed her husband's indifference to her and said she would go home with her family and entourage. Chauda Rani did not prevent her and Salim heaved a sigh of relief and started spending the nights at Rampyari's.

Rampyari was frustrated.

On the other hand, Bilas Khan continued to live like an orphan in Rahmath Khan's house. His father, who used to come every day for riyaaz before the concert, stopped coming altogether. Once when Rahmath Khan had gone to meet him, he had asked, 'Who was that boy with you?'

'One of my relatives,' Rahmath Khan had replied, and had fled from the place. He did not even tell Bilas Khan that his father had asked about him. But one day, Bilas Khan asked him, 'Why doesn't my father come here any more?'

'He'll come. Wait. He'll come a week before the next concert, for riyaaz. Until then, he has eight other children to spend time with,' said Rahmath Khan. He could not help being caustic.

'Why are you so rude to that destitute?' asked his wife.

'That's how things are, aren't they?' ranted Rahmath Khan, 'Who cares for the tabla player? Twice I adjusted the rhythm to his singing but what did I get in return? Everyone praised Miyan Saab. No one even talked to me. Forget about them. Let them be. Couldn't *he* have said a few words? Something like, 'Somehow you managed to keep time when I was singing so badly!?' A purely detached person, indeed! Until the next concert at the darbar, he won't come this way. It'll be all about him and his wives and his beloved daughter until then. Why would he need to come here?'

'Why can't you tell him that his son is in our house?'

'His grandmother and his mother hold me to my promise like a knife. If I tell him, either they will die or I must.'

Rahmath Khan's wife pressed her palms to her ears.

There were no concerts for the next three months and Tansen had no need to visit Rahmat Khan's house.

Initially, Bilas Khan lived in imagined dialogues with his father; as if he had asked him something and his father had replied. He kept to himself, talking aloud at times. He lost interest in everything else. Later, he even lost taste for food; he sat before his leaf, despondent. He had been running a low fever ever since the disappointment at the concert hall. The doctor diagnosed it as typhoid and treated him. But Rahmath Khan was worried. He went to Athrauli and brought back Hamida Banu. By then Bilas Khan's condition had worsened and he was delirious. It did help to have his mother by his side, tending him.

Rahmath Khan sighed with relief, feeling that he had done his duty by the boy.

Rampyari was getting disgusted with Salim's attention. And besides, her desire for Tansen had become acute since the concert. But Salim kept pestering her.

'Why can't you look at me the way you were looking at your beloved ascetic the other day? I can also wear a garland of tulsi beads if you want me to.'

'How did I look at him?'

He imitated her expression, her flowing tears and her *wah, wah!* He also mimicked Tansen's mannerisms and said, 'The sadhu maharaj was looking at you while singing.'

'You were sitting at a height. How could he have looked at you? I was sitting on the floor. He may have looked toward me.'

'How much more he would've looked at you had you been lying on the floor!' he would say, patting her cheek. And as her cheeks reddened, he would say, pinching her chin, 'This is how you blushed even on that day.'

Three months passed this way. Rampyari sent word to Tansen that she was languishing for him. She had also said that she had given up her vow of celibacy on Mondays. 'You've redeemed so many harlots by gracing their homes. Why don't you come to me?' she asked. Neelakanta Bhat garnished his stories as his bid to plead her case. But Miyanji did not respond to her invitations.

'It's a burden to handle my own wives! How can I handle Salim's woman?' was all he had said.

At last, the day of the nuptial festivity arrived. Salim had not shown any interest in it until then but now, he was eager to taste the difference. He had heard delectable stories from connoisseurs and his curiosity was aroused. Until now, his experience had been restricted to liaisons only. And he was losing his interest in them anyway. Of course, the feeling of ownership would be the same but here was the beauty of an untarnished flower. He had connected his wedding with the muddle of his abortive schemes to trap Miyan Tansen and had only contempt for the celebration; he had not even seen his wife properly. When he stole a glance at her during the pre-nuptial ceremony, he was enticed by her long tresses, her slim waist and her youthful body. And besides, here was a new test of his ability to deflower a woman. To prepare for it, he did not go to Rampyari the previous night.

The nuptial celebrations involved only the women of the Badshah's household. Chauda Rani had arranged for a simple music recital for the guests. Invitations were sent to soloists who would like to compete with each other at a jugalbandi. The tabla player who accompanied them would be different and so Rahmath Khan was not invited. Since it was a private concert, it would have been demeaning for such an eminent vocalist as Tansen to attend.

Rampyari knew all this and so she sent Neelakanta Bhat posthaste to Tansen. Her invitation said, 'Miyanji, who will be cleared of all responsibilities during the celebrations of the nuptials, should fulfil my desire. Now, I'm rid of my fear of Salim. He has made me suffer much because of you. If you are a true ascetic, you must fulfil my long-cherished desire. Or else you must throw away the garland of tulsi beads.' Tansen had no excuse; he agreed to fulfil his dharma. And yet he said he would come in disguise to avoid any outcry.

'Why does he say he will come the day after? Why not tomorrow?' she grumbled.

'Don't be rash,' comforted Neelakanta Bhat. 'After all, he has said yes. Let it be whenever it should be—tomorrow or the day after or in your imagination.'

As soon as the jugalbandi began, Salim went in and sent word through his servant, 'Let my wife be sent to me this very moment.' Chauda Rani, as per her dharma, asked that the music recital should go on and went in with her retinue, the bride and some of the Brahmins to perform the arathi to bless the bride. The artistes felt deflated because the Maharani had gone in. However, they completed the aalapana in a hurry and moved on to the song. The staccato of the tabla started. Salim was looking forward to this phase. He had imagined his love-play with his bride against the rhythm of the drumbeats. He asked Chauda Rani to hurry through the rituals. Smiling, she ordered that only one song for the arathi and one nuptial song should be sung. As soon as that was done, the bride and groom were sent to their chamber.

But what happened inside was very different.

Prabhavathi had heard about Salim and Rampyari through her spies and so she started the conversation:

'Rampyari is prettier than me, isn't she?'

Without answering her, Salim leaned to get hold of her. She sprang like a doe and stood on the other side of the bed.

'Give me an answer first.'

'I haven't yet seen your face. How can I answer your question?'

'Now that you've seen it, what d'you have to say?'

'Come closer. I'll tell you.'

'Aren't you ashamed of yourself? After taking my hand with fire as witness …'

'All that fire business was Chauda Rani's. Nothing to do with us. We're Muslims. We see wives only as wives.'

'So, was Rampyari your wife? You saw her for three months, didn't you?'

An hour went by in this kind of bandying. At last, Prabhavathi allowed herself to be caught. But by then the competition between the two singers at the jugalbandi was over and they were concluding with the mangala. Salim was upset that no drumbeats accompanied his foreplay. For the next hour, he somehow tired himself out with lovemaking. And he slept for about half an hour, exhausted. Then, he woke up, opened the door, walked out, called for his horse and rode away.

Prabhavathi remained as she was.

As soon as Tansen walked into her room, Rampyari fell on him and wept.

'Why did you make me wait so long? What wrong have I done? There are six other prostitutes in Delhi who have served you at your feet. Why are you so angry with me? Am I worse than them?'

She sobbed bitterly. By the time he pacified her, Tansen was exhausted. Tansen was not astute. He did not have the art of transforming her sorrow into mirth. He was too straightforward to be a poet; to know the subtleties of being a connoisseur. He had a God-given voice and all he knew was a life dedicated to singing. 'God gives; we receive' was his motto.

Now, he was more bothered with, 'How do I fondle such a holy person? How can I embrace her?'

At last, Rampyari stopped crying. She was able to talk more coherently. But her words tossed Miyan Saheb into a greater turmoil.

'You're a holy person,' she said, 'A devotee of God; an ascetic. I used to be enthralled by your singing. Do you remember? Once during the conclusion of a Monday prayer meeting, I sang a Meera bhajan, *'Mat jaa[14], mat jaa, mat jaa, Jogi!'* I was singing it to you. Couldn't you guess? I didn't want you to go away from me. You're a yogi, a *naadhabrahma*, someone who has seen God in music. Only you can redeem ignorant people like me. I believe you're an incarnation of Narada Maharshi …'

Miyan Tansen did not know whether to laugh or to cry. When Rampyari had raised him to the level of a Maharshi, how could he come down and fool around with her! 'Fine, let her calm down a little and realize that I too am an ordinary person,' he thought, waiting for the right moment.

'Anyway, you've come at last,' she was saying, 'My room has been sanctified by the dust of your feet. How could you have the heart to cast me off to people like Salim? I'm yours. In my deed, word and soul, I'm yours. Did it take you so long to find this out?'

He felt like saying, 'Forget about the word and soul. I've come here to fulfil the deed. Don't restrict me by making me divine.'

He had been there for two hours already. At last, Rampyari was ready. She settled down for an extended foreplay.

Right then, there was a bustle.

---

14 Do not leave

Bilas Khan

The Muslim watchman of her household came running in, stood outside her door and said, 'Prince Salim has asked for his horse. He may come this way.'

Rampyari opened the door immediately.

'If you don't mind, I can lend you my wife's burqa. Panditji can cover himself and go home safely in it,' he whispered.

'Where's it? Go get it.' said Rampyari.

The watchman ran to his room. His wife was sleeping. It took him some time to wake her up. Already they could hear the distant sound of hooves in the stillness of the night.

Tansen was made to wear the burqa and hide in a bamboo corn-bin.

Rampyari quickly rearranged the room, smeared some balm on her forehead and lay down as if she had a headache.

As soon as the front door was opened, Salim jumped in like a hungry tiger. He ran up the stairs to Rampyari's room.

'Pyari, why haven't you slept yet? D'you have a headache?'

'Why did you come now? Isn't your bride at home? You want to foist on me the guilt of separating a newly-wed girl from her husband, don't you?'

'Forget about her. Is your head hurting? Someone told me you weren't well. That's why I came to see you.'

Listening to Salim's smooth talk from his bin, Tansen realized how very naive he himself was.

'Don't pretend,' Rampyari was saying, 'You could've come yesterday. You could've said, "My wife has come home. The relationship between you and me is over. I gave you joy all these days; you gave me too. But the story is over." Lies come so easily to you, anyway. Would your mouth have split open if you had said something like that? I … I, Rampyari, had to hear of your nuptials through others. Isn't that disgraceful? Answer my questions first. Then you may sit on the bed.'

'Pyari, everything has gone wrong with me. I'll fall at your feet. Please don't get angry now.'

'Why should I get angry? Hadn't I had heard of your wedding? Were you embarrassed to tell me about your nuptials? Is it something unnatural?'

'Yes, I can't touch that woman again. It took me an hour. My ardour cooled. But she was not a woman to me.'

'And so, you came here, did you? Just go back. If the Badshah hears about this tomorrow, he'll send me to the gallows.'

'*Pyari*, just this one night. One last night.'

'Just one night then? Give me your word. If my life is threatened, you can't see me even once a month. Beware!'

The door banged shut. Miyan Tansen heard the sound of bolts sliding.

He got out of the bin carefully. The watchman went to open the front door but Miyan Saheb pointed to the back door. He tiptoed towards it and disappeared into the night in the burqa. There was a dog in the backyard. Even the dogs are shrewd in a harlot's house. On seeing the watchman, it went silently towards the open door and crept inside. The watchman closed the door.

Tansen crept warily in the pitch darkness. In his present state of mind, he could not make out the difference between his right leg and his left. He fumbled on, crossed a stream and plonked his foot right into some dung. It got stuck. Fortunately, there was a twig stretching out from the bank of the stream. He caught hold of it and pulled out the leg. But his slipper was stuck deep in the dung. He threw away the other slipper too. And then he thought, 'Now, why do I need that whore's burqa?' and spread it on the dung and crossed over it. He made his way through thorny bushes and reached the street. He looked this way and that to make out where he was. 'If I walk straight ahead on this street, I'll reach Rahmath Khan's house,' he said to himself.

By the time he reached the house, it was around one o'clock. The Delhi cold was severe, the wind was howling, everyone was asleep. There was only one lamp burning. Tansen knocked on the door. Perhaps there was a woman awake at that time. She came immediately to the door and whispered, 'Who's there? Please don't bang the door. The child has just gone to sleep. I'll wake up Khan saab.'

'*Haan*', was all that Tansen said.

Though his loose trousers were messed up to the knees with dung, his face and his chest still had traces of his tryst with Rampyari; he seemed to be in a hangover.

Rahmath Khan came out yawning and stretching, 'Who's there?'

'It's me. Open the door, Rahmath,' said Miyan Saheb.

Immediately, Rahmath was all in a flurry. '*Haan, Miyan! Kholta hun,*'[15] he said as he opened the door.

'I slipped on some dung on the way. My trousers are dirty. Get me some water to wash my legs. And get me your trousers,' Tansen whispered. And then, remembering his slippers, he said, 'And get me a pair of slippers too. I left mine there.'

---

15 'Yes, I'm opening it.'

'*Haan, haan*, come to the bathroom,' said Rahmath Khan. Tansen followed him in. The woman saw Miyan Saheb and stood up.

The glow of the lamp fell on her face.

'Why do I feel I've seen her before?' wondered Tansen to himself and asked Rahmath Khan, 'Have any of your relatives come from Athrauli?'

'Yes,' replied Rahmath Khan, a bit roughly, as he took the lone lamp and walked ahead.

His tone alerted Tansen that Rahmath Khan could be upset about something. 'Did you get the payment due to you from the Badshah's treasury?' he asked. He felt guilty that he had not been in touch with his accompanist. Perhaps that was why he was being rude.

'The Nawab of the household has promised to send it next week.'

Miyan wound a red Kashi dhothi round his waist and washed his legs. He left his trousers in the bathroom and put on the fresh ones Rahmath Khan had lent him. Wiping his feet with the dhothi, he said, as if he was still preoccupied, 'If you're not paid by next week, come to me. I'll advance you as much as I can.'

'Hm.'

'You can pay me back after you get your payment.'

'Hm. That'll be fine.'

'That lady said something about a child being ill. Do you have money to pay the hakim?'[16]

'Yes, I have that much!'

---

16   Muslim doctor

Bilas Khan

'What did the hakim say?'

'He's given some medicine. Beyond this, it is the will of God, he says.'

'Come home tomorrow. I'll give you a letter to the royal hakim. He'll come and see him.'

As they came out of the bathroom, the woman was still standing in the same place as if she was under a spell. Rahmath Khan moved on with the lamp.

'Poor woman! She must be spent from sitting up with the child; she's seeing with unseeing eyes. Perhaps she's his mother,' muttered Tansen as he walked back to the hall. Rahmath Khan followed him, still holding the lamp. Though he had shown some concern, Tansen felt he had not re-established the rapport he had with Rahmath Khan. He had not appreciated him.

'The other day, I felt I came to the end of a bar a half-note too early but you covered up my mistake quickly by readjusting the rhythm. Anyway, there are very few in Delhi who can appreciate the unfolding of a drupad. But that low-down Man Singh noticed it, I think. He seemed to chuckle. "Wah, what a great display of *laya*[17]!" he said later. "*Aap ki dua*[18]!" I replied.'

'Really? I didn't hear it.'

'That's why I have to congratulate you. You played with such verve, handling the burden with ease.'

Tansen might have raised his voice while saying this. Bilas Khan, who had been lying in bed, sat up and screamed, 'Baba! Baba!'

---

17 *Laya* – the distance between two beats
18 *Aap ki dua* – your blessings

His mother hugged him, laid him down gently and patted him to sleep saying, '*So jao beta, so jao.*'

'Poor boy! Perhaps he's delirious and calling for his father because of the high fever. How old could he be?'

'Fifteen.'

'Poor child, he's still young. Come home tomorrow. Get him the right medicines. Don't worry about the expense. Understand? Now give me your slippers.' And with that, Miyan Saheb walked back to his house.

The next day, very early in the misty morning, Rahmath went to Sakina Banu's house, woke her up and said, 'The Badshah has sent for Miyan Saheb.' Sakina Banu was not the type to wake up her husband in such a hurry but she did because the Badshah wanted to see him. Miyan washed his face, changed into fresh trousers and left. They engaged a tonga. As it changed direction, he asked Rahmath Khan, 'Why are we going this way?'

'To my house.'

'But you said the Badshah had sent for me.'

'Allah is the greater Badshah. Who can understand his games?'

Suddenly something flashed across Tansen's mind.

'Your child that we saw yesterday. How is he?'

'Not my child. Yours. He's Bilas Khan.'

'Why didn't you tell me yesterday?'

'Your mother and your wife have wrung a vow from me.'

'And the woman who had sat up the whole night?'

'That's Hamida Banu. I brought her to Delhi a week ago.'

Miyan was silent.

'How's he now? Bilas Khan?'

'He was perspiring towards the morning but his pulse is weak.'

Miyan felt as if the earth had opened under him. He looked bewildered, shattered. And tears gushed forth.

'A man shouldn't be so cruel to another,' he said.

'Who's being cruel to whom?'

Tansen fell silent.

'Who knows the games He plays?' repeated Rahmath.

By the time the tonga stopped at the front door, they could hear the loud wailing from the house.

It had been fifteen minutes since Bilas Khan had drawn his last breath.

Hamida Banu was disconsolate. 'I lived only for him. Allah has taken him away too. Why should I live now? Let me drown in some river or well. Anyway, Ganga Mathe is always there. Let me go,' she wept trying to wrench her hands from Rahmath Khan's wife's grip. As Miyan Saheb entered the room, she stopped crying and went and stood in a corner.

He came in and saw his son, Bilas Khan, whom he had not seen for the last ten years.

Yes, this was the boy who had sat in front of him and silently tugged at his heartstrings. He tried to lift him up and lay him on his lap. But the dead body was heavy; it would not move.

A fifteen-year-old boy with a twelve-year-old body ... This lad had sat there, right in front of him in the darbar. He sat silently but stirred him to the depths of his being. Miyan Saheb could see the boy again as if he were sitting in the concert, staring at him wide-eyed with admiration, mesmerized by his singing and he fell on his son. But the body was rigid as if it had been nailed to the bed.

Then Rahmath Khan's wife, Maamula said, 'As he was dying, Bilas Khan opened his eyes and asked, "Where's Baba? I want to hear him sing." If there's a life force in your singing, you might yet be able to resurrect him.'

Vain hope. But where is the end to such hope?

Miyan Tansen wiped his tears and sat on the bed beside the body. He took the small tanpura that was in a corner. Dawn was breaking. He tuned it and strummed, starting on the aalapana of the Todi raga. But only the first two notes sounded like Todi. The rest of the notes came out differently, rising from the depths of his grief. And with the new pattern of notes, came a suitable lyric.

Raga Bilaskhani Todi was born.

This was Miyan Tansen's original raga; his first musical composition.

But Bilas Khan did not rise again.

The women in Miyan Tansen's family had always been strong-willed; they stuck to their word. Bilas Khan had also become like them. Hamida Banu left for Athrauli the very next day, without speaking a word to her husband, Miyan Tansen.

SARA ABOOBACKER

Between Rules and Regulations

'LE, GIVE ME a bite from that mango!' screamed three-year-old Rauf.

'Why should I? I got it.' Mumtaz was two years older—she continued to suck the mango.

Rauf made a grab at the fruit; but it was Mumtaz's mango. There was a scuffle and then, of course, the crying.

'Ei, Zohra, where are you dying? Can't you hear your children fighting?' Their grandmother, Ameena Bi called out from inside.

Zohra was on the veranda, staring into space, vacantly. Her mother's voice roused her, bringing her back to reality. Heavy with child, she waddled towards her children, whacked them both, grabbed the mango from Mumtaz and tossed it away.

Originally published as 'Niyama Niyamagala Naduve'.

'Shut up!' she screamed as the children wailed louder and thumped them again. They ran inside to their Nani and fell into her arms, complaining.

'May your hand be chopped,' cursed Ameena Bi, carrying Rauf on her hip. But when she saw her daughter stepping inside exhausted, her heart melted and turned to water.

'Ya Allah, why have you yet kept me alive?' she sighed and turning towards Zohra, said, 'Have the pains started?'

Shaking her head to suggest denial, Zohra went to her bedroom, lay on the bed and counted on her fingers. How many months?

That day marked three months since Khader had given her the talaq. What a difference it had made in her life!

Theirs had been a tight-knit family. Though he had a small-time business, Khader never came home empty-handed. He even brought biscuits for the children and some bananas too, sometimes. And of course, both of them had to have fresh fish every day. A life contented with whatever they had.

But the coracle swaying on still waters in the cool breeze was caught in a squall. Everything went topsy-turvy in a moment. And the boatman went missing.

Why did this happen?

Zohra had never been to school. She had worked as a maid until she came of age. She had learnt what it meant to behave like a girl; she had even been beaten by her mistress at work. Whenever she complained to her mother, her reply was always, 'Bear with them, somehow. They've said they'll give you two sovereigns of gold if you work for five years, haven't they? What will you get if you leave now? Who'll marry you if you don't have at least some ear-studs with jhumkis dangling from them?'

Yes, a girl is born only to marry and beget, true. But the hurdles she had to cross before the wedding!

Somehow, Ameena secured an alliance for her daughter. Pawning her fourteen-year-old son, Shafi, as a bonded labourer in her master's house, she got a loan to meet the wedding expenses. She added her earnings to the two sovereigns Zohra had earned and bought her four sovereigns of jewellery, invited a few people, got her daughter married and sent her to her husband's house.

Zohra came home to have her first baby. She had the second in her husband's house. Khader could hardly afford to meet the expenses and Ameena had helped him out as much as she could. Zohra was pregnant again when Rauf was around two. She felt drained, what with two little children and the third on the way. Her mother-in-law never lifted a finger to help her out.

Zohra was in her sixth month when Khader came home, one day, and said: 'Give me your ear-studs and jhumkis.'

Zohra was nonplussed for a moment.

'Why?' she asked, softly.

'Why d'you need to know? Do as you're told,' he snapped.

'I ... I must ask my amma.'

'Why should ask your mother? You're my wife. You must do as I say,' he shouted.

'We have expenses coming. I can't give them to you now,' she said, eyes welling with tears.

'Haven't I seen you through childbirth before this? I'm the one to see to it again. Now, just give them to me,' he shouted.

'I can't give you without asking amma,' Zohra sounded stubborn as she wiped her tears with the edge of her sari.

They had their dinner in silence.

'Look at the kind of girls we get these days!' The mother-in-law grumbled loudly, 'How can she say she won't, when her husband asks for her jewellery? Why would a man want such a wife at all?'

Khader slept on the veranda that night. Zohra tossed about, unable to sleep. His baby stretched a leg or a hand in her belly, to remind her of its presence.

The next day began as usual, with the morning chores.

'Pack up and get ready to leave for your mother's house,' said Khader gruffly, standing at the door.

Zohra stood stunned, but for just a while. She started packing. Her husband was stone-faced; she could not fathom his thoughts. But she was happy to be going to her mother.

Ameena warmly welcomed her daughter, son-in-law and grandchildren. But when she offered him tea with something to eat, he said, 'I don't want anything. I've just eaten,' and left without even talking much.

Ameena was a little anxious about Khader's behaviour; he seemed to have changed.

'What's happened to your husband?' she asked Zohra, 'Did you quarrel with him by any chance?' She sounded like an investigator. Zohra explained everything.

'I slogged for five years as a maid in that house, cleaning children's shit, swallowing my mistress's insults, taking her blows, all to get two sovereigns of gold. Are these mere trinkets to be given away when he says, "Give!"?'

'Even then …' Ameena's voice dragged. 'Isn't he your husband? You should've given them because he asked. You could've told me later.'

Between Rules and Regulations

'How can we pawn it now when we need it later, amma? You don't know what I had to go through when Rauf was born—'

'What can we do, beti?' Ameena stopped her daughter midway. 'Allah has created us only to suffer, hasn't he? Okay, let that be. Why does he need money now?'

'Will husbands ever tell their wives why they need the money?'

'True. Anyway, now that you're here, relax for some time. We'll deal with that later.' Ameena comforted her daughter.

Four days went by ... eight days ... The son-in-law never turned up again.

'Your brother-in-law may have gone away in anger,' Ameena told her son, Shafi. 'Go and soften him up and bring him back.'

When Shafi went to Khader's house, his mother received him with a grumpy face.

'There! Your brother-in-law's come to welcome you back. Go. What more do you need?' she said, taunting her son.

'You've come to take me back, have you?' asked Khader, coming out of his room. 'Your aapa[1] doesn't want me. Her jewellery matters more to her. Hm, let her flaunt them.' He sounded angry.

'It's not like that, sala,[2] began Shafi but his brother-in-law stopped him.

'It's not like that. It's not like this. Go and tell your sister that I won't come. I'll give her talaq if I want.'

'Che, che, what are you saying, sala? Can you give her talaq for such a trivial matter? Come home with me. I'll get the gold for you from her.' Shafi spoke gently.

---

1   Elder sister
2   Brother-in-law

'No need!' Khader shouted. 'Am I a dog to do as she pleases? I'll come when I want. You go now.'

'That's the way to treat her, beta.[3] What? Did she think her husband is her servant?' His mother poured more ghee on the raging fire.

Shafi was not yet twenty; he had barely sprouted a moustache. He had never been through such experiences. And now, he felt a rush of anger towards his sister. Why did she have to be that stubborn? If only she had given away her jewellery when her husband had asked, they would not have had all this rumpus. Totally uncalled for!

He said the same thing to his mother when he returned home. 'Sala's red with fury. Aapa[4] has no sense! Who'll take care of her and her children now?'

Ameena too felt her son was right. What else could a mother do if her pregnant daughter came home with two little children? She had not yet fully paid back the money she had borrowed for Zohra's wedding. She was eager to be done with it and to bring home a bride for Shafi. Now she was worried that the burden of caring for her daughter's family might be foisted on her son.

'Please try and bring him home, Shafi,' Ameena pleaded with her son the next Friday.

'I'll go this evening,' he said.

'Shafi!' someone called from outside, right at that moment.

Shafi thought that was his brother-in-law. He went to the door with his mother behind him and Zohra behind her. That was not

---

3   Son
4   Elder sister

Khader but the muqri[5] who called out the azan for prayers at the mosque. He had come with the talaq Khader had given his wife, Zohra.

'Did this shaitan[6] go to that level?' cried Ameena, sobbing. Shafi stood stunned. Zohra went into the kitchen and sat in front of the woodfire; she was getting ready to harden her heart.

Now Zohra was blamed for anything and everything that went wrong in the house. Her mother and brother scolded her when a crow carried away a chick, when the sugar was finished, when the tea leaves were all used and over … as if she was responsible. The children wept for biscuits and bananas; they had got used to such treats. Zohra wept with them, not knowing how to earn to provide. Hurt at the way her mother and brother pounced on her, she took it out on her children, trying to feel better.

Sometimes, lying on her mat, Zohra wondered what it meant to have a husband. Had she committed such a big crime in refusing to part with the jewellery she had earned, toiling for five years, enduring all that nonsense from her mistress? And, for just that, could he make her and his own children destitute, to live on the bounty of her mother and brother? Does the bond between a husband and wife snap the moment he repeats, "Talaq" three times? Do those words have the power to split them apart forever … even when his baby was growing inside her, even when his blood was flowing in her? Can she too utter those words and free him? Mindless thoughts.

---

5   Teacher of the Quran
6   Devil

Zohra had her third baby; the mother and daughter were a bit relieved that it was a boy. But how were they to survive? What kind of concern will a daughter get who has received the talaq from her husband? When the baby suckled at empty breasts and cried aloud, his mother's tears rolled down his cheeks. Then, Ameena brought some tea in an ounce bottle and the baby sucked it all up. Zohra turned towards the wall and slept.

When the baby was nearing three months, Zohra was at the canal one day washing his clothes when she saw her mother-in-law's distant relative approaching the house. She went inside to tell her mother. Ameena welcomed her warmly, placing a plank on the veranda and inviting her to sit down. They got talking about this and that before Ameena touched upon her woes.

'What kind of a man is your Khader to bring my daughter to this state, Fatima? He gave her the talaq when she was pregnant and didn't send her even a pie to take care of his child. Who's there to punish such men?'

'That's the very reason I came here today, Ameena Bi. He's very sorry for what he did in the rage of that moment. He's missing his children very much. He wants to marry her again. What would you say to that?'

'Hanh!' Ameena opened her eyes and mouth wide. 'What're you saying? Is it that easy?'

'Why not? He can do the iddah,[7] after all, to nullify the talaq, can't he?' suggested Fatima, casually. '... And get married to her again. After all, she couldn't have yet had the three months of periods; the time before the talaq is confirmed.'

---

7   Period of waiting before marriage of a widow or divorcee

'Will girls accept such things these days?'

'Do they have a choice? How will your daughter cope with three little ones? And, what if he wants his children back? What will she have left then? See that you convince her somehow.'

'It's not just a question of getting her to see sense, Fatima. She hasn't yet started having her periods after the baby. She should have it at least once before this one-day wedding, shouldn't she? Some women may not have their periods for nearly a year after childbirth ...'

Fatima stopped Ameena midway, 'Will he wait that long, Ameena Bi? It's a miracle that he wants her back at all. How sure can we be that he won't change his mind again? Just go to some aalim[8] and get her some medicine to start her periods.'

'Is it as easy as all that?' Ameena mused after Fatima had left. 'Having periods and begetting babies go by the rules of nature. Can we tamper with them to suit ours?'

Zohra was furious when she heard the suggestion.

'What? He gives me the talaq and you punish me for it. Who's at fault, amma? He or me?'

'Whoever's at fault, Zohra, it's always the woman who suffers the consequences,' Ameena explained patiently, 'Don't ever forget that. It's good that we do as that woman advised. I'll go to an aalim tomorrow.'

'Amma, you can't do this to me.' Zohra sounded stubborn. Ameena's patience began to fray.

'Hunh!' she ranted without thinking; she was that furious. 'You're always like that. Headstrong. When he asked you for your

---

8   A local practitioner of medicine

jewels, you didn't give them to him. And now, you don't want this way out. If you continue to live here, who's going to take care of you? How long can Shafi do it? Shouldn't we see to his wedding? His family? Or … do you plan to send your children to their father's house and stay here as a servant in your brother's?'

Anyway, Ameena had never seen Zohra's point whenever they had had an argument. And now, she was ready to do whatever she had to, to set her daughter's marriage on an even keel once again. She was willing to oil the machinery however she was forced to; whatever the cost. Her daughter too had to be ready to comply; to make sacrifices.

Though Zohra shrank initially, slowly she was able to see that she had no other choice. Feeding her children was becoming a mounting problem. Added to that was her brother's indifference, his veiled contempt, her mother's scolding. She became aware that this was how it was going to be … and it would only get worse. Feeling cornered, Zohra said yes to her amma's suggestion.

Ameena went to the local quack the very next day. She brought some pills and medicine and gave them to her daughter. And the struggle against a law of nature in a bid to obey a religious law began.

Zohra developed a fever after a few days. Neither mother nor daughter thought much of it. 'Just a slight warmth,' they said.

'The aalim[9] said she should be fine within a week,' Ameena told Fatima when she came by again. 'Let's decide on everything then.'

Zohra groaned with raging fever as the days went by; she developed unbearable pain in her lower abdomen. Ameena could

---

9   Local doctor

not bear to see her daughter suffer. She went again to the doctor and he plied her with more pills, more medicines. She waved a rooster around her head to take away the effect of the evil eye and dedicated it to the dargah[10] with a vow to offer it when her daughter got well.

The next day, Zohra started bleeding. The mother and daughter heaved a big sigh of relief; at last, there was a signal of propitious times to come. But, as the days went by, there was no sign of it stopping. They were bewildered.

One day, Zohra sat up with great effort and called her two elder children and hugged and kissed them.

'Listen to whatever your nani says,' she said to them with great difficulty.

She kissed her baby and handed him over to her mother.

'Amma, your son-in-law who's made me go through so much pain and suffering ... your son-in-law who gave me the talaq ... and wanted to marry me again ... where is he now?' The words struggled out like sighs as she slowly laid her head on the pillow and closed her eyes forever.

The darkening evening enshrouded the house as the children screamed in terror.

'Ayyo, beti, have you gone forever?' Ameena wailed, beating her breast.

---

10 Shrine

NOTES ON THE AUTHORS

A.R. Krishnashastri (Ambale Ramakrishnashastri Krishnashastri), [1890–1968], was born in Ambale, a village in Chikkamagaluru, South Karnataka. After obtaining a postgraduate degree, he worked as a lecturer in Kannada at Central College, Bangalore. He started the Karnataka Sangha in the college and published the paper, *Prabuddha Karnataka*. He was the President at the 26th Kannada Sahitya Sammelana, 1941. He is a recipient of the Kendriya Sahitya Academy Award.

Ajampur Sitaram (pen name, Ananda) [1902–1963] was born in Anavatti, Sorabha taluk, Shimoga District, South Karnataka. Ajampur was the native place of his ancestors. With degrees in Veterinary Science and Botany, he worked in the Department of Sericulture before becoming a full-time writer. He has published *Chandragrahana, Maatagaathi, Swapnajeevi, Joisara Chowdi* as collections of stories, as well as plays, essays and translations.

NOTES ON THE AUTHORS

Hebbalalu Velapanuru Savithramma (1913–2012) was born in Bengaluru. She graduated from Mysore Maharani's College in 1931 with three gold medals. She is well known as a translator of writings by Rabindranath Tagore, Mahatma Gandhi and Anton Chekov from English to Kannada. Her stories have recently been published as a collection, *Samastha Kathegalu*. She received the Karnataka Sahitya Akademi Award in 1975.

Kadengodlu Shankarabhatta (1904–1968) from Mangalore, South Karnataka, was well-known as a poet, a writer of short stories and novels and a journalist. His stories were published in popular anthologies; *Hindina Kathegalu*, 1946, *Gaajinabale*, 1947, and *Dudiyuva Makkalu*, 1952. He was President of Karwar Sahitya Sammelana.

Kodagina Gowramma (1912–1939) was from Mercara, Coorg, South Karnataka. She wrote stories as B.T.G. Krishna. She died an untimely death while swimming.

Koradkal Srinivasarao was from a village near Sringeri in South Karnataka. He was a brilliant student who became a teacher after his Intermediate exam. His story in the present collection belongs to the Navodaya phase of early modern stories in Kannada and yet shows promise of the Bandaya protest literature that followed.

Kulakarni Srinivasa (Kulakarni Srinivasa Konhera) [1911–1971] is from Sadanakeri, Dharwad, North Karnataka. He was popularly known as Natyacharya. He brought *Prema*, a paper published by Pandit Taranath to Dharwad and edited it in a new format. *Sampige*, 1933, is a collection of six of his stories.

NOTES ON THE AUTHORS

Masti Venkatesha Iyengar (1891–1986) wrote under the pen name, Srinivasa. He was born in Malur, Kolar District, South Karnataka. After graduating from Madras Presidency College, he was a lecturer in English before he cleared the civil services exam to become an Assistant Commissioner. He received honorary doctorates from Karnataka and Mysore universities. He was President of Kannada Sahitya Parishad. He was the recipient of the following awards: Central Sahitya Academy award for his collection of Short Stories, 1970 and Fellow of Central Academy, 1974. He was also awarded the Jnanpith award for his novel, *Chikkaveera Rajendra*, in 1983.

Mundakuru Narasimha Kamat (1883–1940) is considered one of the most prolific writers of short stories. But unfortunately, the newspapers in which they were published did not move beyond the district. In 1941, *Andina Avaru* was published as a felicitation volume for early writers in which a memoir about Kamat and five of his stories have been published.

Najanagudu Thirumalamba (1887–1982) was married when she was ten and widowed at fourteen. Her native tongue was Tamil and she was familiar with Kannada, having lived in Najanagudu, in South Karnataka. Her parents were Venkatakrishna Iyengar and Alamelamma. Thanks to her father's encouragement, Thirumalamba wrote devotional songs, stories, novels and plays. They were published in *Madhuravani*, a monthly magazine. Eventually, she published *Sanmarga Darshini*, a newspaper, and *Sati Hitaishini*, a monthly magazine for women, in which she published her novel, *Susheela*, in 1913. She also edited *Karnataka*

Nandini, a monthly newspaper for women. She has won awards from Madras School Book and Literature Society and Karnataka Vidhyavardhaka Sangha. She was honoured by the Central Sahitya Academy in 1980. Shaswathi, a Library and Centre for Women's Studies has been set up in her honour in Bengaluru. She is known as the first woman writer and editor in Kannada.

Panje Magesharaya (1874–1937) born in Bantval, in South Karnataka is one of the earliest Navodaya Writers. He was one of the first to write and publish short stories. With a BA degree, he worked as a lecturer in Government College, Mangalore. He was also one of the earliest writers known for popularizing children's literature. He was an editor for *Kannada Vykarana* and *Shabdamanidarpana*, books on Kannada Grammar and Vocabulary. He presided over the 20th Kannada Sahitya Sammelana in Raichur in 1934. A collection of his writings was published by Orient Longman Limited in 1973.

S.G. Sastry (Sosale Galalapuri Sastry) [1890–1955] writes in his travelogue that his stories were published when he was in London for further studies in Science. His stories were popular for themes of domestic relevance at a time when writers were more concerned with social issues.

Sara Aboobacker (1936–2023) is from Kasargod, South Karnataka. She has written many novels and collections of short stories. Her novel, *Chandragiri Theeradalli* has been translated into many languages. She has received the Karnataka Sahitya Akademi and Karnataka Rajyotsava awards.

NOTES ON THE AUTHORS

Saraswathibai Rajawade (1913–1994) a writer of short stories, novels and plays, wrote under her pen name, Giribale. She is from Udipi and belongs to the first generation of women writers from South Karnataka.

Dr Shankar Mokashi Punekar (1928–2004) is from Dharwad in North Karnataka. He was a Professor of English, well known for his stories and critical writings. He has won many awards from the Central Sahitya Akademi and Karnataka Sahitya Akademi.

Shyamaladevi Belgaonkar (1910–1943) was the first woman writer from North Karnataka. She was considered a feminist writer, focussing on the plight of women who tried to make the best of dubitable situations. She was also an essayist.

Triveni, pen name of Anasuya Shankar (1928–1963) was born in Mysore. She graduated from Mysore University. She has written 41 short stories and 21 novels in barely 13 years. She is well known for her novels like *Bellimoda*, *Hannele Chiguridhaaga* and *Sharapanjara*, which were made into films.

Yarmunja Ramachandra (1933–1955) is from Puttur in South Karnataka. He was a schoolteacher after completing his high school. He was the sub-editor for *Navabharatha*, the daily in Mangalore and *Rashtramatha*, a weekly. He was also the editor of a manuscript newspaper, *Panchajanya*, between 1949 and 1953. A collection of his stories, *Chikithseya Huchchumattu Ithara Kathegalu*, was published in 1954, and of his poems, *Vidaaya*, in 1956.

ABOUT THE TRANSLATOR

Susheela Punitha

SUSHEELA PUNITHA is a Sahitya Akademi Award winner. She received the first Translation Award for English in 2015 for her translation of *Bharathipura* by U.R. Ananthamurthy. *Bharathipura* was also shortlisted for the Jaipur Literary Prize, 2012, and *The Hindu* Literary Prize, 2012. Her translation of *Hundreds of Streets to the Palace of Lights and Other Stories* by S. Diwakar for Oxford University Press (2015) was shortlisted for the Crossword Book Award, 2016.

She was Professor of English Language and Literature at Mount Carmel College, Bangalore, and at Centre for Postgraduate Studies, Seshadripuram College, Bangalore University. She has written stories for children for a UNICEF project, Children for Change, and value-based stories for Tipping Point in the student edition of the *Deccan Herald*. As ELT (English Language Teaching) Consultant for Orient Blackswan, she has written

ABOUT THE TRANSLATOR

Spoken English, A Foundation Course, Parts 1 and 2, and simplified British stories for their Easy Readers' Series.

Her translations from Kannada to English include:
1. *Bharathipura* by U.R. Ananthamurthy (2010)
2. *Asprushyaru* by Vaidehi, as *Vasudeva's Family* (2012)
3. *Dweepa* by Na D'Souza (2013)
4. *Sexy Durga of Doopadalli* by B.T. Jahnavi (2014)
5. *Hundreds of Streets to the Palace of Lights and Other Stories* by S. Diwakar (2015)
6. *Saraswathibai Rajawadeyavara Nenapugalu* (2015); an excerpt for Karnataka Sahitya Akademi
7. *Samboli!: Beware!* by Lakshman (2017)
8. *Krauncha Pakshigalu and Other Stories* by Vaidehi (2018)
9. *Karya* by Aravind Malagatti (2021)

ABOUT THE SERIES EDITOR

Mini Krishnan

MINI KRISHNAN worked with Macmillan India Limited (1980–2000) and Oxford University Press (2000–18), editing textbooks for the Indian school market, and literary translations. She has co-authored textbooks for the Translation Education industry: *Word Worlds*; *Words, Texts & Meanings; Wordscapes;* and *Short Fiction from South India* (all published by Oxford University Press) and edited two volumes of translated fiction for the Aleph Book Company: *Tell Me a Long, Long Story* (sourced from fourteen languages) and *The Greatest Tamil Stories*. She is the series editor of *Living in Harmony,* a programme of peace education textbooks for schools (Oxford University Press).

She is currently Managing Editor of the Tamil Nadu Textbook and Educational Services Corporation, working with twenty English-language publishers to take Tamil to the world through translations of poetry, fiction and non-fiction, and on the editorial board of the Murty Classical Library of India, Harvard University Press.

She writes for *The Hindu* and the *Indian Express* and selects short stories in translation for the *Frontline* magazine.

HarperCollins *Publishers* India

At HarperCollins India, we believe in telling the best stories and finding the widest readership for our books in every format possible. We started publishing in 1992; a great deal has changed since then, but what has remained constant is the passion with which our authors write their books, the love with which readers receive them, and the sheer joy and excitement that we as publishers feel in being a part of the publishing process.

Over the years, we've had the pleasure of publishing some of the finest writing from the subcontinent and around the world, including several award-winning titles and some of the biggest bestsellers in India's publishing history. But nothing has meant more to us than the fact that millions of people have read the books we published, and that somewhere, a book of ours might have made a difference.

As we look to the future, we go back to that one word— a word which has been a driving force for us all these years.

Read.